PERSON
of
INTEREST

PERSON

of

INTEREST

EMERY HARPER

W🌐RLDWIDE®

TORONTO • NEW YORK • LONDON
AMSTERDAM • PARIS • SYDNEY • HAMBURG
STOCKHOLM • ATHENS • TOKYO • MILAN
MADRID • WARSAW • BUDAPEST • AUCKLAND

To my men: Alan, Collin, Aaron, Reed and Zac. Love y'all.

Recycling programs
for this product may
not exist in your area.

Person of Interest

A Worldwide Mystery/May 2017

First published by Carina Press

ISBN-13: 978-0-373-28409-2

Copyright © 2016 by Denise B. McDonald

Printed in U.S.A.

Acknowledgments

Sandy Behr and Amie Stuart, for all the times I emailed, texted or called totally freaked out, you never pushed the ignore button; y'all rock!

John Gwilliam for your awesome pop-culture knowledge.

Dwayne McDonald, finally something just for you.

Pat Mills, thanks for answering my theater questions—I really did learn in your class, I just forgot.

For the moms: Brenda Wood, Betty Brett and Jody Wood, y'all are the best supporters a gal can ask for. And the dads: Don Wood and Richard Brett, you're cool, too.

Maryanne Smith, happy 90th birthday!

Deb Nemeth, you're an awesome editor and you get me, you really get me.

ONE

Go ahead and start the paperwork for my sainthood now. My ex-husband was still breathing while sitting in front of me and asking whether I would help his girlfriend. Out of a bind she got herself into. The restraint alone for not throttling him should qualify as one of the two miracles on the road to canonization. Help her? As if.

Colin Eagan was a lot of things—blond Adonis, football coach and father of our daughter, yes—but dude with a clue…nope. "C'mon, Celeste. All you have to do is sweet-talk Chad into backing off. He likes you and would do anything if you just asked him."

I gripped the back of the sofa, mostly to keep from smacking him upside the head. "Nope, sorry. Not gonna do it." I frowned at the man I'd spent ten years married to—eight years too many. Colin, his girlfriend Naomi Michaels, and I all worked at Peytonville Preparatory Academy, a private school in Peytonville, a suburb of Fort Worth. Chad Jones was the principal, and our boss.

Peytonville Prep was Colin's alma mater; he was working there when we met. Just after we started dating he'd gotten me an interview for a job as the theater teacher. That was fourteen years ago. All in all it was a good job and the perks—summers off and getting to be close to our daughter all day—were great. But it meant no wall of separation from my ex.

After we divorced, I thought nothing of it when Colin

and Naomi started making goo-goo eyes at each other. When he got her a job at our school, I knew I should have moved back to Topeka. It would have been so easy to go home.

Been there, done that. Left my blue-checked dress in the closet and never looked back. But oh how tempting it suddenly was.

"All I'm asking for is a little help here. Chad won't listen to me. We had an argument this morning about it." He stood and paced between me and the front door. "Do it as a favor. For me."

Naomi and Chad had been at odds over her class curriculum. One of the parents didn't like the assigned book *Animal Farm*, said it was political propaganda. The woman had also objected when the cafeteria started serving pizza for lunch as her overweight child had no self-control and we were to blame for his extra ten pounds—plain and simple, she liked to blame and complain.

Still...not my battle. I had no reason to take this matter on. Why couldn't Colin understand?

I watched him as he paced, and paced. As the JV football coach, the man was in as much shape at thirty-eight as he'd been the day we met. Colin had been jogging and I'd run him over with my car—by accident, of course. Fog and too many tears after being dumped led to bad depth perception, his bruised hip and years of Colin Eagan talking me into things I didn't want to do.

To be fair, our daughter was the best decision we'd made together. About the only one.

But no matter how hot he made a pair of double-knit football shorts look—spring, summer or two weeks before Thanksgiving, he wore those darn shorts—it wasn't near enough to jump back into the world of *"C'mon, Celeste..."*

"You're being petty."

Petty? Was he kidding? "No. I appreciate Naomi's stand on the issue, but why do I need to be the one to point it out to Chad?"

"He likes you."

"A little too much." I narrowed my eyes at him. "Do you know how long it took me to get Chad to see I wasn't interested in him?"

Colin's shoulders stiffened. "I knew you'd turn this around to you."

My eyes all but bugged out of my head and my mouth fell open, but only for a moment. "Paige!" I waited a heartbeat and hollered for our daughter again.

"Yes, ma'am?"

"Sweet pea, tell your father bye. He has to go."

My sweet, precocious child righted her glasses on her nose. "Bye, Colin. See you at school tomorrow."

When she'd gone to calling us Celeste and Colin rather than Mom and Dad, I couldn't remember.

"Bye, pumpkin." Colin glared at me and stomped out the front door.

"He's never going to get anywhere if he lets these women lead him around by his—"

"Paige," I warned.

She blinked rapid-fire at me. "I was going to say *nose*."

"Sure you were." I ruffled her bangs.

"When's Uncle Levi coming over?" Levi Weiss, my very best friend, became Paige's honorary uncle the moment she was born. The two were almost as inseparable as we were.

"Any minute now. You need to go get changed into your uniform." Levi had taken it upon himself to give Paige private karate lessons in my living room.

"It's called a gi."

I laughed. "Fine. Go put on your gi."

Her little auburn head bobbed in a nod. "Will do."

I stared after my daughter. Sometimes it was like talking to my mother—always being corrected. I shuddered and hurried to tidy up the living room. Levi has known me too long. He'd keel over dead away if my house was anything less than an F1 tornado aftermath. But at least I tried. Sort of.

I'd just sat down on the sofa when the front door whisked open.

"I have arrived." Levi sashayed into the living room. Only a few inches taller than my five foot four, he seemed larger than life. He was bold where I was reserved and flashy where I was basic. We complemented each other perfectly.

Him and Colin, not so much. They shared a mutual tolerance. Were it not for me, the two men would never run in the same circles much less breathing space. Although he and Colin could be mistaken for brothers with their blond good looks, Levi swayed a little more to the diva side of the road with his meticulously kempt self. And liked to flaunt it in front of Colin.

I smiled at Levi. "He already left."

"Oh." His shoulders slumped and he left off with the sashaying. "Hello, sweets." He leaned down and kissed my forehead. "You ran him off in record time."

"Gee, thanks. Good to see you too, dearest."

Levi smiled as Paige came bouncing back into the living room.

"Hi, Uncle Levi." She straightened her gi. "I'm all warmed up."

Levi unwrapped his leather trench coat and revealed

a matching gi. He glanced over at me. "How 'bout you join us?" He winked at me.

I slapped my curvy size-twelve hips. "And lose all this? I'll pass."

I'd like to claim it was leftover baby weight, but seeing how Paige passed the double digits almost a year ago, Ben and Jerry were the only culprits I could point my empty spoon at. That and an extra-large all-fat, no soy, mocha, choca heavenly delight—or three—every morning.

"Try to refrain from breaking any lamps tonight, please. They're starting to look at me funny at Pier 1 when I buy replacements."

The two gave me a quick wave before they bowed to one another and went through their workout routine.

While Levi kept Paige occupied, I hurried to the computer in my office. Colin wanted me to appeal to Chad's sense of fair play and for kids to read what they were assigned. I shouldn't. Under most circumstances I wouldn't, but Colin knew just how to worm his way into *my* sense of fair play—good, bad or somewhat amicable divorce.

I logged into my school account and popped into the email system. I could easily write up a quick note. But I'd managed to stay off of Chad's radar for the better part of a year now and I was hesitant to give that up even for Naomi's right to actually teach her students.

I leaned back in my chair and stared up at the ceiling as I tapped my pen against my lower lip.

Had Chad been dating? If he had, then my email wouldn't be more than a small blip. I should have paid better attention.

I sighed and dropped my pen. "A quick note couldn't hurt."

WE ARRIVED AT school a little early the next morning so I could see Colin before class. I wanted to let him know that I'd emailed Chad and asked him to back off Naomi's curriculum. See, I could play nice despite what Colin thought.

I glanced to see if Colin's truck was in his allotted spot. It wasn't, although he usually beat everyone to work in the morning. He liked to get in an early work-out; he called it his "me" time.

I hated delaying talking to him, mostly because I would forget and then it would become a thing… Since Colin wasn't in yet, I decided to check in with Chad to make sure he got the email.

"Sweet pea, I need to stop by the principal's office. You go on in." I headed toward the admin part of the building instead of the other end where my office was.

Paige hurried along after me. "You still didn't sign my permission slip." She waggled her messenger bag in the air. "It's due today."

I groaned. I guess the whole beatification would have to wait after all. "Okay, give me a sec." I opened the door to the front office. The administrative assistant's desk was empty. Surprise, surprise, Kelsey Pierce wasn't at her post. I skirted her desk to Chad's door and knocked once before I let myself in. I stopped so quickly Paige rammed right into the back of me.

"Um, sweet pea, go stand by the front door." My voice shook. When she started to protest, I barked out a quick, "Now!"

I waited until she got back across the room, then I took a tentative step into the office. Nausea rolled through my gut and it was all I could do to stay upright as I gripped the doorframe. Up above Chad Jones's desk was none other than Chad Jones. Hanging.

"Paige, I need you to run down to my office. Try calling your dad and then just wait for me. Stay there. Do you understand me?"

I glanced back over my shoulder. Paige's little khaki eyes were wide, but she nodded and ran off in the direction of my office.

I grabbed the phone on Kelsey's desk and dialed 911. When the line picked up, I said, "We need an ambulance or the police at the Peytonville Preparatory Academy on Frankford Boulevard. There's a man, he's, uh, hanging."

I think the operator asked me a question, but to be honest, I had no idea. I was inching closer and closer to Chad. "I think he's dead. He's a weird shade, almost blue. You can't hang and still be alive, right? Should I check for a pulse, though? To make sure?"

"Ma'am, who is this?"

"Celeste Eagan. I'm the theater teacher. Are you sending someone?" I got to the end of the phone cord tether. I stretched out to reach Chad. His wrist was inches from my fingertips. "I should just check for a pulse, right?"

I shivered. I so didn't want to touch a dead body. But if he wasn't dead, they needed to know. My fingers were just right there and…

"Celeste? What the hell are you…?"

Kelsey Pierce screamed. And screamed.

I jumped and dropped the phone.

"WHICH OFFICE, MA'AM?"

I pointed to the door on the right that housed the fine arts department. "That one."

"Okay, wait in there until the detective gets here, please." The young officer held the door open for me. The police had arrived only moments after the ambulance and put the entire school on lockdown. They hustled me into a corner of the room and attended to Chad. And Kelsey, who'd passed out at my feet when she'd seen our boss. I had a bruise on the top of my foot where her head landed.

The first officers on the scene asked me several pointed questions—like did I touch anything in the room or see him before he…got in the situation he was in. I'm not entirely sure how I managed to answer their questions, but apparently I gave them the info they needed as they finally let me go back to the office. With an escort. After I explained that I needed to get to my daughter. Very few students were at school this early, and the ones in the building were tucked away in the cafeteria where they usually waited before the first bell clanged to start the day.

"When can I—"

"The detective will be here shortly."

I nodded and shut the door behind me. The small office that I shared with two other teachers was a godsend after the commotion in the administrative offices.

"Celeste, thank goodness you're here." Rachel, the speech teacher, pushed her hands through her curly brunette hair. "What happened? Paige came in here all freaked out. I couldn't understand what she was saying."

Rachel and the debate teacher, Holly, closed in on me as Paige ran across the room and hugged tight to my waist. I wrapped my arm around my daughter's shoulders and squeezed her to me. "In a sec." I held my hand up to stop questions. "You okay, sweet pea?"

Paige frowned up at me and nodded. "You scared me. What happened?"

"There was an accident." An on-purpose accident, I added mentally. I couldn't shake the image of my boss hanging above his desk. "Did you get a hold of your dad?" When she shook her head, I said, "Go call him again, okay?"

My daughter gave me one more quick squeeze and sat at my desk. When I was sure she was out of earshot I leaned closer to Rachel and Holly. "Chad is dead, I think."

"Wha… How… You *think*?" Rachel stood straight and motionless. Holly paled but didn't say anything.

"He was hanging." I gulped. "Above his desk."

Holly sat heavily back into her chair. Rachel's chin dropped to her chest. It took a moment before she found her voice again. "Seriously?" She shook her head. "You're joking right?"

"I wish I was." I popped open my bag and grabbed out my sweater and shrugged it on, suddenly chilled. "The police are here. They'll be questioning the staff soon, I think." I glanced over at my daughter and hugged my arms across my chest.

"What are they going to do about classes?" Holly finally spoke.

I lifted one shoulder in a shrug. "Canceled, I guess." I leaned against the edge of her desk. Chad had killed himself—I was pretty sure that shade of blue didn't denote health.

It just didn't make any sense. The man oozed self-absorption. I could see him staring at himself in the mirror so long he starved to death, but hanging… I just didn't get it.

"I can't get Dad on the phone."

Dad. She didn't know exactly what was going on, but it scared her enough to knock the kid back into her and call Colin "Dad."

"Then can you try Uncle Levi? Ask him to come pick you up?"

"What about school?"

"Just call Uncle Levi. Please," I added when her lip quivered ever so slightly. I hurried over and gave her a quick hug before she dialed again. "Everything will be fine, sweet pea."

It only took twenty minutes for Levi to wrap up things on his job site. He owned a house-flipping business and set his own hours, thankfully. He left with Paige after I got permission from the squad of uniforms up front. I promised to call Levi with details the minute I learned anything, because he had a ton of questions. But so far, nobody had any answers, just wild speculations. I wanted to look for Colin but the police asked the staff to stay in our offices until they had a chance to speak with each one of us separately. After waiting for three hours, there was a heavy knock on the door. Rachel all but jumped out of her chair. "Come in."

A different uniformed police officer than earlier came in followed by a man dressed in a dark sports coat and khaki slacks. "Ladies, Detective Muldoon would like to speak to you. One at a time, please," the young officer said.

The detective. My chest tightened.

The dark-haired detective looked us over and turned to Rachel. "You first." He walked her out into the hall, the door shutting behind them.

I slid my cell phone from my pocket, but I still hadn't heard from Colin. I was surprised he hadn't even texted me once, if nothing else to check on Paige. Not to mention something like me finding our dead boss in his office was gossip too juicy to pass up. Even for him. I texted him quickly. Where are you? The young officer cleared his throat and shook his head in my direction.

I gave him a sheepish smile. "Sorry."

After a few minutes, Rachel came back in and the detective waved me to follow him into the hallway. As I passed her desk, she snagged my wrist. "He smells scrumptious."

I chuckled and then bit my lip when the man in question frowned at me.

"This way." He motioned to a set of chairs smack-dab in the middle of the hall. When I sat, he poised his pen over his notebook. "Your name?" His voice echoed softly in the empty hallway.

It was eerily quiet in the middle of a school day with no students in attendance.

When I didn't answer right away, the detective cleared his throat.

"Oh, sorry. Celeste. Celeste Eagan."

His gaze snapped up to mine. A quick frown pulled those heavy eyebrows down once again. But just as quickly, he masked any emotion and wrote down my name. He glanced back up, his icy blue eyes a tad bit unnerving as he stared directly at me. "You're the one who called it in? They told me you'd left."

I shook my head. "I came back to my office because my daughter was here."

"Was? You sent her home?" I nodded and he continued. "Was she with you?"

"When I found…um…went into the principal's office, yes, but she didn't see anything. I made sure." Gaw, the therapy that would have followed that—for me. I had a feeling my little analytical munchkin would probably have found it fascinating, hence therapy for me.

"Can you tell me how things transpired this morning?"

This morning. Hmm. I tucked a lock of hair behind my ear and thought through my morning. "I woke up at six and—"

He shook his head. "Just from when you got to the school."

"Oh, sure." I nodded and described parking, walking into the building and on into Chad's office all the way up to the point where the paramedics were sticking smelling salts under Kelsey's nose—all the while I was stuck in the small office with Chad's body only a few feet from me. I'd tried to look anywhere and everywhere that wasn't at the man. I practically had my eyes glued to the top of his desk to keep from seeing more than I wanted. I frowned. I don't know why it didn't register sooner, but there'd been a notepad atop the blotter. It had Colin's name hastily scribbled down in Chad's scratchy penmanship.

The detective cleared his throat. "And you teach?" he asked, breaking into my thoughts.

"Theater."

"How well did you know Chad Jones?"

"About as well as any other teacher and principal, I suppose. I've worked here with him for years."

"And when was the last time you saw him?"

I shrugged. "Yesterday right after school, I guess."

"You guess? You're not sure?"

Very strange questions for suicide. "I honestly don't remember. I see him several times a day, at one time or another, so I just can't say for sure when or where it was."

He jotted down a few more notes in his little notebook. "Do you happen to know a Colin Eagan?"

"Yes, he's a football coach here. And my ex-husband." I twisted my hands in my lap. Had the detective seen Colin's name there? What did it mean? What did *he* think it means? "Is something wrong with him?"

"Why would you ask that?"

Thinking of my father, who was suspicious of everyone, I tried to relax my shoulders and hold the detective's gaze. I didn't want to put anything on his radar that wasn't already there, but my not being able to connect with Colin was making me even more anxious. "No reason. I just don't understand why you're asking these questions."

Detective Muldoon narrowed his eyes. "I wanted to ask Coach Eagan a few questions. And I can't seem to be able to get a hold of him." The man shifted in his chair. "Or his girlfriend, Naomi Michaels."

"Oh, I uh, I haven't spoken with them this morning." I tried not to squirm.

"When was the last time you spoke with either of them?"

"Naomi and I don't really speak. The whole dating my ex makes for an awkward conversation." I smiled and tried to lighten the mood, but the man and his blank stare didn't waver. "Colin was over last night. Around eight."

"Do you often visit with your ex-husband at night?"

My shoulders stiffened. "I beg your pardon, but I don't see how that's any of your business. Or has anything to do with—" I waved my hand in the direction of Chad's office "—anything."

"You wouldn't happen to have a number where I can reach Mr. Eagan, would you?"

I debated telling him I didn't know the number, but he had to know I do—no point in giving the man a reason to distrust *me*. And all he would have to do was get the school directory. I rattled off Colin's cell number and his home number.

Detective Muldoon flipped his little notebook shut and stood. "Okay, thank you."

I stood and hurried back to the office.

"Mrs. Eagan." Detective Muldoon walked over to me, holding out a card. "If you talk to your ex, please tell him I'd like to speak with him."

As I leaned forward for the card, I remembered what Rachel said and took in a deep breath. Sure as shooting, the man smelled of musk, cinnamon and coffee—oh so enticing. To a coffee junkie like myself, you could almost taste the heavenly mixture. I fought to keep from closing my eyes and sniffing again and again.

I realized he was staring at me strangely. I needed to back out of my olfactory orgasm and let the man get back to work. "Yes, sir, Officer." I gave him a quick salute.

"Detective," he quickly corrected me.

I knew that. But he made me nervous. "Oh. Sorry. Detective."

I held onto his card and sat back at my desk, a little stunned by the whole finding a dead body and being questioned by a police detective then wantonly smelling him. As soon as he left with Holly, Rachel pulled her chair beside mine. "What did he ask you?"

"What happened when I found Chad." I didn't see any reason to tell her about the questions involving Colin.

She shook her head slowly. "You okay?"

I pasted on a weak smile. "Yeah, sure." No not really, but what was I going to do? Fall apart? I was, however, more concerned with Colin's absence than Chad's death. Did that make me a bad person? Worse, did I care?

Rachel settled back against her chair and fluffed up her hair. Her brunette eyebrow arched up. She glanced over at the young officer standing in front of the door. "Officer…" She unfolded her thin five-foot-ten body and stood facing the man.

"Starnes," the young man squeaked.

"Officer Starnes, I'm a little confused by all the questions. I didn't realize they sent a detective out to question people when there was a suicide."

Officer Starnes swallowed heavily. "It's standard procedure." He looked over his shoulder at the closed door and lowered his voice. "When the suicide looks questionable."

Questionable? "You think it's not suicide?"

The young officer blushed. "I'm not given all the details." He returned to his rigid sentry stance.

All of a sudden the questions about Colin scared the ever-loving crap out of me. What had he gotten into? The need to find him grew a little more than urgent. I drummed my fingers on the desktop. "Excuse me, how much longer do you think we'll be detained here?"

"I'm sorry, ma'am. That's not my call. Detective Muldoon is in charge of the investigation. I can ask him if you'd like—"

"Oh no, no. That's okay." Once again I tried texting Colin. We need to talk. Now!

TWO

AN ANNOUNCEMENT CAME over the PA. We were to report to the auditorium ASAP. Rachel looked at me and shrugged as we grabbed our bags. It was getting close to the end of the school day—technically. With no kids in attendance it was all up in the air, and we were all still pretty much in the dark as to what was going on. Sure, I didn't think Chad would have hung himself, but murder…in our school was just too unconceivable. But the way they were questioning people… I shuddered every time I thought about it.

Colin had yet to get in touch. I'd surreptitiously called Levi to see if maybe Colin'd tried to check in with Paige, but no such luck. The man, and his skank, were nowhere to be found and with the questions of one Detective Muldoon, the pit of my stomach rolled worse than when Paige talked me onto a roller coaster at Six Flags.

The teachers and staff trudged down the hall with excited, whispered tones like the kids did on assembly day. If it weren't for the death of our colleague and the MIA of my ex, I might have laughed at it all. In the auditorium, Holly, Rachel and I took seats in the back. The new gardener, Danny something-or-other, sat one row in front of us and the entire coaching staff sans Colin in front of him. Several uniformed police officers and campus security along with Detective Muldoon watched us all as we situated ourselves.

Phil Bellmore, the head of the athletic department, turned to me. "Where is he?" he mouthed.

I held up my hands in uncertainty and shook my head. It was one thing for Colin not to return my calls. We could go days without talking to one another when we were between Paige visits, but not to talk to Phil, his immediate boss, on a day when he was a no show... Especially when that day held a suspicious death at our school...

Colin would have a lot to answer for when I got a hold of him. It was easier to work on being pissed than to continue to worry at his absence.

I caught Detective Muldoon watching me. Me. No one else. He wasn't scrutinizing any other Peytonville Prep employees but kept his eyes glued in my direction. I had to tear my gaze from him to keep from getting a full-on case of the squirms.

Vice Principal Mark Hardin stood up on the edge of the stage. "People. People. Quiet down, please." The low roar of the room calmed. "As you all have probably heard by now, we've lost one of our own. Principal Chad Jones is no longer with us."

"Interesting choice of words." Rachel nudged my arm and mumbled, "It's not like the man took a job at another school."

"I know that you've all been questioned. The Peytonville Police Department has promised to expedite their investigation as quickly as possible, but in light of the..." He cleared his throat. "In light of the turn of events since their arrival, the board and I feel it is imperative to shut down the school for a week so they have time to complete a thorough investigation. We will resume classes next Tuesday assuming the police have released the offices to us by then."

Out of the corner of my eye, I saw Detective Muldoon give a slight nod to the vice principal then return his gaze back to mine. Not unnerving at all. Nope.

A titter of comments floated through the teachers. No one outwardly cheered. A man had died after all. But several smiles broke through the crowd. Per our new contracts, any unscheduled school closures not precipitated by inclement weather or medical outbreak—I was one of the committee members that helped institute the policy—were a paid-in-full leave. It had been touted as a way to boost morale, without the board of trustees actually having to pay out. I mean really, what were the chances of the school closing that had nothing to do with a flu outbreak or Texas's icy roads?

Vice Principal Hardin fiddled with the podium mic. "Also, I'd like to introduce you to the lead detective, who happens to be a Peytonville Prep alumnus." The vice principal's circumspect smile morphed into wide grin. "Detective Shaw Muldoon has a few things he'd like to address."

Alumnus? Hmm. Did he know Colin? Was that what all the strange looks were about? He could be about the same age. It was so hard to tell with men. A few lines around their eyes gave them character. A few gray hairs added to the sexy allure. But that could put him anywhere between twenty-five and sixty. My own father was completely gray by the time he was thirty, but Levi, at forty-three, could fool most anyone that he was twenty years younger.

I racked my brain trying to remember classmates Colin had spoken of over the years. No one outwardly came to mind. I shook myself from a mental perusal of his yearbook as the detective started to speak.

"The Peytonville Police Department appreciates your patience in our investigation."

Now that I thought there might be some history in his behavior toward me, I paid closer attention to him as he spoke. He had a calm, almost soothing demeanor. His voice was smooth with a deep timbre. I could see how he might cajole a confession out of a criminal.

"As you know, we have questioned the staff here, but if anyone thinks of anything they'd like to share—" his gaze zeroed in on me again "—please don't hesitate to call us. Mr. Hardin has also provided my department with the staff directory and if need be we may be in contact."

It's not a threat. He's just doing his job. Still, I tried not to squirm. I'd done absolutely nothing wrong, but his scrutiny made me want to confess to any and everything just to get his ice-blue gaze to look away.

Danny shifted loudly in his seat and pulled my attention away from the stage. He tugged at his collar. Coach Bellmore adjusted his ball cap and huffed. Rachel pulled out her compact and put on lipstick.

"What are you doing?"

Rachel dabbed her red lips on a tissue. "I want to talk with the hunky detective before I leave."

"Because?"

She shrugged. "He's single."

"And you know this how?"

"I was on the reunion committee. I thought I'd recognized his name, but wasn't sure until Mark said he was an alumnus."

I frowned and glanced up at the detective—at least he was looking at someone else for a change. "He wasn't at the reunion." Colin's twentieth class reunion had been this previous summer. I'd somehow got roped into going with him since Naomi was out of town. I'd been to the fifth and tenth as well. Never once do I remember seeing Detective Muldoon there. He wasn't the kind of man you could miss even in a crowded room.

"He'd declined. But he'd sent in his bio to be included in the program."

"And out of the two hundred plus students from the 1996 graduating class you remember him."

"Don't be silly." She dropped her lipstick back in her purse and hoisted her boobs skyward. "I memorized *all* the single men."

I scoffed. So loud in fact, every eye in the room turned to me. Lips pressed together in a tight smile, I gave a little wave and a nod. "Yes, I'm a moron," I mumbled. "Knock yourself out, hon."

While Rachel kept the "hunky detective" otherwise occupied, I hurried out of the school. I called Colin's cell five or six times on the drive to Levi's house. I could call Colin's mother to see if or when she'd last spoken to him, but honestly, if I didn't have to speak to her yet, all the better. Colin and I might have parted on amicable terms, but his momma held a grudge against anyone who divorced her son. Being that I was the only one to hold that esteemed distinction, she had a lot of undivided energy to focus in my direction.

At Levi's, on the furthermost edge of Peytonville, I let myself into the 1950s ranch-style house. Levi had been flipping homes in Peytonville for close to three years. When he'd bought this home, he'd fallen in love with it immediately and instead of putting it on the market after his remodel, he put his two-bedroom condo in Dallas up for a sizable profit.

He and Paige were sitting at the kitchen table playing Battleship when I walked through the house.

"Hey, kiddo."

Paige glanced up at me, straightened her glasses on her nose and sank Levi's carrier. "What did they determine?"

"They?"

"The school board." She shifted in her seat and settled her hands in her lap. "They're going to close the school down for a few days. Yes?"

"You scare me, hon." I dropped my bag and pulled out another chair at the table. Levi handed me a cup of coffee and set a plate of double-fudge brownies on the table. "You're a life saver." I took a quick sip of the dark-roasted nirvana, then turned to my daughter. "The school is closed until next week." Paige stood and moved over to my side. I draped my arm around her waist and gave her a quick squeeze. "Tuesday, probably."

"I figured as much." She gave a solemn nod. "I had my project ready for Gateway to Technology." She sighed. "Uncle Levi, may I go out back?"

Levi ruffled her hair. "You go right ahead."

When Paige shut the sliding door behind her, Levi folded his hands on top of the table and leaned in. "Spill."

I hugged my hands around the warmth of the coffee mug. "I don't know where to begin."

"The beginning is always my favorite."

"Funny." I rolled my eyes at him. After another sip of the coffee, I gave him a rundown of everything that'd happened since I arrived at school that morning. "I've been calling Colin all day. He hasn't returned any of my calls. The detective wants to speak with him. And Naomi."

"Why?"

"I have no idea. But there was a notepad on the desk with his name on it."

"You don't think..."

"That Colin drove him to it? Not likely. The two were butting heads on only one issue that I know of and as far as I can tell, Chad was winning that argument."

I picked up a brownie and pointed it at him. "We won't know 'til we get ahold of Colin." I took a bite and the let the warm chocolate soothe my frayed nerves. A decadent, mooshy brownie was the best stress reliever. Ever. I plopped the rest in my mouth and snagged another. Once I'd washed it down with a little coffee, I asked, "Can you watch Paige a little longer? I want to run over to Colin's house and see if I can figure out what the hell is going on."

"Not a problem." Levi picked at the edges of his own brownie. "It's weird that he'd be MIA today of all days. You never know, he could have... Are you getting paid during the closure?"

I squinted at Levi. Around a huge bite of brownie I asked, "What?"

He slanted his head toward Paige coming in through the door.

"Um, yes." I swallowed. "We do get paid. Hey, hon, do you have a key to Daddy's house with you?"

"Yes. Why?"

"I want to run over there and..." I wasn't good at lying to my child. The ten-year-old Mensa candidate saw through any attempts to fudge the truth. Still, I didn't want to alarm Paige with speculation—and up to this point it wasn't even *my* speculation. More of an inference from a police detective. And maybe Levi. "I just do. Please?"

"Okay." She dug through her bag next to the table. "But if you get caught snooping—"

"I'm not going to snoop." Exactly.

"—please tell him you stole the key or something." She held the key aloft. "Naomi made Colin promise you would never get your hands on his keys again."

JUST FOR HOSPITALITY'S SAKE, I knocked and rang the bell—eight or nine times. If he was home and I was interrupting something…good. Not wanting me to get my hands on my ex's keys indeed. I could still hear Levi's laughter followed by a hearty, "Oh no she didn't."

Did Naomi think I was going to use the keys for a nefarious purpose? Maybe try to seduce Colin and beg him to take me back? Ha! Sorry, but too many years of frustration to count to do all over again. No, thanks.

Try to convince the man to grow up was more like it. Unless it affected Paige, I had little-to-no comment where Colin Eagan was concerned.

I knocked again. When no irate girlfriend came flouncing to the door, I tucked the key into the lock and let myself in. "Hello?" I shut the door behind me. "Anyone home? Colin?"

The living room looked as it always did when I came over to pick up Paige. Nothing out of place as far as I could tell. The kitchen, same story. Even though Colin had moved into the modest two-bedroom townhome right after our divorce, I'd never seen more than the front two rooms—why would I?

"Colin, it's Celeste. Are you here?" I paused to listen but other than my own breathing, which I have to admit was a little more rapid than normal—it wasn't every day I walked uninvited through my ex's home— I heard not one peep throughout the house.

I took one tentative step into the hallway and about leaped off the floor when my hip vibrated. My cell. I tugged it from my pocket. Levi's home number lit the screen. "'Lo?"

"Are you in?" His deep voice rumbled in my ear. "Anything?"

"The house was locked up tight." Despite being alone in the house, I lowered my voice to just above a whisper. "So far, I can see he picks up after himself better here than he did when he lived with me."

"I told you, you babied him too much. Leave his junk on the floor and it will find its way to the proper places."

"I am so glad I have friends that don't say 'I told you so' over and over and *over*..." I kept going down the hall. First door on the right, bathroom. Empty. Second door, Paige's bedroom. The only homage to her youth was her obsession with Justin Bieber. His posters adorned all four walls here and at our home. Anytime I bought a new poster or trinket with his face plastered on it, I had to be sure and buy two, so she had one for each parent's house. A shirtless visage of him hung from the key in my hand.

"Talk to me, sweets."

"Bathroom and Paige's room are clear." My heart pounded. "Other bedroom." My hand paused over the knob. For Paige's sake I could do this. I could.

"And..."

The cold metal tingled my palm. "Turning." I opened the door and..."Oh my gawd. You have got to be kidding me."

"What? What is it?"

"Mother fu—" I huffed out a disgruntled sigh. "You know that bedroom set I have been eyeing at Pottery Barn for like a year now? He has it." I slapped my hand to my thigh and couldn't take my eyes off the mahogany-stained wood.

"Not the Valencia sleigh bed."

"Yes." Anger clogged my throat. He had the coordinating rich-brown-and-mint-green comforter with matching curtains. He even had little throw pillows for accent. I turned to leave the room and gasped. "And he has the matching dresser *and* armoire." The room looked like it was the page from the catalog.

"Oh, sweets. I'm so sorry."

"'We just sleep there,' he said. 'Who needs to spend that kind of money on someplace you stay with your eyes closed?'" A scream built. For years I tried to talk him into investing in real furniture rather than the pieced-together cheap crap we'd collected. Once he was gone, I couldn't afford to upgrade more than a piece every here and there. It would take years before I had the house the way I'd like to. "I can't believe him."

"Calm down, sweets." Levi broke through my self-pity. "What's that, Paige?" My daughter's answer was muffled. "Um, Paige says Naomi urged him to buy it."

"Absolutely freaking figures, doesn't it? Tell me again why I married him?"

"Stupidity?" Levi chuckled but stopped abruptly. "Focus."

The police were looking for Colin, and his damn girlfriend, to question them about God knows what to do with Chad's death and I was pissed about furniture. I ran my hand down the cool wooden dresser. It was beautiful furniture.

"Celeste?"

"I'm here. I need to check his bathroom." Between my little outburst and the conversation with Levi, if anyone was in the house, they'd surely know I was there, now, too. No point in stealth or being quiet. "Bathroom, empty. Closet, empty. What now?"

"Garage?"

"Good idea." The carpet muted my steps back through the house. Just for gripe's sake, I knocked a stack of newspapers off the coffee table and onto the floor. And maybe a magazine or two. "Oops."

"What did you do?"

"Nothing. Why would you think I did something? Shame on you." The garage was off the kitchen, two closets and the laundry room narrowing down the last door being the garage. Colin's truck sat inside. I walked around the Chevy and saw no sign of the owner. "His truck's here. Hood's cool."

"So he hasn't driven it in the last few hours. That doesn't tell us much."

"I could push the OnStar button and see if they logged his GPS whereabouts."

"You'd do that?"

I twisted up my mouth in disgust, not that Levi could see me, but the sentiment was just the same. "Like hell. They might tell him *I was here*." I ran my fingers through my hair and retraced my steps. "I'm at a loss. Him being a no-show for work is weird enough. But it looks like he just fell off the face of the earth."

It was time to bite the bullet and call his mom. I could have Paige do it. She has a decent relationship with her grandmother. At the very least the woman didn't loathe her as she does me.

"I'm going to have to call Big Bertha." Her name was really Babette, but that name was far too genial for the woman who never approved of me. So I hit her son with a car and he fell maddeningly in love with me.

Then I divorced him. Was that a reason to hold a steady grudge for nearly fifteen years?

I glanced at Colin's house phone across the room. Big Bertha was more likely to answer if the caller ID came from his number rather than mine. It was amazing how often she wasn't at home when I called for Paige.

As I passed the front door headed for the phone, a heavy knock resounded. I sucked in a deep breath and froze in place. "Someone's at the door. What do I do?"

"Answer it."

"Yeah, no. I'm not supposed to be here, remember?"

"You have a key. It's not like you shimmied down the chimney or something."

The visitor knocked again.

On my tiptoes, I peered out the peephole. "Crap. Stay on the line, Levi." I dropped my phone to my side and opened the door. "Detective Muldoon. What brings you here?"

THREE

THE DETECTIVE LOOKED down at the notebook in his hand, to the number on the door, the notebook again then at me. "Mrs. Eagan?"

"Hiya. How are you doing?" If it sounded overbright and false to him, he didn't show it. He never showed much emotion at all.

He removed his sunglasses and hooked them on the front of his white button-down shirt. "What are you doing here? Is Colin here?"

"Nope." I rocked back on my heels and tilted my head up to look at him. The man was taller than I remembered. Then again pretty much everyone was taller than me. I came up to maybe his chin, if I had my heels on. "Just me."

"Does he often let you hang out at his house?"

"I, uh…" I bit my lower lip. "I have a key." Shirtless Justin hung off my forefinger.

Muldoon's dark eyebrows rose up. "I took you more for a Liam Hemsworth gal."

I don't know what shocked me more, that he knew who Justin and Liam were or that he would joke about it. "Funny." I pasted on a smile. "Were you needing something, Detective?"

"To speak with Colin Eagan."

"He's not here."

He tucked the little notebook in the pocket of his

sports coat. "You'll have to understand if I don't take your word for it."

"Come on in and see for yourself." I stepped aside and let him enter the house. I really wasn't sure of protocol when you invited a policeman into your ex's home. Should I offer him coffee—assuming Colin has any in his cupboards—and give him the grand tour? Did I keep my lips sealed and trail behind him just to observe? Play coy and hop from door to door like Bugs Bunny, saying, "No, officer, he isn't in this closet." Which I supposed only worked had I truly been hiding someone. Still, I didn't know what to do.

After much debate, I hung back as Muldoon went from room to room. He finally came back to the living room and shoved his hands on his hips and stared at the mess on the floor.

"I did that." I shrugged when he turned and looked at me. "Tripped."

"Tell me where he is." He took a step toward me.

"You don't mince words, do you?"

"Not when I'm on duty."

My throat suddenly dried. "I don't know."

He took in a long, deep breath. "You and Cooter." The frown faded from the corners of his mouth.

"What? Who?" I shook my head.

"Cooter Eagan. That was Colin's nickname when we were in high school."

Laughter built. "Why Cooter?"

"He got a lot of…" Muldoon's frown zipped back and his gaze dropped to his feet.

"Tail? You can say it. The man likes women. Doesn't hurt my feelings." At least not anymore. "Some things don't change, I guess." Colin'd never overtly cheated on me, but I'd had suspicions once or twice while we were married. Coupled with the number of women that I knew of since the divorce, it was a fitting nickname. "You never did say why you're here."

"Cooter, um, Colin, is a person of interest in my investigation."

That was cop-speak for a suspect that they didn't have a hold of yet. I watched *Law & Order* and all that. "You can't possibly think he had something do with Chad's death."

"Just a person of interest."

I crossed my arms and did my best stare-down-while-craning-my-neck-back intimidation stare. Yeah, he looked oh so scared. Still, I was a little emboldened. I had snuck into Colin's townhome after all. I was, maybe not successfully, staring down a seasoned police detective. I might as well go for broke. I voiced my concerned opinion—as my daughter's father, the last thing I wanted was for him to be messed up in a suspicious death investigation. "Which essentially means you consider him a suspect."

"It means we need to speak with him." He mimicked my pose, turned up the badass cop routine—and was winning. "Why are you here, Mrs. Eagan? Celeste."

I will not admit what hearing him say my name did to my insides. I had to be three kinds a fool, and too long since a decent date, for him to elicit goose bumps up and down my arms. I tightened my stance to ward off any shivers that might try to break loose.

With the open phone still in my hand, I could hear Levi asking question after question. I'd completely forgotten about him. "I'll call you back." I hung up on Levi and dialed Colin's number. "I need to speak with him, too. About our daughter."

ESPN's *Sports Center* theme echoed through the house. "Weird."

I ended the call and the ditty stopped. I retried Colin's number and again I heard the light music wafting from the kitchen. As I took a step in the direction of the kitchen, Detective Muldoon grabbed my elbow and held me in place. I'd like to say I didn't feel the little spark of electricity. I'd also like to say I listened when he said, "I'll go first."

But I didn't.

I pulled my elbow free and race-walked ahead of him. Under an ad for a local sporting-goods store, Colin's cell phone sat ringing.

Muldoon snatched it up off the counter.

"Hey." I grabbed for it, but the man was fast. "Give me that."

He completely ignored me, of course, and pulled out a plastic bag. He dropped the phone into it and tucked it into his pocket.

"Don't you need a warrant for that?"

"Not when I'm granted access." He took a deep breath. "You let me in. Remember?"

"I don't have any right to give you access to this house."

"You're inside."

"But I shouldn't be. Colin didn't give *me* permission." Oops. Only after that slipped out did it strike me what I'd just admitted. "That means the phone is fruit from the poisoned vine or something? You can't take it." I grabbed for the edge of the plastic bag sticking out of his pocket but missed as he turned away from me. "Give it back." I shoved at the detective's beefy biceps. Too late I realized I'd gone too far. Maybe it was when the frown pulled down those luscious lips—Rachel was right, the man was decidedly hot—or maybe it was when he pinned me up against the wall, frisked and cuffed me.

"Mrs. Eagan?" A young woman in a dark blue Peytonville police uniform spoke to me through the cell bars.

"Yes?"

Keys jangled as she unlocked the door. "Follow me, please."

We walked the short hall from the holding cells to a desk. She motioned for me to sit. Who was I to argue? I sat. Folding my hands in my lap, I tried to look as dejected as possible. It wasn't really a far stretch. I'd never once been handcuffed, fingerprinted and locked away in a jail cell. I was already going stir-crazy. Even if it'd only been about an hour since I was thrown into the pokey.

A couple of minutes later Detective Muldoon entered the room and took the chair across the desk from me. "I still haven't been able to contact Colin Eagan, so I have no one to press unlawful entry charges against you."

"I told you I don't know where—"

His sharp gaze cut off my retort. "I'm going to drop the assault charges I could file against you and let you go with a warning." He eyed me for a long moment then handed me a little brown bag with my belongings. "If you do hear from your ex, please let me know." He again handed me his card. "I'll have an officer drive you back to your car."

Not trusting what might or might not come out of my mouth, I simply nodded and stood. I'd held myself together pretty well at the police station and then in the squad car back to my car still at Colin's house. But halfway home, I had to pull off to the side of the road when my hands shook too hard to keep driving. Ten minutes was all I allowed myself, then I sucked it up, took a deep breath and continued home. I'd already called Levi and he'd driven Paige back to the house and promised to have dinner waiting.

"I'm home." The door separating the garage and kitchen shoved back at me. "What are you—"

"Don't come in here," Levi shouted. "Paige got a wee bit hurt."

My heart beat hard against my ribs. "What's going on?"

Levi might be a lot of things, but stronger than me where my daughter's concerned, not even close. I shoved at the door with my shoulder and pushed through. "Paige?"

I stumbled over my feet but righted myself quickly. Paige sat on the butcher block in the middle of the kitchen with Levi rapidly wrapping her hand. A dark red stain blossomed from her palm.

"Oh, Lord have mercy." I swayed on my feet. I might have failed to mention my extreme aversion to the sight of bloo...

"CELESTE. SWEETS. Wake up, hon."

I tried to shake the woolliness from my head. "Stop slapping me." My cheek burned. I swatted away my friend's hands. I was prone and a little uncomfortable. My eyes fluttered open, but didn't focus on anything in particular.

Levi hooked me under the arms and sat me up. It was none too ladylike, let me tell you. But that was what best friends were for, right? To help you in your most unladylike moments.

"How'd I get on the floor?" I looked from my friend to my daughter and back.

"Mom?" Paige squatted in front of me, her right hand bandaged.

"You called me *Mom*. That's twice in one day." I smiled and ran my hand over my precious child's head. She rolled her eyes and stood.

I zeroed in on her bandage. "What happened, sweet pea?"

"She dropped a glass in the sink and grabbed at it before I could stop her. She's fine. It wasn't too deep. Just bled like hell." Levi grabbed my elbow. "Can you stand on your own?"

"Yes." Despite my affirmation, he helped me back to my feet. "Sorry, guys." It had been a long time since the sight of blood undid me, but seeing my child bleed, yeah, there wasn't enough therapy in the world apparently to help that reaction. "Are you okay, hon, really?"

"I'm fine." Paige tilted her head back and looked down her nose and through her glasses at me. "I asked you not to get caught."

"By Daddy. And I didn't." I snagged her ear and looked inside.

"What are you doing?"

"Looking for the manufacture's date in here, because I know you can't possibly be ten years old."

She giggled. "We made dinner. You hungry?"

"Famished. Doing hard time can take its toll."

"You were in there for one hour," Levi said as I set the table.

"That's an hour longer than you've ever been in jail." We all took our seats and Levi filled our plates with his famous beef stroganoff. My tummy was still a little squooshy after my faint, but hunger outweighed queasy.

"I don't get it. His truck is there. His phone is there. But the man himself is just gone. Poof."

"Did you check his luggage?" Paige twirled her fork through the noodles.

"He has luggage?"

Paige nodded. "He and Naomi bought a matching set a couple of months ago."

The little pang of jealousy had no business niggling at me. We were divorced for good reason. If he'd managed to pick up and start over, bully for him. Me, I didn't want the man back, but I hadn't made the same leap back into the dating world yet.

"I didn't even notice it. But I wasn't really looking for it either."

"What did the detective find?" Levi picked up his glass of wine and held my gaze over the rim as he took a drink.

I shrugged. "Dunno. He took Colin's cell phone. And called him a 'person of interest.'"

Paige's head shot up. "As in, Colin is somehow responsible for Principal Jones's death? Puh-leeze. What's his motivation? He's got none."

"Calm down. *We* know your dad didn't have anything to do with it. But it does look weird with him and Naomi gone. I'm sure he has a logical, not-guilty-at-all reason for missing school and cutting out like he did."

"You could sweet-talk that detective and see if he might give you some info they haven't released to the media yet." Levi waggled his eyebrows.

"And risk further incarceration? Yeah. No, thank you." I plopped a small cube of beef into my mouth and mulled over the options I had. I still hadn't called Colin's mom. And that was all I could think of. "I got nothing."

We all ate in silence, all lost to our own thoughts. Levi snapped his fingers. "I just remembered. You got two interesting phone calls today." He held my gaze.

The look—that you've-been-holding-out-on-me stare—combined with the prolonged silence didn't bode well.

"Are you going to tell me who called?" I pushed a noodle around on my plate.

"Annabelle called."

Annabelle Paulk was the owner of the Peytonville Playhouse. My stalling was quickly coming to an end. She'd called me twice this week already to hire me on as a full-time actor and, as of the last call, she'd sweetened the pot to include a theater co-manager position. A friend of a friend of hers and I were in summer stock together years ago. They'd given me high praise so over the years Annabelle had hired me for minor roles, as much as time would allow with my teaching schedule.

When the co-manager position became available, I was the first person she'd asked.

That meant quitting my teaching position. My comfort zone. I really wanted the job, but it was a scary proposition to give up a career where I'd spent a decade and a half.

Levi knew I was going to take the job, or so he kept saying. But I'd been dragging my heels on actually doing it. I needed to talk to Colin about it, but really what could he say. For me not to take my dream job? He knew I'd been an aspiring actress when I met him. At the time, the jobs weren't coming so I settled.

It ended up being a good settled as I did enjoy teaching. But it was time to move on to something I loved more.

Levi lowered his voice. "Annabelle said she needs an answer by the fifteenth. She needs to audition someone else if you say no. Which would be a huge waste of your talent, if you ask me."

"Which I haven't." I gathered up the plates from the table and took them to the sink.

"You need to shit or get off the pot. The potential for this—"

"I know. It's a great opportunity. As you've mentioned forty bajillion times." I took a deep breath. "The other call?"

"Your mother."

Paige and I rolled our eyes simultaneously. "And?"

"Just wanted to say hi and remind you that you *do* have a mother and her phone is working just fine, *thankyouverymuch*. But you wouldn't know it since her one and only child never calls. And…" Levi leaned against the kitchen counter as I stored the leftovers in a plastic bowl and shoved it into the fridge.

"And what? That sounds a little ominous. Is she okay? Did something happen with Daddy?" I might not want to move back to the same state as the woman, but I sure didn't want anything to happen to her or my father.

"Nothing like that." He frowned. "*And*…she was curious when she was going to meet this new beau of yours."

My new beau? My mind immediately shot to the handsome detective. He could hardly be classified as my beau. I barely knew the man. Not to mention the fact there was no way my mother could have an inkling of his existence. "She said that?" I gaped at my friend like a fish out of water, mouth opening and shutting, no more words more coming out.

Levi shrugged. "Her words exactly." He topped off his wineglass. "I have to say, I was a little peeved I hadn't met this new mystery man. But I figured you'd bring him around when you were ready."

"Shut up. You know I haven't dated anyone." I shook my head and mimicked his stance against the counter and snatched up my own wineglass. "Where in the world would my mother get it in her head I had a *beau*? New or old."

Paige coughed and set down the cookie she was about to shove in her mouth. She pushed back in her chair and stood without so much as "Good meal, Uncle Levi." Very uncharacteristic for the manners-prone child. She backed out of the kitchen.

"Hold it, missy." I set down my glass and shoved my hands on my hips. I narrowed my gaze at the spitting image of me. "You spoke with Grammy the other day."

Paige swallowed heavily. "I did."

"What exactly did you say that gave her the idea I had a new beau?"

"Exactly?" She looked down at her shoes. To Levi and then to me. "The words I used might have been 'Mom's new boyfriend is really great.'"

Levi snorted.

I swatted at my friend and stepped a little closer to my daughter. "Why?"

She waved her hands up in the air and huffed. "She was going on and on again about your cousin Lucy and how great her husband was. How he'd bought her a new car and blah, blah, blah. And how she just can't understand why you can't find a man."

"I'm not looking for one."

"I know that. And you know that. But Grammy can't fathom it."

Fathom? If I hadn't given birth to Paige I might wonder that someone had switched a fully formed adult with a child when no one was looking. "Hon, don't worry about what your grandmother thinks. She also thinks

Elvis is still alive and well and hiding out on the other side of Topeka until the time is right for a big comeback." I held my arms open and only had to wait about fifteen nanoseconds before she ran into my embrace. "Now finish your cookie. I think Uncle Levi was trying to sneak a bite."

The man snatched his hand away from the table. "Nuh-uh."

"You were." I waggled my finger at him.

"Whatever. Hey, why don't I give my guys the next few days off and we drive down to Galveston. For a mini-vacation." Levi tucked his hands into his pockets. "Paige hasn't been there in ages, right, honey?"

"In November?" Paige nibbled on the edge of the cookie. "It's too cold."

Levi chuckled. "Nonsense. Brisk. Invigorating. And you don't have to get in the water. The idea is to go and relax."

"I don't know." I scooped my bag up off the floor, looking for my grade book. "Until I know what's going on with Colin, I hate to run off. Plus, I can get caught up on all my grading. The kids had a major-grade project due last Friday and I haven't got through more than four of them."

"Party poopers."

"Dang it all. It's not here."

"What's that, sweets?"

"My grade book. Can you stay here for thirty more minutes so I can run up to the school to get it?"

"You betcha. Paige and I can watch *The Voice*."

IT WAS DARK by the time I made my way to Peytonville Preparatory Academy. I'd even had to put my sweater back on to ward off the evening chill. It did little however to combat the goose bumps on my arms from my nerves as I walked up to the school. At the far end of the campus, I swiped my cardkey to get in. That door was the closest to my office, and honestly, I had next to no desire to go near the other end of the building where the administrative offices were still cordoned off. I'd worked hard to get those images out of my head. The last thing I wanted to see was the crime scene tape again...

Clip-clop, clip-clop.

I'd been in the school many times after hours, but as the heels of my flats smacked on the wooden floor and echoed through the empty halls, I couldn't stop the shiver that ran down my spine. So what if I ran just a little bit the last few yards to the office for the fine arts department. On my desk sat the grade book. I snapped it up, tucked it under my arm and headed back out the door.

Clip-clop, clip-clop-bump.

What?

I turned to see what had made the extra sound. The shadowed hall didn't reveal anything but my own cowardly self. Not one to sit around and wait to spook myself half-silly, however, I hightailed back out of the school. The door snicked shut behind me, but before I could turn to the parking lot I ran smack-dab into a warm mooshy wall.

"Holy hell." I jumped back and, in tripping over my own feet, fell into a heap on the well-manicured grass along the sidewalk.

"Mrs. Eagan? Are you okay?"

I fought off the instant urge to scream as a gloved hand wrapped around my upper arm and hoisted me to my feet. The only thing that kept me from not cutting loose with the shrill defense mechanism was the fact the man knew my name and helped me up—what would be the point of doing that if he intended to hurt me. I might have been reaching, but the whole thing caught me off guard and there was a tingle of recognition from his voice, not that I could see him well. The man stood under the safety light that hung above the door, illuminating him from behind and half-shading his young face.

"Danny?" I gaped at the gardener when I finally recognized him. "What're you doing here?"

"Trying to catch up on work." He waved a wrench in his other hand. "I had a list a mile long to take care of before school got closed. What are you doing here?"

"I have a list a mile long of papers to go through." I copied his words and waved the grade book in my hand. Not one to overstay my welcome, and frankly a little creeped out by literally running into someone at school, it was time for me to leave. "Um, good night, now."

As I backed away, he stared at me a little longer than need be. I'd like to think my crown of copper-red hair glowing under the fluorescent safety lighting and my figure shrouded in shadow and mystery was cause for his perusal—vanity picked a weird time to rear its head—but seeing how we'd run into each other at least once a day since the school year began and he'd never once given me a second glance in daylight… I didn't want to know what had changed.

Finally, Danny nodded and walked around the back side of the building. That was my cue to hustle my butt to the car. I pushed the key fob to unlock my car door when I noticed lights on in the administrative part of the school. Stranger still was the dark form that passed in front of the window.

I snagged the cell from my pocket. I should call 911, but what if Danny was working on something?

"Only if he's Superman and could fly around the building that fast." It could be the police, investigating. And I would just be getting in the way. But what if some yahoo broke in hoping to snag a few hundred dollars' worth of equipment while folks were otherwise distracted?

I moved closer to the school, wanted to peek in the windows and see who it might be, when the light doused. I stopped cold in my tracks and waited. And waited.

I typed in 911 to my cell phone. I had my finger poised over the send button, torn between staying to see who emerged and getting in my car and skedaddling. Skedaddling would have been the smart thing, of course, but my momma always said I was too curious for my own good.

Finally, Kelsey Pierce came flouncing out of the building as casual as you please. She had her blond hair uncharacteristically pulled back in a ponytail and was dressed head-to-toe in form-fitting black with a large bag tossed over her shoulder. Given the peculiarity of her late-night visit, I would almost call it a burglar getup if it weren't bejeweled with hundreds of rhinestones and dangling gems. Coupled with her usual platform heels, she looked like she was headed out to a club rather than sneaking around the school after hours. Not odd at all. Nope.

"Kelsey?"

"Christ almighty." She shifted the big handbag on her shoulder and grasped her chest. "Celeste, what are you doing here?"

I lifted the black book from under my arm. "Grade book. You?"

"I, uh…" She glanced back over her shoulder. "I needed to get a few things from my desk. I was a little out of it when I left this afternoon."

"Yeah." I reached out and gave her a quick pat on the arm. "How're you holding up?"

There was much speculation as to what exact kind of dictation the bottle blonde took for the man over the past two years as every one of her memos had a minimum of three typos. In the first paragraph.

Kelsey sniffed. "I'm okay." Her voice wavered and belied her words. "Wasn't it just so awful?" She flung herself into my arms and cried. And cried. And cried.

I patted her shoulder. "There, there." So much for blocking out the images of Chad in his office. In all my years—other than on TV of course—I'd never once seen a dead body. At my grandparents' funerals, I held back *just* far enough not to see inside the caskets—I'd like to remember them the way they were *thankyouverymuch*. And I'd thankfully never had any cause to come across one elsewhere. Until this morning.

Kelsey continued to cry and I was at a loss as to what else to do. Consoling a grieving coworker wasn't something they covered in the teachers' manual.

At close to nine o'clock at night, we stood in the middle of a vacant lot. Only my little Nissan graced the area. While the neighborhood was fairly safe, I couldn't stay there all night.

"How did you get here? Do you need a ride home?"

As if in answer to me, a car came to a screeching halt a few feet away. Kelsey sniffed and swiped at her eyes. "Nope. Thanks. See ya." Gone was the inconsolable admin. Kelsey climbed into the dark muscle car and gave me a quick finger wave as it sped away as fast as it had pulled in.

"All righty then." I shut off my phone and walked back over to my car. A shiver once again danced its way down my spine as I tucked my cell in my pocket. "Nope, not strange at all. And no need to contact the police."

FOUR

I JERKED UPRIGHT in bed at the pounding on my front door. "What the…"

Paige came into my room, rubbing her eyes. "What's going on?"

"I don't know, hon." I glanced at the clock. It was barely six in the morning—on a day when I didn't have to be at school. Someone better have a damn good reason to wake me. "Go back to bed."

My daughter grumbled and followed me down the hall to the front door. I pulled the curtain aside. The sun had yet to rise but under the corner streetlamp I could see a beige sedan at the curb. At the door, all I could make out was a large form. Very large. A tingle of recognition skittered through me.

I groaned and pulled open the door. "To what do I owe the remarkably early honor this morning?"

Detective Muldoon blinked rapidly after I flipped on the porch light. His gaze traveled from my bare toes up to my pink polka-dotted nightie. I was completely covered, but still the man swallowed like I'd flashed him or something. I shifted to hide my saggy boobs behind the door. In a bra they looked great, but in my nightie they were droop city, the drawback of a full figure and no silicone. Things went where they wanted, not where you paid to have them sit on display.

He shifted. "I didn't mean to startle y'all."

"Uh-huh." I glanced sideways at him. Who was he

trying to kid? "Pounding on my door at the crack of dawn might make it hard to believe."

"Who are you?" Paige squinted.

I sighed. "The detective in charge of Principal Jones's death investigation. Why don't you go grab your glasses and head to the kitchen? I'll get breakfast on as soon as I finish speaking with him. Okay?"

Paige narrowed her eyes more for a moment then turned and headed back down the hall.

"Your daughter?"

"Family pet. Cute little booger, huh?" I gripped the edge of the door harder. "Came around one morning begging for food and I decided to keep her."

The corner of his mouth quivered, didn't so much move up in a smile as it hinted it could. Did the man ever smile? For a moment, I wondered what it would take for him to tip up his lips. What could make the hard detective break his even harder demeanor and relax?

Whether he did or not though was really no concern of mine. Especially when he showed up on my front porch before the sun did. "Are you going to cite me for not having her city tags up to date?" I motioned in the direction Paige went.

"Are you always so chipper in the morning?" His dark eyebrows arched upward.

"Did you *need* something, Detective?"

He pulled out his ever-present notebook. "I'm wondering where you were between eight forty-five and nine fifteen last night."

"I, uh. School." I bit my lower lip. "But I'm guessing you must know that already or you wouldn't be here. Did something happen?"

"What were you doing there?" There he goes answering a question with a question. Did they learn that in detective school? He did it an awful lot.

"I forgot my grade book."

A little yappy dog walked by on a leash. My neighbor slowed down and didn't even try to be discreet as she stared at me, in my nightie, and the detective all sharp-dressed. "If I invite you in, will you promise not to go rummaging through my stuff like you did at Colin's yesterday?"

"If you don't give consent, then no, I can't search."

"No consent. No searching." I stood away from the door and held it open for him. "Come in, have a seat and I'll make some coffee."

"No need."

I scrubbed my hand through my hair. "You may not need it, but I certainly do."

Detective Muldoon nodded and I showed him to the living room.

In the kitchen, I pulled some frozen pancakes out, heated them up for Paige, then started a pot of coffee. The microwave dinged as she came in dressed in a light blue terrycloth robe and matching slippers. "Sit, eat," I told her when I set her plate and the bottle of syrup on the table. "Detective Muldoon is in the living room. I'm gonna go change clothes real quick."

I peeked my head around the corner. Muldoon was sitting on my sofa, his elbows on his knees, hands clasped in front of him. He looked over at me, his lip quivering again. "Not touching a thing."

"Good boy. I'm going to get dressed. Won't be but a moment, I swear." I ran to my room and threw on a pair of jeans and a pink T-shirt—so what if I put on my best Victoria's Secret bra underneath? It made me feel bolder, as well as supported, and the detective was none the wiser.

Muldoon was in the same spot on the sofa where I'd left him. "Coffee?"

"Sure. Black, please."

"Coming right up." Coffee I could handle. I doctored mine up with a touch of sugar and a seriously generous helping of pumpkin spice flavored creamer. Before I could face the detective and his questions, I drank half of it down right there at the kitchen counter, then re-filled my cup and redoctored the concoction. "Paige, hon, did you get enough to eat?"

"Yes. May I go in there while you speak with the detective? I've seen it on TV but never in real life be-fore." She blinked up at me all sweet and innocently.

I took one more fortifying sip. "Seen what?"

"An interrogation." Paige said it so earnestly I nearly spit pumpkin spice coffee all over her.

"It's not an interrogation." At least I hoped it wasn't in any official capacity. "He just has a few questions to ask."

Again, she blinked her khaki eyes up at me. "The difference being?"

"The difference being, I'd prefer that I don't have little ears sitting in on it." I wiggled one of her ears before I tapped the tip of her nose. "There's no telling what he wants to discuss."

She sighed. "Okay."

Once in the living room, I handed Detective Mul-doon the full mug. "Here." He stared down into the mug for a long moment.

"Oh, for heaven's sake, I didn't poison it." I snatched it back and took a sip. A very hot sip. "Ow."

"Yeah, kinda why I was waiting."

"Mmm-hmm." I sat in the chair across the room, the sofa a little too close quarters to share with the man. I sipped my own drink, way less hot, and waited for him to start. When he didn't, I said, "We've established I was at school. How would you know I was there?"

"The cardkey log."

I frowned. "Why would you check the cardkey log?"

"Someone broke into the school last night and ransacked the principal's office."

I paused with the cup against my lower lip. "Wha…" I set the mug on the table. "You can't think I'd… I didn't… What?" I asked when his eyebrows pulled down lower and lower into a tight V.

"What were you doing there?"

"I told you. I went to get my grade book." I picked up the offender smack-dab in the middle of my coffee table and waved it at him. "Since we're home for a few days I thought I could get caught up with my students' projects, but I left this on my desk. I went in, grabbed it and left. I certainly didn't ransack the front offices." I settled my head back on the chair. "You don't *really* think I had anything to do with it, do you?"

"You were there." He took a tentative sip of his coffee.

"I wasn't even near that end of the building." I narrowed my gaze at him. "Besides, I was hardly the only person up at the school last night."

One dark eyebrow rose. "You were the only one who logged in using a cardkey."

"That's impossible. I saw Kelsey up there."

"The administrative assistant? Inside the offices?"

"Well, no, not exactly. I saw the light on in the main admin office. *Someone* was inside. When the lights went out a few minutes later, Kelsey walked away from the building."

"Did you see her leave through a specific door?"

"No." I sat forward and leaned my elbows on my knees and mimicked his stance. It was quick, but I'd swear I saw the good detective dart his gaze down my shirt, checking out my prettiest secret before his eyes met mine.

He shook his head and sat up straighter. "Go over exactly what you did when you got to the school. Please."

"I pulled into the lot." I ticked off the items on my fingers. "Went into the building."

"Hang on." He set his mug down and pulled out his little bitty notebook. "By which door?"

"The northeast entrance right over by my classroom and office."

Muldoon wrote something. "Go on."

"I ran down the hall." Finger tick three.

He glanced up at me. "Why?"

I shrugged. "It's a little spooky being in there late at night all by myself considering…" I picked up my coffee and took a long sip. "I unlocked my door." Tick number four.

"With the cardkey?"

"No, a key key. Only the school entrances have the electronic locks. I snagged my grade book." I waggled my thumb at him. "That's it. Well, then I ran back out of the school. Through the same door." I gave him a long look. "I'd have to be pretty stupid to use my cardkey to gain access, then rob the place, don't you think?"

"People do any number of things for any number of reasons," he said off-handedly as he looked down at his notes.

Another non-answer.

"But no, you don't look that dumb." He raised his gaze back to mine.

"Thanks. I think." I leaned back in my chair. "I should mention I did run—quite literally—into the gardener."

Muldoon tapped the end of his pen on the notepad. "Does he have access to the inside of the school?"

"I don't know. There's a separate building out back that serves as his office. I don't know what his card-key can get into. Sorry. You could ask—" I started to say *Principal Jones*. Maybe for the first time, it really hit me that the man was dead. It was almost surreal to lose a peer I saw nearly every day.

A sudden chill raced over me. I wrapped my arms around myself, then frowned. I rubbed my hand where Danny had grabbed my arm. "He left a huge grease stain."

"Who did?" Muldoon frowned and gave a quick headshake. "What?"

"Danny. Left a stain on my pink sweater."

"You wear a lot of pink."

My cheeks heated. He'd noticed that? Growing up with auburn hair and hazel eyes, my mother dressed me in all neutrals. Said I clashed otherwise. I always felt a little drab. My answer to that when I got old enough to buy my own clothes was a pop—or more often an explosion—of color. As of late, pink was my go-to pop. And the detective noticed.

Before I could comment—and really, what was I going to say, *aw geez, it's so sweet you noticed*?—he shook his head and asked, "May I see it? The stain."

"On my sweater?" Duh. I gave myself a quick mental slap and stood. "Sure." I ran back to my room and grabbed it off the back of the chair. I'd planned to take it to the cleaners to see if they could get the stain out. It's my favorite sweater. When I came back, I started to give it to him but pulled back quickly. "Is it because you don't believe what I'm telling you?"

His outstretched hand still hung there. "Why would you think that?"

"Oh, I don't know. The skeptical look on your face that pulls your eyebrows down. Or the way you keep staring at me and then jotting down quick notes in your little notebook. Or maybe the fact that you arrested me for no reason yesterday. Take your pick."

"I had reason to arrest you."

I harrumphed and shoved my sweater at him. He looked it over, took a couple of notes, looked it over again, took more notes, then set it on the coffee table. "Was the grease on both his hands?"

"I don't know. The other was holding something so it could have been. I didn't stop to ask him. Unless you own a dry cleaner on the side, I don't see why you care about it."

I was getting snippy. I couldn't help it.

"Can we get on with this?" I resituated myself in the fat club chair. I started ticking off points with the other hand. "I fell. He helped me up. As I was walking to my car, I saw a light on in the admin part of the building. I got closer and I could see someone walking around." I finished my tale with Kelsey's weepy behavior and the awesome car that picked her up. "Do you believe me? That I had nothing to do with the break-in up at school?"

He ignored my questions, used up a few more pages and tucked the notebook back into his pocket. When he finally met my gaze again, he only held it for a moment more, then stood and started studying the pictures that lined the fireplace mantel. "How did you and Cooter, um, I mean Colin, get together?"

I stood and joined him on the other side of the room. "I ran him over with my car."

He chuckled. His face was hidden, so I missed any smile that might have accompanied it. Dang it.

"I really did hit him." I edged closer, but when he turned, the same flat expressed covered his face.

Oh well.

"Seriously." I nodded when he looked at me in disbelief. "It was an accident. I swear, Officer." I crossed my arms up under my breasts. I didn't *mean* to shove them up—at least not much.

He swallowed all nervous-like just as he had when I'd answered the door earlier. He opened his mouth to speak when the doorbell rang.

"I'm not usually this popular so early in the morning. Excuse me." I didn't even bother to look through the window. I mean, I had a detective standing in my living room. As soon as I unlocked it, the door swung open and Colin waltzed right on in.

"Colin? Where have you been?"

"You will not believe the last couple days we've had."

The first thing that went through my mind was the use of *we*, then Naomi flounced in behind him and gave me a quick I-don't-want-to-be-here-any-more-than-you-want-me-here smile. Her long, light brown hair was the most unkempt I'd ever seen it, pulled up in a messy yet stylish ponytail. She was dressed for anything from a day at school to a luncheon with girlfriends, making a pair of black stretch pants and a shiny tunic look alluring. Did I mention how much I hate her?

The second thing that occurred to me was Colin was considered a person of interest by the aforementioned detective in my aforementioned living room not twenty feet away. I hadn't so much as blinked when Muldoon pushed past me.

"Colin Eagan, you're under arrest for the murder of Chad Jones."

"Murder?" I gaped at Muldoon. "I thought it was a suicide?" And he thought Colin did it. "You're way off base. I promise you." I tried to reason with Muldoon, but he wasn't listening to me.

He grabbed Colin by the wrist and had him flipped around, face pressed against the wall before Colin could react. Naomi was not so subdued. She smacked Muldoon on the back of the head with her überexpensive coordinating handbag.

"Back off, Conan. Colin didn't do anything."

Muldoon slapped a pair of shiny silver cuffs—a feeling I wouldn't want to repeat, let me tell you—on Colin and turned to grab Naomi, who was winding up to swing again. "Miss Michaels, I presume." I nodded confirmation. "That's assaulting an officer." He snapped a matching pair of cuffs on Naomi, then whipped out his cell phone and called for assistance.

"Celeste? What in the hell is going on?" Colin frowned and toggled his gaze between me and Muldoon. He gave quick sneer, then scrunched up his face. "Shaw? Shaw Muldoon? Is this some kind of joke?"

Paige came running at the commotion. "You can't arrest him."

I grabbed my daughter and hugged her to me. The last thing she needed to see was her dad in handcuffs. "Colin, don't say another word. I'll call the lawyer and have him meet you at the station."

Colin looked me square in the eye. "What did he mean by Chad Jones's murder? He's dead?"

I didn't know how much I could, or should, say. I didn't want to get Colin in trouble by my words. I looked at Muldoon for any kind of go-ahead. His skeptical frown came back, however, and slammed across his face. He was watching us both to see what we knew and what we told each other, either through body language or out-and-out words.

I really needed to lay off all the cop shows on TV as my mind raced with all the thugs incriminating themselves with one little word or two.

"Do not speak, Colin." I bent and whispered reassurance in Paige's ear and asked her to run back to her room. Thankfully she minded with no argument.

Once Paige rounded the corner, I turned to the other woman in the room. "Naomi, calm down."

She'd fallen into a heap on my foyer floor and was blubbering loudly. Mascara streaked down her pale cheeks.

"Naomi, who's your lawyer? I'll call for you, too."

"Same as Coll's."

Coll? Between that and seeing my ex arrested in my home, it was a wonder I didn't whack her upside the head. But then Muldoon would have to arrest me too and I didn't want a repeat of that.

Naomi's caterwauling drowned out any conversation as the red-and-blue lights lit up the foyer.

"Where are you taking him?" Outside I tried to keep pace beside Muldoon as he dragged Colin down the sidewalk to the awaiting officers. "Same station you hauled me off to yesterday?" I didn't even try to hide the bitterness in my voice.

"Yes."

"You were arrested?" Colin paused as they were

shoving him into the back of a black-and-white squad car. "What did you get us into?"

"WHAT DID *I* DO? I didn't do jack, you odious jerk."

"Shh." Coz—Colin's lawyer, Peter Cosgrove, who also happened to be his cousin—waved a long, bony finger at me. While he and Colin shared the same blond hair, slate-gray eyes and a height right at six feet tall, that was all they had in common. Colin was tight and firm, Coz was lanky and gangly. Colin was boisterous and self-confident. Coz—while a force to be reckoned with in a courtroom—was quiet and reserved. He was a good guy and remained friendly with me since the divorce, unlike several other members of his family.

Yet again I'd had to call Levi to come over and watch Paige. It was bad enough for her to see her dad get cuffed and shoved into the back of a squad car, but to see him locked up like any old criminal...her young psyche—regardless of her IQ level—shouldn't have to bear that image.

We'd had to wait almost two hours for Coz to arrive at the station, during which time the rest of us sat impatiently—well, okay, I sat impatiently—and waited. The detective did whatever detective work he did when he wasn't locking away members of the Eagan family.

Muldoon, Coz and I, as well as two uniformed officers, were all crowded in the small front office of the Peytonville police station. I will say I rather enjoyed not being in the back in one of the small cages. Still, being in the vicinity of the cages made my knees wobble a wee bit with claustrophobia.

"My client has an ironclad alibi." Coz gripped the edge of the counter.

"Both clients," I whispered.

"Pardon?" Coz's blond eyebrow tilted upward.

"Naomi said you're her lawyer, too."

When he rolled his eyes, I hid my smile—not the time or the place.

"Yes, *both* my clients have an alibi."

"I haven't given you a timeframe, yet, Counselor." Muldoon's nostrils flared as he took a deep breath and exhaled.

Coz sighed. "Fine. When did this crime allegedly take place?"

Muldoon regarded the tall wiry man for a long moment. Whatever kindness or gentility he'd had at my home, even if briefly, was replaced with an edge that sent a chill down my spine. I hoped never to be on the other end of that stare. It was unnerving at the very least. And totally sexy at the worst possible time. I'm sure I'd melt into a puddle if he turned it on me. He finally said, "Somewhere between late Tuesday evening into early Wednesday morning."

That was the first detail I'd really gotten on Chad's death other than the fact that he was indeed dead.

Coz nodded in his lawyerly manner and pulled out several sheets of paper from the dilapidated leather pouch that hung from his shoulder. He shoved them across the counter at Muldoon.

"What am I looking at here?"

"Ms. Michaels's ticket for parking illegally. The receipt from the towing company. In Little Rock."

"Arkansas?" I grabbed Coz's sleeve. "He went to Arkansas Tuesday night?"

Muldoon frowned. "You said he was at your house."

Oh, no, no, no, he was not going pull me back into this. "He was. He left at eight."

Coz nodded. "He was at Mrs. Eagan's. An hour or

so after his return home, Ms. Michaels received a call that her mother had suffered a heart attack and had been rushed to the hospital. In Little Rock, Arkansas. They left immediately."

"And didn't tell anyone where they were going?" Muldoon asked Coz but kept me pinned with his eyes— with *the look*—dammit.

"Quite the contrary. They notified their boss, the late Chad Jones, of their immediate plans and the need for substitutes for their teaching duties for at least one day. Possibly two."

"Convenient."

"Not for Ms. Michaels's mother." Coz tsked. "She is in stable condition now by the way, not that you asked."

Muldoon's cheeks reddened. For real, the man blushed. He tossed the papers back onto the counter. "This proves *she* was in Arkansas. There's nothing here showing me that Colin, Mr. Eagan, was out of the state at the time of the murder."

Murder. I was still having a hard time wrapping my brain around that.

"Oh, for heaven's sake." Coz adjusted the strap of his bag on his shoulder. "I can get affidavits from the hospital staff."

Muldoon flattened his hands on the countertop. "You do that."

"And Ms. Michaels?" Coz scooped up the papers and shuffled them. "When will she be released?"

"She assaulted a police officer." Muldoon's clear blue eyes slammed to near slits.

"She didn't realize you *were* a police officer." I couldn't believe I'd just defended her. Again. "She sees you manhandling Colin after coming home from her mom being in the hospital… C'mon, Detective. You let me go."

Coz swung his gaze over to me. So many questions hung in his eyes. I gave him a little headshake that said, "Later."

Muldoon eyed me for a long moment then walked through a door that led to the holding cells. A moment later he returned with Naomi in tow. The bedraggled woman launched herself at poor Coz. "Thank you, thank you for getting me out of there."

"Wasn't me." He pushed her to arm's length and darted his gaze to me.

"You." She slammed her hands on her hips. "First you get me thrown in there, then you expect me to thank you for getting me out."

I scoffed as if I'd swallowed a bug—I would much prefer swallowing a bug than being near her. I settled my hand on Coz's arm. "Please let me know if there is anything else I can do."

"You call me, if need be." Coz glanced in Muldoon's direction. "For absolutely anything."

"Don't help her. She got us into this mess. I'll bet she told the detective Coll's name, address and all of our information. She probably pointed him at us."

"Okay then." I nodded and turned to go while Coz lectured Naomi on the significance of keeping her mouth shut standing in a police station lobby.

"Hang on, Mrs. Eagan. I'll walk you out." Detective Muldoon rounded the counter and was at my side before I could even protest. Neither of us spoke as we headed across the small lot and to my car.

Morning had rolled in and was pushing into a warm, sunny day while the drama in my life quadrupled. It was almost insulting how the day kept to its schedule when I didn't know what was next in line for me.

I jingled the keys in my hand as we stopped at the driver's side door. "I know Coz would have my hide for saying this, but I hope you know I didn't have anything to do with Chad's murder. I know you can't just take my word for it. What Naomi said..." I shook my head. I was on a ramble and couldn't stop. "That's just mean-spiritedness talking. She's a harpy. She's never liked me, feels threatened by what Colin and I had—not that I would ever repeat that again. Once was enough, trust me on that. She can't seem to understand that. So she makes these little snipes an art form. And I don't know why I won't shut up. Did you want something, Detective? Is that why you walked me to my car?"

I pressed my lips together tight—not one more syllable would leak out. The detective stood so close I had to crane my neck back to look up at him. A smile split his face. I almost did a double take. The man had teeth after all. I wasn't sure. The few times his lips hinted at a skyward tilt had been brief and close-lipped.

The smile fell away and he stepped back. His body morphed into his police stance—shoulders squared, chin up, feet shoulder width apart, hands loose on his hips. I always assumed they stood like that to have quick access to their weapons and be ready to take off running, but I truly had no desire to find out for sure. "I had a couple of my men check with the administrative assistant and the gardener. Both deny being up at the school last night."

FIVE

"THAT'S NOT POSSIBLE." Levi gawked at me over the top of his coffee mug. We sat at my kitchen table, our usual contemplation spot, be it on world issues—as if—or whatever grievance one of us has suffered.

"That's what I said." I ran my finger over the brownie in front of me. Even chocolate held little appeal. "I offered to let him come back to the house and search for anything that might be missing from school." Not that Muldoon'd let on what was taken. I suspected he wanted me to produce a different alibi. Not that he'd said so, but it was the look of something akin to disappointment on his face when I didn't. As if he were offering me a chance to redeem myself.

Levi waved his hand at me. "And?"

"He didn't say much of anything, just glared at me then walked off."

Levi nodded. "Probably figures you've already hidden it."

"Levi! I didn't take *it*. I don't know what *it* is." I lost my appetite and shoved my brownie over to my friend. He ate the entire thing in one bite. "Whose side are you on?"

He wiped crumbs from his mouth. "I'm on your side, sweets, always. I'm just saying, think like him for a minute." He snagged my hand. "Did he or did he not show up on your doorstep first thing this morning. Stuff like that is meant to rattle a suspect."

I jerked my hand away. "Now you're calling me a *suspect*?"

"Listen and focus." He tilted his head down like a parent talking to a child. "The man is doing his job. We both know you didn't do anything, but he doesn't. He has to look at everyone involved. As far as they know, you killed the man, then maneuvered the situation to look like you found him."

I opened my mouth to argue, but Levi held up a finger.

"If it were anyone else—if it was Naomi—you'd wonder if they had anything to do with it. Right?"

I slumped my shoulders. "Fine, yes. Whatever."

"And to make it worse, you're the only one at the school last night who logged in with your keycard. Because, because—" he repeated when I tried to interrupt "—because you're actually an honest, law-abiding citizen. And *we* know it wouldn't occur to you otherwise. He doesn't know you."

I got up and paced behind my chair. "But how is he going to get to the bottom of anything if the other folks are lying to him?"

Levi shrugged. "He will figure it out. *Let him do his job.*"

"And in the meantime live under suspicion?" I laughed. "If only I could help him along somehow." I grabbed a rag and wiped down the table. "And exactly how am I supposed to do that?" I asked more to myself than to Levi. "If they would just tell the truth." I balled up the rag in my fist. "Yeah, if neither of them had qualms lying to Detective Muldoon, do you honestly think they're going to talk to *moi*—the person they lied about?"

Levi rubbed his temples. "You're not making much

sense right now. Maybe you need a nap. Or a shot of vodka." He let out a long-suffering sigh. "They may never tell the truth."

"To me. Or the detective. But maybe I can get them to open up. To someone else."

He stood and snagged the rag from my hand to finish wiping down the table. "And who might that be?"

"Me."

"You said—"

"Me. But not me. I'll go in disguise."

"Excuse me?"

"What do I do for a living?"

"You're a teacher."

"*Theater* teacher. Duh."

"Maybe you need a straitjacket." He tossed the rag in the sink. "You're crazy if you think you can waltz right up to someone—in disguise—and get them to tell you something."

"I think it will work. What have I got to lose?"

He rounded the table and stopped right in front of me. "I'd say your sanity but it seems to already be gone."

Why was it insane? I had the playhouse at my disposal which was filled with costumes and makeup. And they wouldn't be expecting it. It could work. But what to wear?

"Hello." Levi snapped in my face. "Where'd you go just now?"

I shook myself. "Trying to figure out what would be the best disguise to use on Kelsey."

"I can see this will happen with or without me." Levi slowly nodded. "Someone has to watch over you, so how are we going to do this?"

"We?" I raised an eyebrow. Levi was a lot of things, but his ability when it came to acting was as good as my willpower and java. As a supportive BFF he was, however, perfection.

His smile fell. "You, I meant you."

I could have dragged it out, made him sweat a little. But as I needed him to babysit Paige while I was sneaking around all dolled up, I broke. "*We* will need to get *me* all made up."

His smile returned and he all but vibrated with energy. "And how do we do that?" I had him hooked.

I waggled my eyebrows at him. "Paige, honey?"

"Yes?" my daughter called from somewhere in the house.

"You want to go for a ride up to the playhouse for a bit?"

"Knock, knock." I peeked into Annabelle's office. Levi and Paige were looking around the stage. Knowing my daughter, she was standing in the wings pretending to direct. She liked to be in charge. Who knows where she got that from? "Anyone here?"

A thump and muffled "Hang on" came from the closet on the far side. A moment later, Annabelle emerged, her arms loaded down with fabric. "Celeste, honey, hi. How are you?" A huge smile slashed across her face.

Annabelle was a tall woman, close to six feet with no shoes on. She had the most gorgeous jet-black hair that she usually kept in a shoulder-length bob. And a figure to die for. One could easily hate her when they caught a glimpse of her seafoam-green eyes and long, long lashes, but the moment you spoke with her, you couldn't help but fall a little in love with all her Southern charm. Not that I'd admit it aloud, but I did have a weensy bit of a girl-crush on her. She was a sweetheart through and through.

"What're you doing here in the middle of the week?" She shifted the large bundle in her arms.

"Let me help you with that." I hustled over to her side and removed the top few layers.

"Thanks. These are going to the costume shop." She motioned her head for me to follow. "Have you made a decision?"

"Actually, I have. If you still want me, I'd love to have the job."

Annabelle smiled over her shoulder at me. "That's wonderful."

We stowed the material in the appropriate cupboards. As soon as our arms were free, Annabelle scooped me up in a huge bear hug. "I am so excited to get you full-time."

The warm fuzzies rushed through me. It would help to combat any of the fear and trepidation that would come with leaving a career-long job.

"Are you excited?" she asked when she finally released me.

I smiled up at her. "Absolutely."

"I only ask 'cause your eye is twitching and you're only smiling with half your mouth." She gave me a playful wink.

"It's a little scary." I ignored the shivers at the base of my spine. "But scary in a good way."

Annabelle smiled. "You'll love it, I promise." She'd told me how she'd quit her job ten years earlier. She was a CPA for a large internet company. She hadn't once regretted her decision. If she could leave such a lucrative job... "Is your ex okay with watching the little one until your contract at the school is up?"

"Not a problem." Or at least I hoped it wouldn't be once I told him.

She shut the door to the costume shop. "I have some paperwork you need to fill out. You up to doing it now?"

"I have Paige and a friend with me." Just about then we heard a rash of giggles coming from the stage door at the end of the hall.

"Bring them on back to my office." Annabelle headed to the opposite end from the stage door. "I'll show them some of the new prop jewelry that was donated recently."

Half an hour later, I had a cramp in my hand, but I was "officially" a full-time employee of the playhouse. Paige, Levi and I toured all the different departments and wound up in the makeup room.

Annabelle was putting away one of the kits with the extra hair pieces when Levi nudged my arm. "That would be fabulous for a disguise," he whispered in my ear. "Ever gone out in drag?"

"SIT STILL." LEVI rolled his eyes and smooshed a mustache against my lip.

I'd given Annabelle a brief—and extremely edited— version of what had happened at school and why I'd like to "borrow" some of the playhouse's wares. I wasn't sure if I should be worried she'd agreed so readily and didn't ask any further questions.

Levi tapped the tip of my nose. "Say something."

I swatted his hand away. "If you don't stop bossing me around…"

"I meant in character." He tsked and moved away. Worried I might smack him again?

I cleared my throat, took a deep breath and lowered my voice. "You best be getting off of me, boy. I don't take too kindly to being manhandled." I'd thrown in a Midwestern accent for full effect.

Levi blinked at me several times. "If it weren't for your eyes, I'd swear one of my mother's bridge partners came over for a visit."

"What's wrong with my eyes?" I scooped up the hand mirror. It was a little disconcerting to see someone who resembled my grandfather looking back.

"Nothing's wrong. I just know you too well."

I bit my lip then smacked my lips when I got some of the pancake makeup in my mouth. "If Kelsey recognizes me..." We'd decided I'd go see her first. I knew where she spent her free time—everyone in the entire school knew where she was when she wasn't working— at Grind Effects. She made my coffee addiction look cute and manageable in comparison.

"She won't recognize you. I promise."

"Uncle Levi." Paige came running into the kitchen. "Oh. Sorry. I didn't know we had company."

Yikes. I turned my back on my daughter. I didn't want to confuse her in the getup. "I'll be going now." I reached for my purse on the back of the chair when Levi cleared his throat. I glanced up at him and he was behind Paige, shaking his head.

"Here. Why don't you use my car?" He tossed me the keys to his Lexus. Kelsey would know my—well, "Celeste's"—car. Still, I didn't want to drive around in a pink—even though he said it was some weird champagne color—Lexus.

"Okeydoke. Bye."

"Bye, *Celeste*."

I stuttered my step and turned slowly back to my bright daughter. "How did you know?"

She rolled her eyes. "Your walk, for one. Your

smell—you always wear the Lacoste perfume. And your eyes. I'm ten, not blind." She shoved a hand on her hip and arched an eyebrow in a move that mimicked me to a haughty T. "Is Uncle Levi going to have to bail you outta jail?"

"I, uh…" Not a question I'd have ever expected to hear coming from my child. Worse, yet, it wasn't an unreasonable question. And despite my "No. Of course not," I wasn't sure if that was true.

IN THE PARKING lot of Grind Effects, I sat in the car and bolstered my nerve. "Think of this as an acting job. Nothing more. Nothing less. You can do this."

When I got out of the car and walked up to the building I was mindful of what Paige said. I altered my gait to match that of a much older *man*. Not that I'd ever played across gender before, but there was always a first time.

In late afternoon, Grind Effects wasn't too terribly crowded so I spotted Kelsey right away. I walked near her once, then on the second pass, I bumped her arm and made her drop her coffee. "I'm so clumsy. I do apologize." We both grabbed for some napkins and bent to wipe up the mocha-latte stain on the marbled linoleum.

When she looked up at me, and into my eyes, I held my breath as I waited for her to point to me and call me out. Instead, she smiled and said, "No problem."

"Please let me buy you another."

Kelsey dabbed at the spilled coffee on the floor. "You don't have to do that."

"I insist." We both stood as the young barista came over with a mop. "Can you get my friend another white chocolate latte?" The coffee scents surrounding me made my system quake for caffeine, but I was afraid the heat would make my mustache fall off. "And a bottle of water for me."

"Yes, sir."

Kelsey looked at me oddly. Was I busted so fast? "How'd you know that was what I was drinking?"

Because you always drink it, I started to stay. But not wanting to sound like a weird stalker, I fumbled with, "I, uh." I sniffed. "It has a distinctive aroma."

"Wow, you really know your coffee."

"Eh." I did that typical male shrug and tucked my hands down in my trouser pockets. I had several outfits way in the back of my closet that ran on the masculine side. Thankfully, I never throw anything out. With a man's wig—I didn't even bother to ask Levi where he'd gotten it—and some body parts strategically placed or significantly flattened, I was getting the hang of being a dude.

I dropped a couple of bills on the counter. "Keep the change for the mess I made." Then I turned to Kelsey for a quick, "Enjoy your coffee," before I feigned interest in the rack of CDs for sale.

"Would you like to join me?" Kelsey sat at a scarred wooden table, coffee in hand. "Sorry, I didn't catch your name."

A *name*? I hadn't thought of a name. "Levi." She'd met my friend once or twice when he'd been my "date" to a couple of the school functions over the years. Let's hope the name didn't jump out and—

"So, Levi, do you come here often?"

Did people *really* use that tired old line? "I've been here a time or two." I quickly racked my brain to turn this in the direction I needed. I had to find out why she lied about where she was last night. Taking a chance,

I said, "I was here last night." I sat in the chair across the table.

Kelsey's smile fell away. "Oh, hmm. I'm usually here every night. But I missed last night."

"That's too bad. We might have run into one another."

A shadow crossed over us. I started to dismiss it until Kelsey's cheeks paled and she started fidgeting in her seat. What the hell was that all about?

"Ms. Pierce?"

Muldoon. My heart stutter-stepped. He glanced at me for a moment, did a double take, frowned, then looked back at Kelsey.

"Detective." Kelsey laced her fingers together on the tabletop. "Are you following me?"

"No, ma'am. But I do have some follow-up questions." He whipped out his notebook, then settled his other hand on the back of an empty chair. "Do you mind?"

The twenty-something turned off her flirt mode and was in the agitated mode we all knew from school when we tried to get supplies from her—you'd think she paid for them out of her own pocket the way she hoarded pens and pencils. "Do I have a choice?"

Muldoon started to tuck the notebook back in his pocket. "I could ask you questions down at the station if you'd prefer."

Kelsey sighed. "Fine. Sit. Whatever. Levi, will you excuse us for just a moment, please?"

"Oh sure." I nodded and moved to another table two seats away, still within earshot but with my back to Muldoon. I took a long sip of water. All the damn makeup was hot as hell. Add in my nerves at Muldoon's appearance, and it was a wonder I didn't spontaneously combust in the middle of November.

"Can you give me a reason why Celeste Eagan would say you were at school last night if you weren't?"

"Jealousy."

"Ugh." Water shot out my nose as I coughed.

"You okay, Levi?" Kelsey asked.

I waved my hand in the air as I dabbed at my mustache. Too much water and it would curl up on my lip like a sun-dried caterpillar.

Muldoon resumed his questioning. "And why would that be?"

"She had a thing for Chad. I mean Principal Jones."

A thing, my ass. I shoved my water bottle to the far side of the table. Better not risk injury by choking to death. Or hurling it at the bimbo's head.

"And did Principal Jones return the sentiment?"

"Heavens, no. He and I had been dating for the last year."

If I'd have been a cartoon character, my eyeballs would have bugged out of my head and probably knocked the water bottle to the floor.

"And this would make Mrs. Eagan lie to the police about you, why?"

"I don't know. You'd have to ask her. She's always had it in for me. I tried to be friends but, well, it got to be uncomfortable with her always hitting on Chad."

"Did Mr. Jones ever say anything to Mrs. Eagan? To get her to stop?"

"He didn't want to cause a scene. He was afraid she would run to the board and start complaining."

"If he had a legitimate beef with her…"

"Do you know who Coach Eagan is? Of course you do, you were up at school interviewing everyone. He's a big deal at Peytonville Prep. He made it into the NFL, believe it or not. But he hurt his knee or something like that and couldn't play."

"Yes, I know," he replied with a dry, irritated tone.

"Well, the board absolutely loves him. Chad was afraid they'd take Celeste's word over his because of Colin. So not to lose their game-winning coach… Chad just put up with all her advances."

I couldn't believe what I was hearing. Colin stand up for me? Not likely. And since when was Chad afraid of the board? But seeing how I was some loosey-goosey man-eater hitting on poor Chad, I suppose it was all possible—when hell froze over and turned purple.

"Can you tell me where you were last night?"

"I was here, of course. I am always here. Just ask anyone."

Liar, liar, pants on fire.

Lot of good knowing the truth did for me. I couldn't exactly lean over and tell Detective Muldoon that she'd just admitted to me—old man me—that she hadn't been here. That would blow my cover and get me back to square one with Kelsey.

Despite her claims, we'd always been civil to one another. There was no reason for her to throw me under the bus unless she had something to hide. For the briefest moment, I wondered if she'd had anything to do with Chad's death. But seeing her reaction when she walked into his office, I doubted it. She was not that good of an actress to pull off those kind of hysterics. Something, though, kept her lying lips moving.

And then, in the blink of an eye—or rather, I'd guess the bat of long eyelashes—she went from defensive witness back to bimbo floozy. She turned on her charm and was mercilessly flirting with Detective Muldoon.

With her simpering and him all but breathing down my neck—I might be a touch paranoid, dressed up as a man while he was mere tables away—I decided to cut my losses and get the heck out of Dodge. Pronto. A crowd of teenagers came in making a loud enough ruckus to draw people's attention to the other side of the room. I scurried from the table and out a side door. I was fumbling with the keys to the Lexus when a hand clamped down on my shoulder.

"Excuse me, sir. May I ask you a quick question?"

I turned and faced Muldoon but didn't meet his gaze. "Yes?"

"Did you happen to see Ms. Pierce here last night?"

"No, sir. I just ran into her today." Ha. I didn't lie to the good detective. Maybe omitted a thing here or there, but I did not out-and-out lie. It shouldn't make a difference as I was dressed up as a man—that pretty much was a lie in itself—but in my warped little mind, it mattered.

"Oh. Okay, thanks." He looked me over for a long minute. "Have we met? There is something familiar about you."

Sweat rolled down the back of my neck. "Do I look like a hardened criminal to you?"

Muldoon chuckled—close-lipped, of course. "No, sir." He tucked his hands in his pockets. "But looks can always be deceiving."

SIX

"THAT WAS TOO CLOSE." I handed Levi the short-haired wig. "Forget the gardener."

He'd set up his computer at my kitchen table. The eBay website up, I wondered how many little tchotchkes would be whisking their way to his house. He held up a finger, typed something into computer, then closed the lid. "Kelsey didn't recognize you, did she?"

I ripped the mustache from my lip and tossed it onto the table. I poured myself a cup of coffee and added the necessary tweaks before I took a long sip. "No. Kelsey was all smiles and eyelash batting. Muldoon, however—" I motioned at Levi with the mug "—was awfully suspicious."

"He's a cop. It's his job to be suspicious." Levi stood and refilled his own coffee. "It was a fluke you ran into him. Nothing more."

"I guess." I'd already told Levi what I *did* learn. And what I didn't. "She is knee-deep in something. I just don't know what. Not only did she lie to the police, but she lied *about me* to the police. It's just so odd. Colin has no sway whatsoever with the board. He's not even the head coach."

"And you never once made a pass at that man, so don't let it get you all bent out of shape."

I scrubbed at my flattened hair. "You're right. You're always right."

Levi chuckled. "Stitch that on a sampler and let's

move on. Mmm." He snapped his fingers together. "I forgot to tell you, Colin called. The police haven't dropped the charges but Coz got him out on bail."

"That's good."

"He wants Paige to come over for a bit. Something about being locked away makes a man reprioritize." Levi studied his nails. "If you ask me, I think he's a little freaked out about clearing his name."

"That's ridiculous." I removed the sports coat and hung it on the back of the chair before I untucked the shirt tails from the trousers. "Colin has never been freaked out about anything in his life that didn't revolve around football."

"Really?" Levi's eyebrows twisted comically. "He didn't try to insult me even once. Was—" Levi paused and waved his hand "—polite even."

"That's not like him."

"I know, right."

I sighed. What started out as me trying to clear my name just morphed into me trying to make sure my daughter's weekend visits with either of her parents weren't surrounded by armed guards and barbed wire.

Colin would be fine, though. Once the affidavits came through, Detective Muldoon would look to someone who had the means and opportunity to hurt Chad.

If you listened to Kelsey, someone like me…

"How're we going to find Danny's home address?"

AFTER A GOOD night's sleep I almost chickened out, but too much time on my hands, an empty house and a best friend who made my flair for the dramatic pale in comparison, and I was up to my hair follicles in costumes again. At least I got to dress like a woman. I shifted the fanny pads under my skirt. I shook my head. Levi said it added authenticity to the getup.

How Levi found Danny's home address—it wasn't in the school directory—I didn't bother to ask. The young gardener lived right next door to an assisted-living home. We decided it was best if I pretended to be a lost little old lady to get him talking. Yeah, it sounded better when I was in front of my mirror adding wrinkles and blemishes.

I should've used my own car. My woolen skirt, Peter Pan collar shirt and funky shawl didn't really mesh with Levi's pink Lexus, but, like with Kelsey, we were afraid Danny might recognize my car. I parked the Lexus on the street in front of Danny's apartment building just before noon.

Of course, the man had to live on the third floor. Despite the chill in the air, I was huffing and puffing with little beads of sweat at my temples by the time I got to the landing. My plan to pretend to be confused and in the wrong place lost any validity as I passed umpteen apartments to get to his. Hell, I'd just have to wing it.

I knocked and waited. Then I knocked again. Sure, it was presumptuous that he had nothing better to do than wait at home for the theater teacher in disguise to show up and question why he lied to the police. I knocked for a third time when the apartment next to Danny's opened.

"He's gone." A scraggly guy in his mid-twenties peeked his head into the breezeway.

"Gone?" I patted my chest. "Oh my, really?"

"Yep. Said something about needing tape, I don't know." The guy scratched his hairy chin.

I fought to keep from rolling my eyes. "Gone? To the store?" I tucked my little man-hitting purse on my elbow as I was considered wielding it at the boob. "Did he mention when he'd be back?"

"It's not like I'm his secretary or anything. You probably passed him on the stairs." Without so much as a goodbye, the guy eased back into his apartment and shut the door.

I hadn't passed anyone on the way up, but with all the stairs surrounding the building, he could have gone down anywhere. "Damn, damn and damn again." Each and every step back down to the ground floor, I cursed Danny—and his neighbor—for making me go up and down three flights. My brain went into overdrive trying to remember what kind of car he drove. And then it hit me, or nearly did, when I stepped into the lot.

"Watch it, lady." Danny's red Jeep whizzed past me and onto the street.

"Hey." I waved the gray leather purse in the air. "Wait."

When he didn't stop, I hoofed it over to the Lexus. You can't believe the stares an old lady gets sprinting down the block. "What, you've never seen an octogenarian run before?" At least that's what I'd have said if I hadn't been so damn winded. I guess I shouldn't have given up my gym membership.

Once behind the wheel, I peeled out onto the street and in the direction that Danny had headed. I finally spotted him two intersections up, stopped at a light. Traffic was heavier than usual so early in the afternoon. I tried to weave up into a better position next to him, but couldn't catch a break.

When a spot opened beside me, I cut into the next lane and floored the sedan. Two car lengths behind Danny and I was digging in my purse for my cell. Maybe if I hadn't been looking down, I'd have noticed the light in front of me changing. That and the police car on the cross street. I will say he had no trouble seeing me. And once he turned on the colorful flashing lights, there was no mistaking him anymore.

I pulled over and watched Danny's Jeep get farther and farther away.

"Double damn."

I snatched my wallet from my purse, rolled down the window and waited. It wasn't until the uniformed officer came to my door and said, "License and insurance please," that I realized I was in deep, deep doo-doo.

"Well, you see…"

A COUPLE OF hours in the Fort Worth Police lockup and I'd earned a new respect for the Peytonville PD cages. They were vastly more private. And it didn't take three hookers and a swearing biker chick to convince me. They also smelled worlds better; I hazarded a glance at the offending biker chick.

"Keep your eyes to yourself."

I nodded and looked anywhere that wasn't at Matilda—her name was stitched on the front of her leather vest. As well as tattooed on her well-honed biceps. I have to tell you, it was darn hard not looking at her, though. She was gorgeous, and minus the tattoo and burly vest, she could be a supermodel.

From my precarious perch on the end of the wooden bench, I made an effort to keep my eyes trained on the bars or the floor. The cell was larger than Peytonville's. All in all, my tour of holding cells across Texas better be coming to an end very soon. It was becoming tedious.

"Mrs. Eagan?" a young female officer called.

I stood and white-knuckled the bars. "Here. Right here."

Triple damn. Detective Muldoon stood next to the guard. "That's not her." He looked back at the guard, confused and a little bit irritated—his typical expression when he was around me.

I cleared my throat. "Actually, it is."

His jaw literally dropped to his chest before he regained his composure. "Celeste? What the..."

"I can explain. I swear." Just get me the hell out of here, I mentally begged.

The corner of his mouth quivered. He gave me a head-to-toe once-over, then squeezed his lips together. He looked like he might just walk away. But if I just had a chance...to explain. To him.

When the policeman pulled me over—because, really, when you hand him a license that has one set of statistics but you're sitting in a borrowed Lexus that's not on your insurance card while dressed as an eighty-year-old gray-haired granny, he tends to stop listening—I gave up trying to explain. There was no way to convince him not to drag me in to jail.

To be fair, the arresting officer did drive me to the assisted-living home first to see if they'd lost me. For some reason he wasn't buying anything I was telling him anyway. When they'd declined to claim me, I was then taken to the downtown Fort Worth precinct where I was fingerprinted—second time in less than a week—and frisked and, despite their only slightly veiled laughter, asked to remove anything that wasn't real body parts. Wig, padding, fake teeth and all went into a bag and left me drooping.

Still, they didn't ask many questions. Which makes one wonder how often they see this.

I didn't want to call Levi. The "I told you so" would have never ended. Colin, oh God, I couldn't tell him. He was watching Paige and I'd sworn to her I wouldn't end up in jail again. What a liar I am. Plus, I did not want Colin to see me like this. As I contemplated who else I could call, an officer found Muldoon's number wedged between my Macy's card and a doctor's appointment reminder. I asked them not to call Muldoon, but I got the impression they'd rather pawn me off to a different police department. Rude.

The guard came to the cell, keys in hand. For a long moment she just stared at me, then she unlocked the cell and released me. As I passed, she whispered, "Girl, you have your hands full with that one." She all but purred.

If Muldoon hadn't been standing with his hands on his hips and those killer brows smashed down tight over his eyes, I might have asked what she meant by that, but truth be told, I didn't think I wanted to know. And I was more than ready to put as much distance between me and any uniformed law enforcement personnel. Matilda waved her fist at me when I glanced back over my shoulder.

A shudder ripped through me as I turned to Muldoon. "I don't even know where to begin."

Muldoon took hold of my elbow. "Let's keep the confessions to nil until we get to my car, please."

"Your car? I appreciate you getting me out, but—"

"They towed your car, whoever's car that was." He waved a sheet of paper at me. "So unless you want to walk back to Peytonville…"

"I uh, no, thank you. I appreciate the ride."

We stopped and gathered my belongings. Neither of us spoke through the halls and the parking garage of the downtown precinct. It was the quietest ten minutes I'd had in a long while. Finally, we were nestled away in his car—a black Camaro. Of course he drove a Camaro. The inside smelled of leather and Muldoon. I closed my eyes and breathed in the comforting fragrance. It would be so easy to get lost in the cocoon of Muldoon, even if it was just his car. And only briefly.

So close to succumbing to a little nap, I opened my eyes and sat up straighter as Muldoon drove through downtown Fort Worth. The soft, lulling rock song on the radio transitioned to head-banging grind and ruined whatever moment I might have imagined—or hoped for.

Muldoon sighed. "Can I take a guess? You went to talk to Danny Eems to see why he contradicted your claim that he was at the school the other night."

"How'd you…"

"I am a detective, Celeste." He reached over and turned off the radio. "You were picked up a few blocks from his building. You're dressed like—" he took his eyes off the road and glanced at me for a moment "—a bag lady?"

"A granny. You'd had to have seen the whole outfit for the full effect." I shook the bag with my fanny pad, wig and teeth. "Since he lives next to the nursing home, I thought I could pop in and get him talking."

"Did it work?"

"I'd just missed him." I dropped my gaze to my lap. "I saw his Jeep—the little prick nearly ran me over, no respect for the elderly, I tell you. Anyway, I was following him. When I got pulled over for running through a light."

"Hmm. That wasn't the brightest thing to do, you know. You could have…" Muldoon jerked the wheel and pulled off to the side of the road and up to the curb in front of an office building.

"Figures you can find a parking spot on a Friday afternoon." I tried to joke but my throat was suddenly dry.

"Stop, Celeste." A horn blared behind us as he slammed the car into park and shut off the engine.

I gripped the bag in my lap tighter. "Okay. Sorry."

"Look at me."

I turned my face to his but didn't meet his gaze. Muldoon snagged my chin and tilted my face up higher. "In the eyes. Look at me."

I did.

He narrowed his gaze at me. "Goddamn, Celeste. The weird-looking guy? At the coffee house?" He released my face. "I knew there was something familiar." He slammed his fists on the steering wheel. "For someone who claims to be innocent, you're not doing yourself any favors here. What were you thinking?"

"That Kelsey and Danny lied. And I wanted to know why. Because I *did* see them up at the school." I took a deep breath. "I didn't do anything wrong but I don't know how to prove it. I don't even know what was stolen from the school. But I can tell you Kelsey told me she wasn't at the coffeehouse last night—and by me I mean the 'weird' guy me." I used finger quotes when I said *weird*. Anything to keep from fidgeting in front of Muldoon. "And for the record, not weird at all. Distinguished. She was digging on him. Me. Whatever.

"But that's not the point." I waved my hand. "Before I could get any info, you showed and started questioning her. She told *you* she was there. I'd bet if you asked, the folks there would say they saw her because when you frequent a place, people just assume you're there."

I shook my head. "And before you ask, I know this because a few years ago I broke my leg and missed two weeks from the Grind Effects I frequent. When I showed up on crutches, no one even knew I'd been gone, they just assumed it was same old same old and couldn't have been more surprised to see me with a cast." I ran my fingers through my hair.

He glared at me for a long moment. "Finished?" When I nodded, he said, "The people working at the coffeehouse hadn't seen her. They didn't, I repeat, did *not* verify *her* alibi."

"So that was all for naught. Figures. Women like her would be missed. Of course she would. She's pretty and perky and dumb as a stump. Me not so much. I'm smart, can carry on a conversation without referring to myself in third person, and no one looks twice at me." I was working myself up to a full head of righteous indignation.

"Look, Celeste, I can't say I understand why you're dropping yourself smack-dab in the middle of my investigation, but you have to back off and let me, and my department, handle this. If you're innocent—"

"If? See, this is what I'm talking about. I am innocent."

"If you're innocent, we'll figure that out."

Right, I wanted to say. I thought of Colin being arrested. Hell, even myself getting arrested. Twice. People were lying, my boss was dead. Muldoon and his department didn't seem to be any closer to the truth than I was.

"You need to back off."

"I'm not sure that's possible."

"You don't think I can do my job?"

"I'm sure you're a great detective. But I think whatever crap is going on between you and Colin—and don't give me that look, you all but sneer every time you say his name—I don't think you can be completely objective. I know the players involved—"

"Do you even know what's going on?" His hands tightened on the steering wheel.

"Apparently not. Tell me." I turned in the seat toward him.

Muldoon held my gaze for a moment, then restarted the car. He pulled back into traffic before he spoke again. "Last warning. Back off or you're going to end up in jail. Again. Don't make me have to arrest you myself and keep you locked up until the end of the investigation."

MULDOON PARKED IN front of my house. Early evening darkened the street, but it didn't take a trained observer to see my front door hanging wide open. "Where's your daughter?"

"At Colin's. She's staying with him for a few days."

He reached for the driver-side door. When I started to open the passenger side, he grabbed my wrist. "Stay in the car. Do you hear me?"

"Yes." I nodded and gulped. He had me a little bit scared.

I released the door handle. Muldoon closed his with little more than a click. He had his gun unholstered before he reached the front porch. It took all I had to stay put while the detective was out of sight. I could imagine any number of things befalling him inside the house, from a burglar to my great-grandmother's throw rug in my office.

It seemed like an eternity before the porch light lit as well as the one in the foyer. Muldoon emerged and waved me to join him.

My legs were shaky as I hurried up the walkway. "I'm afraid to ask, but how bad is it?" I asked in a whisper when I was within whisper-earshot.

"Messy. But nothing's broken that I can tell." He

settled his hand at the small of my back and ushered me inside.

Muldoon flipped on the light to the living room. From the foyer I could see every stitch of furniture out of place. Cushions littered the floor. The club chair was lying on its side. Even the damn pictures hung askew.

"Did you turn on your alarm when you left?" He motioned to the control panel by the front door.

Sliding the cell phone from my purse, I snapped several pictures. "It doesn't work."

He pulled up short as his dark brows slashed down together. "Celeste."

I tucked the phone away. "The house was hit by lightning during a storm several years ago. It fried the control panel and a bunch of the appliances. The insurance didn't cover it by half."

"And you didn't think to replace the alarm?"

"Haven't needed it." I was getting defensive, but it was not the time to yell at me. A book skidded off my toe when I moved away from him. Not a single book was left on the shelves. "Why? Why did this happen?" I glanced around my living room. DVDs were strewn everywhere, too. All the knickknacks and picture frames had been removed from the mantel and were piled in a heap next to the fireplace.

I jumped when he spoke quietly, his breath feathering across my ear. "Can you tell if anything is missing?"

"At first glance? Absolutely not." Someone could have stolen half my possessions but I wouldn't be able to tell with them spread out everywhere.

"Let's go from room to room and see if you can tell if anything's gone. But don't touch anything. Okay?"

Muldoon followed me through the house but didn't so much as breathe too hard. Just listened to me gritch at the mess left behind. I looked in closets and under beds and not one single thing seemed to be gone. All the high-ticket items were still in place. "The other laptop's not here," I said when we walked back into the hall. "But Paige usually takes it with her when she visits her dad." I mentally ticked off things worth stealing. The heirloom jewelry I'd inherited from my grandmother when I got the rug was still sitting in my jewelry box next to my engagement ring. I was saving that for Paige if she wanted it later. The diamond earrings I'd splurged and bought myself last Christmas were still there as well.

I searched one more time throughout the house and as far as I could tell, all was present and accounted for. "What would someone be looking for?"

Muldoon leaned his against the arm of the sofa. "You tell me?"

"I haven't the slightest clue." I slammed my hands on my hips. "I don't know what was stolen from the school—assuming this even has anything to do with that." I turned my back on Muldoon and walked farther into the living room.

"Nothing we know of."

I swiveled on my feet. "What?"

Muldoon picked up a sofa cushion off the floor, righted it into place and sat. "We don't know what, if anything, was taken."

"Then why did you come barging in here first thing the other morning?"

"I knew you'd been there. I thought maybe if you had taken something, I could rattle your cage enough to tell me what it was. Then Cooter showed up." He leaned his elbows on his knees and dropped his head to his hands. "This is the most screwed-up case I have ever been involved in." He sighed. "I have no business telling you this, but I'm afraid if I don't, you're just going to keep nosing around trying to figure out what's what."

I flipped over my club chair and sat. Then I stood again and yanked the godawful granny dress off over my head. Clad in a pair of spandex biker shorts and a tight T-shirt, I sat back and waited for the detective to continue. "What?" I asked when he peeked at me through his fingers. "It was uncomfortable. Are you going to tell me? Or do I have to go digging through my trunk and find another snappy outfit to get my own information?"

Muldoon leaned back on the sofa. "I don't understand how someone like you wound up with Cooter Eagan."

I'd heard the comments when Colin and I got married. *He can have anyone. Why'd he marry her?* It hurt then. Coming from Detective Muldoon, it was like a slap in the face. "What's that supposed to mean? You don't think someone like me can snag a man like him?"

"Quite the opposite. How did he land a woman like you?"

Heat infused my cheeks. It wasn't often that someone other than Levi took up the cause of me. Not that I was a mope-ish, poor-me sad sack, but still it was nice to think I was worthy in the good detective's eyes. I gave a quick mental shake. He was still the detective determined to put someone behind bars for Chad's death, and if it turned out I was the most viable suspect, I didn't think he would bat an eye at throwing my butt in the clink.

He looked at me somewhat expectantly and I remembered he'd asked me a question.

"I told you. Nightingale effect. I ran him over, then nursed his wounds. I mean, I didn't *really* hurt him that bad. He just wrenched his bum knee a little. But you get the idea." It wasn't love at first sight, or rather first hit. At least not on my part. I didn't want to admit that to anyone. He was attractive, sure. Over the years, I got a lot of looks that said I'd married up while he… no one seemed to know why he married me. "Believe it or not, he was funny." I paused with my hands at the tops of the knee highs. "We laughed a lot."

"I think it was something more than that. I do have to give the man credit. I'd always figured he'd marry some airhead sycophant."

"I don't know whether I should be insulted or thank you." I slipped the knee-highs down my calves, a little unnerved at his eyes following my every movement—but he was a cop, maybe he couldn't turn off the scrutiny. "I don't get why you dislike him so much. I don't ever remember him mentioning you, but clearly something in the past went on between you two."

"High school was high school. Boys competed against each other in every area. And Colin and I were no different."

"But that doesn't explain all the animosity." I settled back into the chair.

Muldoon held my gaze. "I was at Peytonville Prep on scholarship and he never let me forget it." He dropped his head to the back of the sofa and rubbed the bridge of his nose. "Snide remarks here and there. Shoving stuff in my locker. Hiding my football gear. Stupid shit. Never-ending but stupid shit."

"I'm sorry."

"Not your fault."

"Still." I shifted and tucked my feet up under me. I sat quietly for a long moment. How did one apologize for something their ex did? "It must have been hell to go to school with him. Then you come into this case and who is smack-dab in the middle of it? I didn't know him then, but he's not a bad guy now."

His head shot up. "You divorced him."

I waved away the comment. "Apples and oranges."

"Whatever you say." Muldoon shook his head and stood. "I still shouldn't let it affect my job."

He held out his hand to me. When I grabbed it, he pulled me to my feet. I didn't want to examine the little rush of jitters that skittered down my back. Probably left over from being locked up twice—right, and eating Krispy Kremes standing up eliminates all the calories. Muldoon held onto my hand a fraction longer than politely required. A slight tint darkened his cheeks.

What the hell was that all about?

"I'm, uh." He let go and slipped his cell from his pocket. "I'm gonna call the fingerprint guys out to dust, but I doubt we're going to get any hits."

"Can I go wash my face real quick." I scratched at a flaky patch of makeup on my cheek. "It's getting itchy."

"No, sorry. We need to get back out and wait." He guided me back out the front door onto the porch.

"Gotcha." I looked longingly toward the bathroom as I followed him back out the front door. An itchy face should be my penance for such a stupid idea. "We don't want to contaminate the scene, right?"

Muldoon laughed. Out loud. Straight white teeth flashing and all. "Something like that." Before long, we were accompanied by several members of the Peytonville police force.

It was hours before I was finally left alone in my house. I righted some of the furniture but left the bulk of it for later when I could keep my eyes open. Despite my nerves when I crawled into bed—with all the lights on—I slept better than I had since Chad's death. First thing the next morning I was, however, awakened abruptly by a phone call.

"THANKS FOR COMING by so quickly." Annabelle locked the door behind me. She'd called, frantic, half an hour earlier. "When the alarm company called me I knew I needed to get some help." She walked me back to the far end of the theater into a short hallway I hadn't seen before. An acrid smell wafted over us as we hurried through. "My apartment is through here."

"You live here?"

Annabelle smiled. "I own the building. As much time as I spend here, I figured I might as well build an apartment onto it. Save myself from paying mortgage to a place I was rarely at."

"Makes sense." I crinkled my nose as the smell got worse. "What happened?"

"I have a date tonight and I was rehearsing dinner." Annabelle pushed open the heavy door into a small living room. "And it was a good thing. I set the food on fire. Twice. The second time, it set the alarm off in the theater."

A thin haze hung over the small, square living area. A half wall separated it from the kitchen, where pots and pans littered the countertops.

"And you called me because…" I still hadn't quite figured that out yet. But as I was all alone, with Paige at her dad's, my Saturday morning was wide open until I met Levi for lunch—after he picked up his car for the impound lot. That conversation hadn't gone well.

Annabelle turned and faced me. She wrung her hands in front of her. "You're a mom. You were married. Surely you know how to cook. Something. Anything." A half grimace, half smile tilted her mouth. "Please tell me you know how to cook."

I bit back a laugh. "I do."

"Oh, thank God. Takeout is the strongest culinary

skill of anyone else I know. And you owe me one—you said so yourself—when you borrowed the mustache. If you don't mind, I'd like to collect on that. Pretty please." A decided whine had entered her voice.

Coming from anyone else, it would probably grate on people's nerves. But as with just about everything with Annabelle, it was charming. She could do no wrong. Other than cook, apparently. I won't admit that made me feel a little better.

"I don't know how fancy I can make it, but I know a few surefire meals."

Annabelle squealed and bobbled up and down on her feet. "Thank you, thank you."

"First order of business, we need to air this place out." She and I went around and opened as many windows as possible to get some of the thicker smoke out.

We ran to the store and grabbed the ingredients for my famous—and by famous, Paige and Levi raved over it—pot roast. I convinced her to buy a crockpot once I assured her it was foolproof. She picked out a wine. That, I had no clue about. Any wine found in my home was Levi's doing. He'd often leave a sticky note on the bottle with a list of what it would go with. I found I went through the dessert wines more often than any of the rest. Go figure.

Annabelle also grabbed several scented candles in case the smoky odor hadn't fully dissipated by the time her date arrived. We had just put away the last of the groceries when she leaned against the edge of the counter. "How did your undercover work go?"

I shrugged. It was a little embarrassing to admit that I probably caused more problems than I solved by trying to ferret out the truth from two lying coworkers. "Eh. Not quite as I'd planned."

Annabelle looked down at her hands and picked the color off of one long nail. "So you didn't learn anything that could help you?"

"Not really." I frowned. "Why?"

She straightened away from the counter and chewed the edge of her lip. "I didn't want to alarm you at the store. And I wasn't entirely sure until we got back here, but…"

"But…" That little squiggle of fear snaked down my spine.

"I think someone's following you."

SEVEN

"WHY DO YOU keep looking over your shoulder?" Levi snapped his fingers in my face.

"I'm being followed."

He grabbed the arms of his chair. "What? Where? Show me. Should we call the police?" He was panting by the time he finished speaking as he scanned the area around us.

I, myself, took a long, deep breath. "He is the police."

Levi's head swiveled slowly—comically so—back in my direction. "I beg your pardon."

"Detective Muldoon. He's sitting over in front of the shoe store." Levi and I were having lunch at the Grind Effects around the corner from my house—they served the best sandwiches around. I picked at the crust of my ham on wheat. "He has been all morning." It was one of the reasons I'd suggested a table outside on the sidewalk. I wanted to make Muldoon watch me eat while he was hunkered down in his car. That and it was a nice, enjoyable cool autumn afternoon. But mostly the watching-us-eat part.

The night before, I'd had police crawling all over my house for hours dusting whatever surfaces they could take fingerprints from. I think that was more Muldoon's doing. They didn't seem to need or want to work so hard for a break-in that appeared to have no loss of property. Luckily for me, they had my prints on file already and I didn't even have to go in to provide any. When Annabelle had called, I'd been able to forget everything for just a little while. Until she mentioned I'd been followed. At first, I was terrified that the bad guy had tracked me down for God only knows why. I was equally afraid for Annabelle. The last thing I wanted to do was drag her into something she wasn't even remotely involved in, other than by knowing me.

Annabelle and I snuck out the back of the play-house—*sneak* being a subjective term as we simply walked out and down the back alley until we could see the front of the building to where she'd seen the man park. Had I not caught a glance of the jet-black hair as the man sat a few blocks over from the playhouse, I might have called Muldoon and told him.

How silly would it be to call the man tailing you to tell him there was a man tailing you? He probably would have laughed his ass off. He was smart enough to use a different car, though, than the one he'd picked me up in from the Fort Worth PD the night before. For a brief moment, I had half a mind to charge right up to him and tell him to shove off.

After leaving the playhouse, I'd made several stops around town running errands that I didn't necessarily need done on a Saturday when I could relax—just to see if he was, in fact, following me. And sure enough, Muldoon didn't miss a single stop I made. I have to admit, he was good. Had I not known what car to look for, I might never have realized I was being followed.

When I'd gotten home from Annabelle's, with Muldoon in tow, it had taken two hours to right my home back to livability. Every crevice was scrubbed, dusted or wiped. It hadn't been that clean in well over a year, but I figured I might as well go hog wild since I had to straighten it up anyway. All the while he sat. In his car. Watching my house.

I will say Muldoon had offered to stay and help the night before, but that was all a little too cozy for me. Not to mention he had on his cop face. And as he never once came right out and said I was off the suspect list, I wasn't about to take the chance he would be snooping through my stuff looking for the don't-know-what-was-stolen items.

Maybe if I had accepted his help, he wouldn't have been so inclined to watch me all morning.

He'd called the case crazy. That was for sure. There'd been a murder staged to look like suicide. A break-in where nothing appeared to be taken. People lying about their whereabouts. Another break-in that *might* or *might not* be connected. It was enough to drive someone batty—or dress themselves up pretending to be someone else to get information.

I sighed. "I guess I moved up from the general list to the short list."

"Why?" Levi took a long sip of his drink and trained his gaze toward the shoe store.

"Well for starters, Coz called me this morning to let me know Colin's affidavits came through. Colin was, in fact, in Little Rock with the hussy. The doctors there were kind enough to provide him with a strong alibi. And he'd used his credit card to pay for several things and they provided the receipts to back it up."

"So, he's off the hook. But that still doesn't answer why you're not."

"There's no telling. Maybe he thinks I'm in on something—whatever *it* is. Maybe he thinks I did it and he's watching to see what I'll do next. Getting arrested twice has shot my credibility. Thanks for not talking me out of dressing up. That went real swell."

"Thanks for getting my car impounded. I spent all morning in Fort Worth." He balled his napkin in his hand.

"I spent hours in lockup. I think we're even." I pushed my plate away, no longer hungry.

Levi stared past me. "Which car exactly?"

"The tan sedan. He's got dark hair. Has on those mirrored sunglasses cops like to wear." I motioned to my face.

Levi clapped his hands together. "Mind if I go get a good look at him?"

"Knock yourself out. But if you wind up in jail, I'm not bailing you out. I've seen the inside just a few too many times."

"I will be the model of discretion."

"I'm sure." I rolled my eyes and sipped my caramel latte as Levi headed down the street. I vowed not to turn around. I didn't want to see what he might do and whether or not he could be discreet as he tried to take a peek at Muldoon. *Do not give into temptation* was the little mantra playing in my head while he was gone. And I didn't. Which, truly, was a miracle.

Naturally I jumped when I heard a throat clear behind me.

"You lose something?"

I swiveled in my seat. Muldoon had Levi by the collar of his shirt and directed him back to his seat across from me.

"Why, Detective. Fancy seeing you here." I kicked the chair next to me out. "Why don't you join us?" I slid the remainder of my sandwich over to him.

"Since I'm here." Muldoon plopped down on the wire mesh chair and waved away the offered food.

He trained his gaze in my direction, though with the mirrored sunglasses I couldn't really tell for sure where he was looking. I fought off the urge to check my reflection, fluff my hair. I didn't think he'd be too terribly amused.

"Colin has alibied out," he said finally.

"I know." I looked away and took another long sip of my coffee. I needed to do something, anything, other than having to come up with some inane conversation with a man who was legally stalking me. In my periphery, I saw a small muscle in his jaw tick. Was he annoyed with me?

Muldoon set his elbows on the edge of the table and steepled his fingers in front of him. "No hits on the prints at your house."

I nodded. "Just like you predicted."

Levi kicked me under the table. I toggled my gaze between him and Muldoon. I stopped on Levi. "Levi Weiss, my shadow. I'm sorry, I mean Detective Muldoon. Muldoon, Levi." The two men shook hands, Muldoon a little more grudgingly than Levi. The two stared at one another for a long moment. Sizing each other up? Comparing the vast differences?

Levi was wearing a lemon-yellow argyle sweater with roll-cuff khakis and his favorite tan Cole Haan loafers. Muldoon was wearing his cop-wear, also dressed in khakis, but his were stiffly ironed with sharp pleats and all. He wore his typical—at least every time I'd ever seen him—button-down shirt, navy sports coat and a pair of brown lace-up dress shoes, the kind with thick rubber soles. Better to chase a bad guy, I'd guess.

Before either started growling at each other, I tapped

Levi on the arm and stage-whispered, "Would you be a dear and go get me another." I waved my empty cup at him.

He made some strange sucking noise with his teeth and stood. "Yep-a-roony. Can I get you anything, Detective? Black coffee? A life?"

Muldoon slipped his glasses to the end of his nose and stared down the man with a gaze that could probably fell any bulky criminal. Unfazed, Levi tilted his head to the side, his face awash in mock innocence as he waited for the detective's response. "Black. Thanks."

The moment Levi walked out of earshot, Muldoon leaned close. "If I was confused about you and Cooter, you and that guy—" he hitched his thumb in the direction of the café "—that, I do not get at all."

"Jealous much?" I meant it as a joke but when the man started stuttering and tripping over his words, I couldn't help but wonder if I'd hit the nail there. But that would just be...silly. "He's my friend." I didn't need to explain. Why was it any of his business? But once I started, I couldn't shut up. "My best friend. My very gay, very best friend. I'd bet money he's working up the nerve to ask *you* out."

He wasn't really. Levi's type was... He liked them a little younger and malleable. Muldoon was too much of a type-A personality, too used to being in control, too...everything.

"I—uh..." More stuttering.

I managed to rattle the big bad detective. Why? Not that it mattered. I wasn't walking into that minefield for anything. "Look, if we're going to play this, you following me all day, let me give you my schedule so you don't have to practically run folks down when I make a yellow light."

"I didn't…"

"Yes, you did, at Western Center. You should be expecting a ticket in the mail in two to four weeks." I gave him a quick smile. "Seriously, you're totally obvious on a stakeout. You're one of the biggest men I've met."

Muldoon leaned back in his chair. His glasses still perched on the tip of his nose, he looked over the top at me. "I'm only six-five."

"Only…" I scoffed. "Detective, your height and all that black hair, you stand out just a wee little bit, you know."

He shrugged. "If you'd just promise to stay out of my investigation…"

I crossed my fingers under the table. "Oh, I promise. Absolutely."

Muldoon snorted and checked the cell phone at his hip. "Right." He stood and glanced in the direction Levi'd gone. "Behave. I'll…see ya around."

"I'm sure you will."

A few minutes later, Levi returned, coffee in hand. "Where'd he go?"

I shrugged. "Jaywalker down the block."

Levi handed me a cup and a plastic container that was tucked under his arm for the rest of my sandwich. He flopped down in the other chair and sipped the coffee he was still holding.

I transferred the leftovers to the container and frowned at my friend. "You don't like black coffee."

"It's not. I got a pumpkin spice latte." He looked at me over the top of the lid. "You have a way of running folks off."

A COUPLE OF hours after lunch, I was unloading groceries and turned the TV on. I'd already followed up on all the messages on my voice mail—not that there were very many. I had several hang ups, a call saying "This call is not from a debt collector..." which I deleted before hearing anything else, and the time and date of Chad's funeral—the next morning at nine.

I was excited. Not about Chad still being dead. That was just...wrong. No, I was looking forward to the funeral because I'd have all the players I knew of in one place. I could ask a few discreet questions and try to figure out what the hell was going on. Number one on my questioning list was Chad's ex-wife, Julia. For so many years she'd put up with his philandering. The teachers had always speculated on the whys and hows of her unwavering support of her husband, but no one knew for sure.

The day we discovered they were getting divorced the speculation grew tenfold, but no one had ever learned any details. Chad had kept pretty mum about the whole thing.

Next on my list were the two liars. Kelsey and Danny would hopefully be there. Surely neither would ditch the funeral of their boss. It was bad form, and if anything *was* going on, their absence would throw suspicion on them further, wouldn't it?

I really didn't have any business poking my nose in Muldoon's case. I could hear his voice in the back of my head saying so. Colin was in the clear. I hadn't done anything wrong. Whether it came to be that I'd have to prove it remained to be seen. Already someone had broken into my home. It could have been coincidence. But, statistically speaking, what were the chances of a random break-in on the heels of my boss dying and a break-in at the school? Slim to none? Or was that just my way of coping, making myself feel safer?

Though really, which was safer? That or a random break-in in a neighborhood that had so few? It put me on edge. Why would my house be targeted? It was smack-dab in the middle of the street, not the easiest to get to or from without being seen. No one could see in from outside so my hodgepodge furniture was not to be coveted. I really didn't have anything worth stealing. The only thing I did eventually find missing were some old home movies—and Paige could have very easily misplaced them or taken them to Colin's with her. She liked to watch them.

And if it was tied to Chad's death, then why me? I didn't have anything to do with it. I didn't know who did. I couldn't imagine what would make me stand out as a conspirator to the police or the "bad guy," and again, nothing I could tell was stolen. Was my house ransacked to scare me to back off? Had I hit on something close to the case?

Nothing that I'd learned made a difference or made sense.

I had to stop dwelling on it all, though. I was starting to spook myself. With Paige at Colin's, my house was eerily quiet and a little depressing. I was reaching for the remote to change off the early-edition local news show and find some sappy chick flick when a familiar name caught my attention. "… Kelsey Pierce was found dead in her apartment. A spokesman for the Peytonville Police Department has declined an interview while they are still in the early stages of investigation. There has been much speculation as to how her death may tie in to that of her boss, school principal Chad Jones, earlier this week."

I dropped the carton of orange juice I was holding. Kelsey, dead? That wasn't possible. I'd just seen her two days earlier. I ran to the front door and searched for Muldoon's car. I'd seen him when I'd gone into the grocery store, but I'd managed to forget about him by the time I left and headed back home. When I needed to ask him a question, he was nowhere to be found.

I snatched up my purse and dug through my wallet until I found his card. He didn't answer so I left a message.

I'd paced my living room floor twenty-four times— I counted—before Muldoon returned my call. And that was only to hear a brief, "I'm headed to your house. Sit tight."

It took another four trips across the floor and back before my front bell rang. I let him in and while I didn't know him all that well, the look on his face was indeed grim.

"What's going on?" I hugged my arms to myself, trying not to let my wild imagination run rampant. Knowing another coworker was dead, I was more frightened than I had been in a long, long while.

Muldoon settled his hand in the middle of my back and guided me to the sofa. "Sit. We need to talk."

"Gaw, you're not going to accuse me of killing Kelsey now, too, are you?" I was being facetious; I didn't know how or when she'd died. It could have been an accident or natural causes—if a twenty-something could die of natural causes. No reason to jump to all sorts of conclusions. Still, my legs were a little wobbly, so sitting was good. "It feels like every crime committed in the last few days is pointed at me and only me."

Muldoon sat next to me, his knees snugged up next to mine. "We know you weren't the one who killed her."

"So she was murdered? Why? How?"

"I can't really go into details." He glanced down at

his hands balled in his lap. "Her apartment was ransacked."

"Like mine?"

He nodded.

What if I had been at home? Or Paige for that matter? Nausea aggravated the back of my throat. "I did notice something missing."

Muldoon looked up at me with a frown. "Why didn't you tell me?"

"I'm telling you now."

He rolled his hand at me impatiently. "Well?"

"DVDs. When I'd righted the DVD case and put everything back, it wasn't quite normal. I didn't actually realize it until later this morning, but some of them are missing."

"Which ones?"

"Home movies of Paige when she was little."

"Were they labeled?"

"What difference does that make?"

"Answer the question." He was using his cop voice again.

I stiffened my shoulders. "Yes, Detective, they were labeled. Sort of. They were in those plain cases you can see through, and had the years written on them."

"Is that all? Not titles or names?"

"Just the years. We knew who was on them." I gave him my best "duh" look. "Paige could have taken them with her to her dad's." The look on the detective's face said otherwise. I slipped my cell from my pocket and lickety-split texted Colin and asked him to check with our daughter.

My brain went into overdrive. Why was Muldoon asking these questions? "What do my missing DVDs have to do with any of this?"

My cell vibrated. "Paige doesn't have them."

Muldoon nodded. "We found some DVDs at Kelsey's apartment."

"What was on them?"

He gave me a long look. "I can't share that information."

I scoffed and stood. "You won't tell me this. You can't tell me that. I am in this one way or another."

His cell rang. He tucked it next to his ear, listened for a minute and answered, "Got it." Then he pocketed it. "I have to go." He got up and walked to the door. "Don't know if I told you, Colin alibied out."

"Yeah. You mentioned it this afternoon when you were tailing me." Yes, I sounded a little testy. I had every right to be pissed. Some weird stuff was going on, with my ass mixed up in the middle of it all. I had no clue how to protect myself. I didn't know who or what I was protecting myself from. So I slammed the door on the detective as he walked out.

What, like he can arrest me for a noise violation or something? Let him try.

I WENT THROUGH every inch of the house again, hoping to find something else missing that would make sense. Why would someone, anyone, steal home movies? There was nothing special on them—well, to me they were, they were Paige.

Nothing made sense. And I had to make it make sense. I needed to grab last year's yearbook. All the main characters were in the yearbook—well, those I knew of. I mean really there could be a world of people involved who I didn't know, but if I thought about that, my head would explode. Now if I could only remember where I'd stashed it.

I dug through my closet and came up empty-handed. Then I ransacked the spare—formerly known as Colin's—closet. I didn't find last year's yearbook but I did find a box of Colin's from his high school days.

Out of curiosity, I grabbed his senior year from the pile and found the graduating class of 1996. I spotted my ex without even looking at the names. He'd beefed up some over the years but for the most part he still looked the part that his caption read: *Colin Eagan, football captain, most athletic, most handsome and most likely to cause a wedgie.*

"Some things don't change."

The senior class wasn't very large, just over two hundred students. My senior class was closer to eight hundred—so easy to get lost in the crowd when you wanted to. I found the *M*s. There he was. Shaw Muldoon. Even at eighteen he had a presence about him. Strong. Brave. And no-nonsense. The caption under his picture read simply: *Valedictorian.*

A little shiver ran down my spine. "Sexy and smart." And so not the point.

The K-12 annual sat heavy in my lap when I remembered that Chad Jones started his teaching career at Peytonville Prep. He'd been there for a few years, moved around some, then came back to the school eight years earlier to take over as the principal. But I couldn't remember when he started. I flipped to the back to the index to see if there were any pages with him. No Chad Jones. But another name—or rather six—caught my attention, Six Muldoons. I paged back and forth through the listed entries.

Looked like Detective Muldoon had a pretty large family—there was no mistaking the resemblance from one Muldoon to the other. All blue-eyed and raven-headed. He and his brother Finn, according to the class dates, were ten years apart and bookended four sisters: Regan, Darcy, Claire and Alana. From Shaw to Finn, the Muldoons aged backward by two years, the youngest, Finn, at eight years old with his gapped-tooth grin.

"Wow, four sisters and a brother." I couldn't imagine. I was an only child with only one cousin and it looked like Paige would be an only child—not that I dwelled on that fact, most days. Colin was also an only child. He had lots of cousins but it wasn't the same thing.

All very interesting, but none of it pertinent to getting my ass out of the sling.

I set the book back among the others and shoved the box back into place. A little more digging in the closet netted no current books. Next, I went into Paige's room. A pang of loneliness knocked though me again. She'd only been at her dad's for a day and I missed the heck out of her.

Paige had to have looked through the book. Where would it be? I stood with my hands on my hips and scanned the room. If I were a ten-year-old, where would I put a school yearbook? I dropped to the floor and lifted the bedskirt. She might be a precocious child but tidy? Well, she'd gotten that—or lack thereof—from yours truly. One shoe, several dolls, a stash of books—she'd gotten into my romance novels again—and several articles of clothing cluttered under the bed. I pawed through it all until I hit pay dirt. Last year's yearbook.

It wasn't hard to figure out why she'd hidden it. A flower was pressed between the pages of the sixth grade class. A bright pink heart circled one Caleb Capps's picture.

"Ah yes, the crush."

While my little, sweet child was only ten, being in

the seventh grade put her in the midst of much older kids. Boys specifically. I would be a little more worried if the boys were the least bit interested, but they barely liked the girls in their own grade—having the junior high and high school kids all together, most of the newly turned teens drooled over the almost-out-of-school girls. A Mensa candidate ten-year-old two grades ahead of her own peers wasn't even on their radar. But that was an issue for another day...

Carefully, I thumbed through the book and went to my office. I pulled a notepad out from my desk and took both to the kitchen. I sat at the table with a pint of ice cream at my elbow. A spoon in one hand, my favorite purple felt-tip pen in the other, and the faculty section of the yearbook open in front of me, I let my brain kick in to sleuth mode. What were the connections?

What did I know? I took notes as I thought things through.

Chad Jones was murdered. But staged to look like suicide.

His office was broken into. At last mention, the police didn't know what if anything was taken.

My home was broken into. First glance, nothing missing. Further searching, DVDs were gone.

Kelsey was murdered. DVDs found at her home.

Muldoon never said what was on the DVDs or what they had to do with mine. Hell, he didn't even mention if they were mine. But with the questions he was asking they couldn't be mine or he'd know what they looked like and what was written on them. Nor had he said how any of it tied into Chad's murder.

Was I jumping to way too many conclusions here?

I scooped up a spoonful of frozen yummy and shoved the spoon in my mouth. Chad didn't have a TV much less a DVD player in his office. The police had confiscated his laptop. That much I did learn from Coz when he'd finally called that morning. Apparently the police found an email Chad had started to send out to a couple of subs the school frequently used.

And I was involved all because of the email *I'd* sent on Naomi's behalf. I shook my head. No good deed goes unpunished.

I pulled the spoon from my mouth, held it aloft. "May God strike me down if I ever lift a finger to help that woman again!"

"A little on the dramatic side, don't you think?"

"Mother fu—" I leaped off the chair and almost three feet in the air. "Levi, what the hell is wrong with you, sneaking up on me like that?"

The man didn't even have the decency to look the least bit sorry for scaring the ever-loving hell out of me.

"I knocked. Three times." He took the spoon from me, dipped it into my ice cream and had the pint finished in a few bites. "My favorite, thanks." He handed me the empty container and spoon.

I looked inside. Not even a single chunk of chocolate left. "Glad I could oblige."

He rolled his eyes. "Whatchya working on?"

"Trying to figure out what's going on. I made a list of what we know." I passed him the notepad and tossed out the empty pint.

"Don't forget your run-in with the two peeps up at the school," he said when I returned.

"One of whom turns up dead."

Levi's eyes widened. He hadn't heard the news so I told him what I knew.

I sat back down. "I'm not sure if I should be mad or scared."

"The two don't have to be mutually exclusive." He leaned his hip against the table. "I'd be mad as hell if someone kept blaming me for crimes I didn't commit. I'd be scared I couldn't get out from under it. And scared that whatever caught up to your boss and Kelsey might catch me unawares."

"Great, thanks. You always know just how to cheer me up, don't ya?" I gave him a quick, wan smile.

"I'm just saying." He tapped the pen onto the notepad. "Chad's enemies?"

"I've no clue." I shrugged.

"Ex-employees? Anyone holding a grudge?"

"No grudges that I know of." I leaned my head back to look at the ceiling while I thought. "Mrs. Farris. But she retired. She was close to eighty." Who else? I gnawed on my lip. "Bobbie Jacoby. She didn't renew her contract at the end of last year." I named off two other teachers who'd quit abruptly, which was weird. "Jerry Pullman." I sat up straight. "He was fired."

"Really. For?"

"Dunno." I shrugged. "They just said he was 'let go.'"

"The vaguest of the vague. Which helps us not." He gave me a sideways glance. "So what do we do next?"

"We?"

"Yeah, duh. Have I not been outstandingly helpful up to this point?"

"I landed in jail."

His eyebrows rose. "I didn't tell you to run a light."

"Twice."

"Mere formalities." He studied his nails. "None of which can be tied directly to me."

I rolled my eyes. "That doesn't make you any less culpable."

Levi waved away my comment. "Anyhoo...what's our next move?"

I sighed. That was the thing about best friends, they might egg you on to do stupid things—that wind your ass up in jail—but the really best friends will be right beside you planning the next adventure.

"Next move? Find something appropriate to wear to a funeral."

EIGHT

"WHICH ONE IS the widow?" Levi peered over the rim of his dark glasses then shoved them back up on his nose as he stood beside my car door.

I ran my hands down my black suit skirt when I got out of the car, then slid my arms into the three-quarter-sleeve jacket to cover my pale pink camisole. The cool morning air swept around us and lightly rustled the small copse of trees that lined the cemetery. I looked for police presence, seemed like I couldn't go ten minutes outside without seeing a police officer or two lurking about. If they were at the funeral, though, I didn't see them.

"Technically she's not a widow but his ex-wife." I scanned the small crowd. Fewer than half the staff were present at the cemetery, along with a handful of people I'd never seen before. Of the people I did know, most were looking at me and talking behind their hands—like our students do.

"What's up with all the little looks and sniggles under their breaths?" Levi leaned in close, voicing my thoughts.

"Not a clue." I tucked my clutch under my arm. It was getting to the point of unnerving, being the center of attention at someone else's funeral, but I spotted Julia Jones and pushed aside all other thoughts. She wore a black sheath dress with some feathered neckline and looked appropriately solemn. The matching hat… It was a little over the top for a funeral. But who was I to judge? "There's the ex. Black dress, dead bird on her head."

"Is that what it is? I thought maybe her dress threw up."

I guess there was a fine line between paying respect for the dead and sending off your ex-spouse with a proper *see you in hell*. Again, not my place to judge.

"Come on." I tugged Levi's sleeve and dragged him behind me.

"Julia."

She turned toward me. An instant frown pulled down her mouth. A feather shook loose and fluttered between us to the ground. She didn't so much as glance at it, just kept her haughty gaze pinned to mine. "Celeste."

Her usual tanned complexion was waxy and a little too made up for morning. Her dark eyes showed no hint of tears or sadness, just resignation. A plucked-too-thin brown eyebrow arched up expectantly.

"I am so sorry for your loss." I patted her arm, but she shied away from me so fast she almost tripped over her own feet. "Is something wrong?"

"It's bad enough Chad is gone, but for you to be here…" She shook her head, and a few more feathers came loose. She then whispered to the woman next to her and left me standing with my mouth gaping open in confusion, looking like *I* was molting.

"What in the hell was that all about?"

I slammed my mouth shut and shrugged. Sure, I found the body and was questioned by the police, but she couldn't possibly think I had anything to do with Chad's death. Hell, how would she even know about the interviews? It was too ludicrous to consider that she saw me as a murderer. "Some days I think everyone around me has lost their ever-loving minds."

"Present company excluded, of course."

I waved at Levi. "Sure, whatever. Oh, there's Colin and *her*." I headed in their direction at a pretty good clip. "Hey. Where's Paige?"

Naomi looked down her long pointy nose at me. She wore a tan wrap dress that matched her caramel highlights perfectly. She'd have been breathtaking if her five-inch heels weren't sinking into the ground, making her wobble like a child playing dress-up. "This is hardly the place for a child," she said as she tried to gracefully right herself.

I sighed and turned my attention to Colin. "I didn't expect you to bring her here. But I am curious as to where *my* daughter is."

Colin swallowed heavily. "At my mom's."

Should have known. There were plenty of Eagans who would jump at the chance to watch Paige for an afternoon. Colin would, of course, have to take her to the one Eagan who couldn't stand me—the woman threw a party the day our divorce was finalized. I received a "you're not invited, but…" announcement. What a peach.

Naomi nudged Colin in the ribs. Some not-so-subtle power struggle was going on.

I didn't care, didn't want to know. "Levi, let's—"

"Um, Celeste?" Colin snagged a hold of my elbow. I waved Levi off as he stepped forward ready to drop-kick my ex if need be. "We need to talk."

Uh-oh. The four most dreaded words every woman fears. But we were long since divorced. They had zero power over me anymore.

Colin walked the two of us off to the side, away from

several staff members who were trying to look like they were not eavesdropping.

"Under the circumstances, Naomi and I…" Colin swallowed hard again. "Um, I think that it's best if Paige stays with me for a little while."

Oh, how wrong I was. The result of those four little words could tear a hole right through me in an instant. I fisted my hands at my sides. "I beg your damn pardon?"

Colin ran his hands though his hair, then settled his hands on his hips. "Look. We both want what's best for Paige, right? With your house being broken into—"

I'd had to tell Colin what happened. After my cryptic email about the DVDs he'd been too curious to blow off.

"—and in light of all the allegations going on, I think keeping her with me for a little while is best." He glanced down at his feet and back up at me. "I don't want to be a dick about it, but if you force my hand, I am prepared to play hardball."

I opened my mouth, shut it. Opened it again, but was at a complete loss as to what I wanted to say. Or do.

My first instinct was to punch Colin. How dare he threaten me with my child? But deep down a little niggle said that he was right. When it came down to it, Paige's well-being far superseded anything and everything. "Okay."

"I'm not trying to be… What? Okay? Just like that?"

"Give me some credit, Colin. Did you expect me to make a scene and tell you no?" I held in a sigh.

He shifted from one foot to the other and looked past me quickly before squaring his gaze back on mine.

"You did." I glanced back over my shoulder to Naomi. Through gritted teeth, I said, "Paige comes first. Nothing else matters. I will always do what's best for my child. And protect her."

He tucked his hands in his pockets. "I knew that. I mean know that. For what it's worth, I'm sorry this has happened."

The minister called everyone over to begin the grave-side service. With the tension in my shoulders threatening to strangle me, I decide it was time to hit the road. I was afraid I might just upchuck my morning lattes right then and there and frankly I wasn't looking to give people anything else to talk about.

"Can I call her?"

"Of course you can. And stop by whenever you want."

Naomi made some strange, choking sound at his offer.

"I'll pack a few extra things for her and bring them by later tonight." It took all my will to hold the tears at bay.

"That would be great. Thanks." Colin patted my arm and turned back to Naomi. She waylaid him with all the reasons why that was a bad idea. Colin glanced back over his shoulder. "Seven thirty okay?"

Glad to know his balls were still firmly intact and hadn't been forfeited to his new girl, I pasted on a weak smile. "See you then."

I motioned for Levi to follow me and headed back to the parking lot.

"Funeral's that way, sweets."

There didn't seem to be enough oxygen getting to my lungs. I took in a heavy breath. "Paying my respects has lost any appeal."

"What happened with Colin? You turned about four shades of green."

"You weren't eavesdropping?"

He shrugged and waved his cell at me before tucking it in his suit jacket pocket. "I tried but I got a call on a prospective property."

That's the man I knew and adored. The only thing that would keep him from putting his nose in someone else's business was making money.

He skipped along beside me, his breath huffing a little as he tried to keep pace. "Are you gonna tell me what happened? Or do I have to go over there and ask Colin?" He shuddered dramatically.

I sighed and slowed to a brisk my-life-is-so-screwed-up gait. "He's going to keep Paige with him for a little longer."

Levi frowned. "How much longer?"

"At the moment?" I stopped at my car, sat on the bumper, took several deep breaths and adjusted the heel strap of my shoe. "Indefinitely."

Levi's mouth worked open and shut. Little more than squeaks came out.

"Yeah, pretty much my first reaction, too."

"He can't do this."

"He can and is." And I wasn't planning to fight him on it. There were too many variables still unknown in Chad's case. And I had inadvertently—well, not really inadvertently since I was potentially being accused of his death—thrust myself into the investigation, as Muldoon reminded me at every turn.

He'd gone so far as to stalk me to see if I'd stay out of it all. My mind flashed to Annabelle. I needed to remember to call her and see how her date went. It had been so long since I'd got the first-date jitters I couldn't even remember. It was easier to focus on her life rather than mine; hers seemed so much more manageable, if totally un-relatable.

I'd put off dating for so long since the divorce. Work

and Paige took up most of my time. Work had gone to hell and Paige was with her dad, leaving me more alone than I had been in years. I could admit to myself, but not quite yet to Levi, that I seriously needed to rethink my no-dating policy.

Muldoon's face popped forward. While the idea of him was very appealing, he was too dedicated to his job. I sighed and pushed it all from my mind. It was time to get back home and go over my notes again. I had nothing better to do between the funeral and school on Tuesday.

I reached for my purse to get my keys and knocked it loose from under my arm. It fell to the ground at my feet. With a heavy sigh, I bent to retrieve it. "I know you don't want to hear this but I have to say I…" As my fingers seized the small black clutch, a little red blinking light under the car caught my attention. "Shit."

"You shit? Metaphorically, right?" He took a step back.

I was frozen, could not get my brain synapses to fire. The breath stalled in my lungs and dizziness swept over me.

"Celeste, sweets. Are you okay?"

Not really. Not with a bomb strapped to the undercarriage of my car. I didn't want to move. Weren't bombs triggered by movement? Or was it ignitions? A scene from a movie popped into my head. A police detective was sitting on his toilet and found a bomb. If he moved…kablooey. Yeah, I wasn't about to move. Without so much as twitching, I swiveled my head to the side to look up at him. "Phone?"

Levi frowned and stepped back another length. He pulled his cell from his pocket and waggled it at me. "Why?"

"Under my car."

"What's under your car? Sweets, you're acting stranger than usual." Levi bent and looked at what had captivated me so. His eyes grew larger and round. "Dialing 911."

He chatted away with a police dispatcher, flailing his arms wildly as he explained the situation. "B.O.M.B. Under her car." He paused and rolled his eyes heavenward. "I don't know what kind. I've never seen one before." He raked his hand over his face and dropped to the ground beside me. "I don't know. It's a little black box. Red blinking light. There's a couple of wires and duct tape." He nodded several times. "Mmm-hmm. Mmm-hmm. A little green bubble-looking tube. Are you sure?" Levi's voice creaked. "Sweets, whatever you do, do not move. Do you hear me?"

"Yes." I tried to keep the hysteria out of my voice. I wanted to jump up and run as far away as I could. Out of the parking lot. Out of Peytonville—hell, out of Texas. My back was starting to cramp and my thighs were on fire. My body was not meant to stay half bent over for so long. Worse still, my nose was all atingle. I released my purse and rubbed at my nose, but the tingle built to a tickle. "Oh, sneeze."

Levi shot to his feet. "You can*not* sneeze."

Sirens echoed in the parking lot.

I squeezed my nose shut. Could not, would not sneeze.

"Sit tight, sweets, they're coming."

"Like I have a choice." It came out all nasally and whiney. I hated that.

"Don't bite my head off. I didn't put that contraption under your car." Levi's pissiness pulled my attitude up short.

"I know. Sorry."

I had no concept of time as all sorts of commotion surrounded me. At that moment, I was thankful I was bent in half and not able to see all the gawkers wondering what's what. Levi moved farther away, replaced by someone resembling the Pillsbury Doughboy, but with my limited sightline, the entire town of Peytonville could be staring down my neck and I wouldn't know. The Doughboy moved closer and held a long pole with a mirror on the end.

It eased under the rear of the car. I caught a glimpse of my reflection. Hanging upside down was not my friend. My cheeks were puffed up under my eyes. My chin morphed into jowls. And I could practically see my puny brain up my nose. Luckily, no one else could see me.

A pair of rubber-soled dress shoes eased into my line of sight. "Celeste?"

I was *not* hearing my name called by Detective Muldoon. I couldn't be.

I closed my eyes and counted to ten. "Nope. Still there," I said when I opened them again and saw the same pair of dark Rockports just on the edge of my periphery. I tilted my head ever so slightly. "Hi, Detective. How's your day been? Mine? Just freaking peachy."

"Detective, you need to get back," someone called from the other side of the car.

Muldoon did not, however, listen and came up to the end of the car. He squatted next to me. His knee crackled slightly. "I heard the call over the radio. A potential bomb at the Jones funeral. I thought to myself, what are the chances it's Celeste? But no. There's no way she could get tangled up with a bomb at a funeral." Humor and a wee bit of fear laced his words.

"I strive to be a challenge a minute."

"And you have succeeded brilliantly." He let out a deep breath. "Are you okay?"

Tears welled up in my eyes. "Not really." I sniffed—my sinuses felt like they were going to explode. "How bad is it?"

"Do you want the absolute truth?" He reached forward and touched the tips of my fingers with his but didn't try to hold onto me.

I was so very thankful for the contact. "Um, how about seventy-five/twenty-five."

"A little iffy. There's a bomb strapped to the undercarriage of your car and it appears to have a motion trigger. The slightest movement could set the thing off."

"I wanted seventy-five percent optimism."

"It was."

"O-okay." The tears made the sneezing potential flee. My nose was too stopped up to do much of anything. "What's going to happen?"

"They're clearing the area as we speak. There was another funeral going on at the far side of the cemetery as well as Jones's."

"And then?"

"Once the area is secure, the bomb squad will snatch you off the car and see what happens."

Another officer called to Muldoon and he stood.

A half sob, half hiccup caught in the back of my throat. "Muldoon. Shaw."

"Yeah, babe." He leaned toward me.

"Do me a favor. If things don't…" My voice shook. I took a deep breath. "Please make sure Paige knows how much I love her."

"I've seen you with her. Trust me, she knows."

"Promise me."

"I will. But we're gonna try damn hard so that I don't need to." As he turned to walk away, the device started beeping.

"Shaw, what's that? Why's it making noise?" From my vantage point I could see the light blinking wildly.

Muldoon dropped to the ground next to me again. People scrambled around us. He looked up at me. "Change of plans." He wiped his hands on his pants. "Y'all get back. Get back. We're going to have to move her now." He squatted in a sprinter's stance. "Look at me, Celeste. When I count to three, I'm gonna grab you up and run like hell. Got it." He took hold of my elbows. "One, two—"

"Shaw, you can't—"

"Three." Muldoon hauled me up on my numb legs and flush up against him, then dragged me across the parking lot.

It lasted an eternity as I waited to feel shrapnel and pain shoot through my back. It was almost anti-climactic when we landed in a heap, then were covered by heavy blankets. Muldoon wrapped me up tight against him, covered me with his very own body. No one had ever protected me so well. It sparked every little-girl rescue fantasy I'd had when I still thought a man could make the world right. Granted they were more of making a boring old life more exciting. Never once had I dreamt of a car bomb—be careful what you wish for.

His heart pounded wildly against my shoulder as he tucked me under him more securely.

We waited. And waited.

No kablooey.

His heavy, warm breath rustled across my forehead. I will admit, I snuggled closer to him, let his strength just envelop me. I needed that moment, to myself, surrounded by him to let my heart come out of humming-bird range.

After what seemed like a few minutes—but really it could have been seconds or hours, I didn't know, I was so out of sorts—I said, "You can let me up now." My muffled voice only wavered a little.

If he said anything, I honestly couldn't say. Everything from my knees to my eyelashes quivered with the adrenaline rush. He rolled to his side, taking me with him, and pushed aside the blanket. Several hands reached in and helped us to our feet, then guided us farther away.

Muldoon stood in front of me and cupped my face in his huge hands. "You okay?"

"Someone put a fake bomb under my car." It was more or less a statement. Not a question.

"Celeste, look at me." Muldoon's grip tightened on my face ever so much.

I shifted my attention to his blue gaze surrounded by dark, sooty lashes. He had gorgeous eyes. Eyes women would long to have focused solely on them.

"Celeste?" Muldoon shook me slightly.

"What?"

"God, you sure do manage to get in the middle of it, don't you?"

I opened my mouth to tell him not on purpose, but a deafening, hot blast stopped any and every cognizant thought. I slapped my hands to my ears to try and close off the painful boom as Muldoon grabbed me and yanked me back to the ground underneath him again.

Just as quickly, the sounds dissipated. Car parts—my car parts—rained down on us and all the emergency personnel in the lot. An acrid stench filled the air. I tried not breathe too deep.

"My car blew up." The mantra repeated over and over in my head. And maybe aloud. I can't really say for sure what I said—I was in the throes of a meltdown as whatever parts of me hadn't been shaking before took up the scared-spitless shimmy.

Muldoon shook nearly as badly as I did. We sat up and glanced at what was left of my little sedan. I wasn't sure how my insurance agent was going to take the news.

Shaking my head to clear the bells, I looked at Muldoon. His hair fell across his forehead. When I reached out and pushed it back, my hand came away a little moist. I glanced at the dripping digits. Something red coated them. My gaze snapped back to his forehead where a huge, nasty gash slashed sideways up into his hairline. "You're bleed…"

NINE

"CELESTE, CAN YOU hear me?"

I heard him, whoever he was. It sounded like he was at the end of a tunnel—with a sweater over his face, voice all woolen and muffled.

"Celeste?"

Pain radiated from my biceps. "Yeow." My eyes fluttered open to see a strange man standing over me. "Did you pinch me?" My words slurred like it was three-dollar Appletini night. "Why would you do that?"

The young EMT—I finally got a glimpse of his nifty uniform—smiled down at me. "Sorry. Didn't have time to grab the smelling salts." He flashed a penlight in my eyes. "Can you tell me what year it is?"

"Why? Did you lose your calendar?"

The man frowned. "Checking for a possible concussion, ma'am."

"Ma'am? That's what you call old women. I am not old. Do I look old to you? Actually don't answer that, you look like you're about twelve so to you I just might be." Such an odd conversation to be having—somewhere outside. Not that I was completely sure where outside we were, but I could feel the breeze across my face. A pungent odor permeated the air. A bonfire? I doubt it. I couldn't remember the last time I'd gone to a bonfire.

All sorts of commotion blotted out the ambient

noises. Should that be a clue? I closed my eyes again to consider the possibilities.

"Ma'am? Celeste, I need you to work with me here."

I cracked an eye open and gave the young man my best withering look—with one eye open. Call me *ma'am* again, will he?

"She didn't hit her head. It was the b-l-o-o-d," Levi said from somewhere over the EMT's shoulder. "Made her faint."

"Levi. What are you doing here?" As I asked, *here* came screaming back to me. My car. "Are you okay?" I struggled to sit up. The horrendous explosion echoed in my ears. Little-bitty pieces of sedan had sailed across the parking lot. Shrapnel caught Muldoon. "Where's Muldoon? Is he…" My throated seized.

"Detective Muldoon is getting taped up." The EMT went through a battery of questions—all of which I answered truthfully—well mostly—with a minimum of sarcasm. I mean really, if I lied about how woozy I was, how was he to know? I didn't want to be poked or prodded any more than was absolutely necessary.

When he finished, I finally got to get up off the hard cement parking lot. Levi rushed over and hugged me until I couldn't breathe. "Oh my gawd, I thought you were a goner. When it blew…" Tears laced his words. He kissed the top of my head four or five times, making so much noise several eyes darted in our direction.

"Making a scene." I pushed at him.

"I almost lost you. I can make as much of a scene as I want." He gave me one last—louder than the rest—smack square on the mouth and loosened his death grip on me. He did not however relinquish all hold of me as he kept my hand tucked in his.

It was my first chance to get a good look at the area.

My car—what was left of it—was pretty much on top of the car in the next slot. Was it too much to hope that the little red Mercedes belonged to Naomi? Probably bad karma to even think it so I shook away that little bit of hope.

Several cars in the vicinity had charred sedan parts sticking out of them. Several fire trucks, three ambulances, six squad cars along with news vans crowded the edges of the lot. Yellow crime scene tape wrapped its way around a perimeter.

A handful of gawkers graced the other side of the tape. I thankfully didn't see Colin or Naomi. Julia Jones was talking animatedly to the woman beside her, feathers floating around them. A few other teachers stood next to her. The algebra teacher held his cell phone out. Recording my adventure for the next faculty meeting?

I turned my back on the entire scene and found Muldoon walking toward me. "Are you okay?" I asked at the same time he said, "Are you hurt?"

"I'm fine," we both said.

Without thinking, I wrapped my arms around him and hugged him. "I can't thank you enough. If you hadn't been here…" The tears I'd been holding back fell in buckets. And buckets. Muldoon held me close and rubbed my back, all the while muttering calming words. When my shudders and sobbing ratcheted down to mere sniffles, he let go of me.

"Did they check you out? Do you have a concussion?"

Heat flamed my cheeks.

"She faints at the sight of blood." Levi was more than happy to drop that little foible any chance he could get. My ass was almost blown to Dallas and he thought my hemophobia was funny.

Muldoon's eyebrows rose, then he flinched and reached for the white dressing.

His wound all covered, I was good to go. I gently touched my fingers to his forehead. "Does it hurt bad?"

"Not too. Couple of butterfly bandages." Someone called to him and he glanced over his shoulder. "If you're up to it, we need to ask you a few questions."

"I guess. Sure."

He guided me toward a squad car. "Detective Bush will debrief you on what happened before and after you discovered the bomb."

"What? Why can't I just talk to you?"

"We need someone who can be objective."

He likes me. Heat bloomed in my cheeks. "You can't be objective?" I wonder what the waiting period was after nearly getting blown up before asking someone out. *Gaw.* I had no business thinking of my lackluster dating life and how Muldoon could make up a lot of distance in that race.

"No." He rubbed at the tape on his bandage. "Not when I was part of the rescue."

And with that, I was left at the gates again.

He was part of the rescue. How did he always manage to stay so distant from a case, victim or a crime? I guess it was his job. I was just part of another case, part of the job, not a potential lust connection. Maybe I did need to get checked out a little more thoroughly. I could have a concussion. I tenderly fingered the bump on the back of my head. It could explain the delusions of chemistry between the detective and myself.

Detective Bush, short, stubby and not the least bit attractive—not that it mattered—stood by his car waiting to escort me down to the station. Without so much as glancing back at Muldoon, I slipped into the backseat of the cruiser and was driven to the Peytonville police station so I could be subjected to a new round of questions.

Wonder if they'll name a wing after me.

IT WAS EARLY evening by the time Levi finally dropped me off at home. He'd had one of his employees swing by with his car as we were left to hoof it when my sedan exploded. He'd offered to stay with me, keep me company, but I needed some alone-time to sort through my thoughts.

I'd spent the better part of three hours going over, and over, the morning and up through the bombing with Detective Bush. Then I'd gone around and around with my insurance agent, who didn't believe me the first ten minutes of our conversation. Once I started spouting off the phones numbers for the police and fire departments and who he needed to contact, his demeanor sobered. And as I feared, my premium was going to blow up as high as my car had.

I wanted to use the rental car option in my policy, but the insurance agent was hemming and hawing. I got the impression he wasn't going to approve the claim; I was a sudden liability. And I couldn't just go out and rent one. I had no current driver's license. It was in my purse. Unfortunately, it had been destroyed in the blast. Along with the rest of the contents of my wallet: all my credit cards and bank card. Poof. Gone. My cell phone and my two favorite Clinique lipsticks were also disintegrated. My car keys and house keys had been blown to kingdom come, too. Not that I had a car to go with it. Thankfully Levi had a spare set to the house. He'd run out and had copies of the house key made while I was at the station.

Did I mention what a good friend he was?

Once home, and alone, I plopped down on the sofa, kicked off my scuffed shoes—my two-inch black mock-crocodile wedges were not meant to outrun explosions—and propped my feet up on the coffee table. The home phone rang for the umpteenth time since I'd walked in the door. Thank goodness for voice mail. One reporter after another wanted a statement or comment. Their pestering was nothing compared to Detective Bush's grueling line of questioning, which I had no choice but to answer. The reporters, I didn't have to tell squat.

When it rang again, Colin's number popped up on the caller ID. I didn't really want to speak with him either, but he could be calling about Paige. I snapped up the receiver next to me. On a sigh I answered, "Hey, Colin."

"Finally. I've been calling—"

"I was otherwise busy, as I'm sure you know." I rubbed my left temple. Since the bombing, the ringing in my ears had lessened and some of the Eau de Burnt Car had dissipated, but a low pain radiated from my skull and I thought of a campfire every time I sniffed.

"Your car exploded." Just a statement. No question or demands for answers.

I rolled my eyes. "Can't get anything by you."

"You see why I'm keeping Paige with me?"

I could picture him standing there: legs spread shoulder-width apart, the phone to his ear with one hand, the other smashed on his hip. It was his coaching stance—minus the phone-to-his-ear part, of course. Which doubled for his mad stance, disappointed stance and his are-you-gonna-eat-the-last-slice-of-pizza stance. Not to mention his I-told-you-so-stance. He didn't like to mix it up.

I should be pissed, but I was too tired to argue—plus he had a valid point. "Did you want something?"

"Are you okay?" His voice softened. "I mean really okay?"

Did I tell him the detective all but accused me of planting the bomb myself? Bush hadn't come out and said it in so many words, but his line of questioning led that direction. Did I tell Colin I didn't know what I'd gotten myself into and was scared of what was to come next? Did I confide in a man I used to share all my secrets with? A man who now had a new confidant and would not, could not, do so in return.

"I'm okay," I said finally. "A little frazzled but otherwise okay." For the most part it was true—physically. No point in worrying him with anything more than the obvious issues—being on a suspect list and my car blowing up. I didn't need to unburden myself that bad. He couldn't help me any more than I could help myself. As long as he kept Paige safe, that was all that mattered.

He didn't speak for a long moment. "Paige wants to speak with you."

I closed my eyes. "Did you tell her?"

Colin huffed. "It was all over the news."

I should have known.

Paige got on the phone. "How are you?" She was a little breathless. "Was it incredible when the car blew up?"

"I'm good, sweet pea. It wasn't near as exciting as the news made it sound." Which was a total lie and I didn't even know what they'd said. But unless someone stood that close to an explosion, there was no way to do it justice. "How is it at your dad's?"

"Colin is fine, but Naomi…" She sighed. "I will be glad when their relationship runs its course."

I couldn't help but chuckle. "Please don't say that around Naomi."

"I would never be so callous."

"I'm sure you wouldn't." I removed the clip from my hair. My carefully coiffed hair hadn't withstood the blast. When I'd gotten a good look at myself at the station, I was a cross between the Mad Hatter and Medusa. Thankfully a young, female police officer had taken pity on me and given me a clip from her desk.

I'd had a beautiful leather-tooled clip in my purse. And we know how that turned out.

"I should go." Paige lowered her voice. "Naomi cooked dinner and is waiting beside the table. If she doesn't stop trying to frown like that, her Botox will wear out."

I knew it, I wanted to shout, but all the fire and fight faded away. "I love you, sweet pea. You be good for your dad."

"Love you, too. Stay out of trouble, please." Most kids would be on the receiving end of that comment.

We hung up and the phone instantly rang again. "I'll be careful, I swear."

"Sounds like it's a little late for that."

I dropped my feet to the floor and sat up. "Mom. Hi."

"You're in an explosion and questioned by the police and you don't even bother to call." The woman tsked through the phone.

"How did you…"

"Your cousin taught Dad and I how to watch news feeds from Dallas on the internet."

"Damn Lucy." It wasn't bad enough she'd tell on me any chance she got when we were kids, now she was getting me in trouble from nearly five hundred miles away.

"I knew I'd see you on there one day. What happened? What are you subjecting my granddaughter to down there?"

I'd rather take Bush's questioning over my mother's any day. I was a full-grown woman with a child of my own and she could still make me feel like an awkward teenager who didn't have enough sense. "Paige was nowhere near the explosion. It happened at Principal Jones's funeral."

"What kind of people do you associate with?"

You have no idea. Apparently no one did. "I'm fine, by the way. Thanks for asking."

"Well, of course you are. If anything terrible had happened, that good-for-nothing ex of yours would have called."

"If he called, he'd be good for something then, right?" I'd defended Colin to my mother so many times, it had become second nature. Not that he'd necessarily needed or wanted to be defended—then or now—but it was habit. "Well, look at the time. I've gotta go. Give Daddy a kiss for me."

She was still yammering away with some outrage or another when I hung up. I'd have to remember to call Daddy in the morning when my mother was up at one of her clubs.

Until then, a hot bath and a glass of wine would do the trick. I eased up from the chair and dragged myself into the kitchen. I'd just poured a very generous helping of merlot when the doorbell rang.

I'd told Levi to leave me be. I love him, but come on.

I stomped to the door, wineglass in hand. "What?" I hollered when I snatched the door open.

A man wearing a pair of jeans and a starched green button-down shirt took a step back. "Celeste Eagan?"

He looked only a couple years younger than myself despite his boyish freckled cheeks. He ran a hand through his short-cropped sandy-blond curls.

I had a bath to run and a drink to gulp. I was a little impatient when I said, "Yes?"

"Hi, I'm Kellen Schaeffer with the *Peytonville Gazette*. I was hoping you could answer a few questions."

Super. The day that couldn't get worse nosedived. "I'm sorry, I don't have anything to say to you." I closed the door, or at least tried to. The reporter put his hand up and stopped it before I could get it more than halfway shut. Then he wedged his foot at the bottom. I gripped the edge to slam it as soon as he moved his loafer-clad foot.

"Wouldn't you like to go on the record and give your side of the story as to how your car blew up at your boss's funeral?"

As if. "Nope." I held his gaze but he didn't back off.

He glanced at a Muldoon-looking notebook. "Even with the rumors out there that you—"

My hand slid down the edge of the door. "Rumors? It just happened this morning, how can there already be rumors?"

"—set it yourself to throw off suspicion of your involvement in the man's death?"

Sure, Detective Bush's questions had leaned that direction, but why was the media? "What?"

He didn't blink, laugh or shout *just kidding*. Just waited for me to comment.

The wineglass sat heavy in my hand. I slugged down the contents, to lighten it of course. As soon as I did, Kellen Schaeffer scribbled something on his notepad. Super, I'd be a lush suicide car bomber tomorrow morning when the paper came out.

"Would you like to comment on the connection between the break-in at your home and Kelsey Pierce's home? How her death is tied into all of this?"

My house? Her house? "How do you…"

He hid a smile—almost. "I have my sources."

I arched an eyebrow heavenward. A little bit of wine, and my eyebrows were loosey-goosey. "Mind if you tell me who those sources are?"

"I can't do that." He shook his head and chuckled lightly.

"Of course not." Yeah, I didn't expect him to.

He leaned in a little closer. I could smell his woodsy cologne. "I've also learned you were arrested twice this week."

I blinked several times, trying to figure out what to say. The arrests weren't necessarily a secret but to have some reporter, a very cute reporter—I'm sorry, the wine was really kicking in and I couldn't help but notice—standing on my front porch, giving me a rundown of my worst week in the history of worst weeks was…a little too freaky. "It was nothing. I wasn't actually charged with anything." Fingerprinted, mug shots taken and questioned, but ultimately let go, and that's really all that mattered. Right?

"I appreciate you giving me the opportunity," I said in my best saccharine voice. "But I think I'll pass."

The reporter nodded and tucked the notebook in his back pocket. "Okay. If you change your mind—" he held out a business card "—call me. Anytime. My cell number's on the back." When I didn't take it, he tucked it into the empty wineglass in my hand, winked and turned to leave.

"Mr. Schaeffer?"

"Call me Kellen."

"Can you just give me a hint how you got my name and info?"

He paused. "Hmm. Tit for tat maybe. Call me when you want to talk."

I LEANED FORWARD in the hot bath, and bubbles lapped over the side. I loved my tub. It was one of the few additions I'd made to the house when Colin moved out. It could probably fit four people it was so huge—not that I'd tried, mind you. It had a whirlpool and I'd sprung for the deluxe tiled steps and surrounding ledge in a delicate soft pink ceramic. I'd even painted the walls to match the darker veins in the tiles. It was heaven.

I checked the clip in my hair—might as well use the thing since I had it—and snagged my refilled wineglass. I'd emptied the rest of the bottle into it just before I slipped into the tub. I took a long sip, and then set it back on the edge of the tub. Warm water and a warm buzz. Just what the doctor ordered.

The CD player in the corner played Michael Bublé's "Crazy Love." The sweet tropical scent of the soy candles I'd placed around the bathroom pulled me from the crappy Texas autumn and transported me hundreds of miles away. It would have been stellar if I had some piña coladas rather than wine, but you make do with what you have.

One more deep sip and I sank down in the water up to my neck, leaned my head on the little tub pillow and closed my eyes, letting the day melt away.

The front doorbell rang.

"You have got to be kidding me." No more reporters. I wasn't in the frame of mind to hear their accusations or be "allowed" to speak on my own behalf.

The bell rang again, followed by a swift knock.

"Go away," I halfheartedly yelled and dunked myself under the foamy water. I could barely hear Michael's sexy voice, but the warm cocoon soothed the ache in my temple as well as the tension in my neck.

An odd bang echoed even under the water. Weird. I emerged from the water, and bubbles covered my face. When I swiped the suds away I yelped, met face to... metal with the barrel of a gun pointed at me.

TEN

"MULDOON? WHAT THE hell are you doing?" I stooped lower in the bath and crossed my arms. Thankfully the bubbles kept the majority of me hidden but I wasn't taking any chances.

He walked into the bathroom, gun still drawn, and peered around the door as well as in the cabinets under the sink. "Why didn't you answer the door?"

I narrowed my eyes and glared at him. "Who are you looking for, the Ty-D-Bol Man? He skipped out a few minutes earlier. If you hurry, you might be able to catch him." I narrowed my gaze further. "Again, I'm asking, what the hell are you doing in my house?"

"Why didn't you answer?"

"Isn't it obvious?" I cupped a handful of water and threw it at him, none of which actually hit him, just splashed all over my floor.

"Don't move." He slinked back out the door before I could so much as blink.

"Not to worry, Detective," I hollered after him.

Muldoon came back a few minutes later and shoved the gun in a holster under his arm, inside his jacket. He flipped the light switch on and slammed his hands down on his hips. And stared.

Modesty be damned, I uncovered whatever might be peeking through and grabbed my wineglass and drank. When I downed the rest of the wine, I waved the stemmed glass at him. "Care to explain?"

He sucked in a long breath and released it before he said, "All the lights were off."

I rolled my eyes. "Since when is that a crime?"

"You didn't answer the door."

I flicked more bubbles at him as comment.

"The officer sitting on your house saw you go in. When you didn't answer…" Muldoon closed the lid of the toilet, sat and swiped his hand over his face. The white bandage stood out starkly against his tanned skin and dark hair. He looked a little disheveled. In the few days I'd known Muldoon, he'd never been anything but spit-and-polish tidy. Sitting in my pink candle-laden bathroom, he looked rough around the edges and a wee bit haggard.

"You were worried?" A warm rush spread through me, then turned quickly to bitter cold. "Why am I still being watched? Do you honestly think I'd set a bomb under my own damn car? You must be crazy." I ended my tirade with a very ladylike hiccup.

Muldoon looked up from his perch. "How much have you had to drink?"

"Never you mind." I thrust my chin out in the haughtiest manner possible while sitting in a tub with bubbles disintegrating by the second. "Unless you're here to arrest me, I'd appreciate it if you'd leave."

He shook his head in a slow deliberate motion. "No arresting. But I'd rather not leave."

I crashed my hand into the water, sending more streams of water onto my floor as well as speeding up of the demise of my bubble cover. "Why?"

"There is still potential danger." His brows knitted together with a frown.

"From me? Or against me?" I lifted my foot and pushed it against the faucet to turn on the hot water.

When nothing more than cool water came out, I turned it back off, not wanting to wait while it warmed up, hoping Muldoon would just leave so I could get out of the tub.

"Why won't you take any of this seriously?" Again he took in and let out a long breath. "Do you not get the severity of it all?"

"Of course I do. My damn car blew up. It's doesn't get much more severe than that. But why are you so focused on me? What could I have possibly done to warrant so much scrutiny?" I waved my hands in a flourish and knocked the wineglass off the edge of the tub. It shattered into a billion pieces and I stared at it for a long moment. Anger was running through my veins, and the broken glass was the last straw.

I slammed my feet down in the tub and thrust to standing. "Look here, *Detective*, I am tired of being scared. I am tired of being looked at as a victim. Hell, I'm *really* tired of being looked at as a criminal. I want to make sure you hear me on this: I have done nothing wrong."

Muldoon lifted his finger and opened his mouth.

"Okay, fine, sure, I was 'arrested,'" I said with finger quotes. "One was bogus and you well know it. The other, there was nothing to charge me with. As a matter of fact, I have not been charged with one damn thing. You will not tie me to Chad's death. Listen up good, Detective, I didn't do it. You will not tie me to the bomb under my car either. I don't know the first thing about bombs or explosives. Not that I would attempt to throw off suspicion by putting my life—or anyone else's life, for that matter—at risk. Got that?"

Muldoon stood. A smile crinkled the corner of his mouth. He snagged the pink bath sheet from the towel rack and came next to the tub. He leaned forward—so close in fact I could feel his breath on my face—and wrapped it around me. "You might want to cover up."

Oh crap. Heat drained from my cheeks so fast I could feel it. I hoped against hope I was not standing completely nude in front of the lead detective out to put my ass behind bars.

I glanced down at my very wet and very naked body. Lumps of soap suds clung to various body parts but not near enough to cover up any particular part. Not a thing was left to his imagination. He got to see the full glory of my birthday suit.

"I, uh, sorry." I grabbed the ends of the towel and tucked myself deep inside. I was too shocked to do much of anything else.

Muldoon pushed his jacket sleeve up to his elbow, reached past me and pulled the stopper. His rough jacket brushed against my thigh and I thought I might go up in flames right then and there. Whether from embarrassment or lustful heat I couldn't say. Nor could I say which was worse. The next thing I knew, though, he'd scooped me up and lifted me out of the tub.

He walked into the hallway, held me for a moment, his gaze fiery as well when it locked onto mine, then set me down on the thick carpet and pushed me at arm's length—literally and figuratively. "Why don't you go get dressed? I'll clean up the broken glass."

How could a man turn you on and right back off again so quickly? And look not the least bit affected afterward?

On wobbly legs, I hurried to my room and slumped into a pair of denim jeans and a hooded KU sweatshirt. I stopped off at the linen closet to wrap a towel around my wet hair, then found Muldoon sitting on my sofa in the living room. "Did you get it all cleaned up?"

His elbows were on his knees, his fingers laced together in front of him. "Yes."

"Thanks." I curled myself up in the club chair and shoved my hands in the front pocket of the hoodie.

"Do you own any non-pink clothing?"

I eyed the detective for a long moment. "You didn't come over here to ask about my fashion tastes. Or clean up after my clumsiness." My cheeks heated and I narrowed my gaze. "Did you break my front door?"

Muldoon leaned back, tossed his arm over the back of the sofa and crossed his ankle over his knee, all casual as you please. "It's fine."

"Why are you here?"

"Someone blew up your car." He held my gaze. That was one thing I really liked about Muldoon, he didn't shy away when he spoke to people. He held your gaze. Kept it all real, if a little blunt. He finally asked, "Do you know who?"

"According to a reporter, I did it to throw off suspicion of my involvement in Chad's murder. Didn't you know people are speculating about that?"

"What reporter?"

I shrugged. "Kelly or something."

"Kellen Schaeffer?"

I had to think back on that—it was almost a full bottle of wine and totally embarrassing moment earlier in the evening. "Sure. That's it."

Muldoon closed his eyes and took a deep breath, then looked back at me. "What else did he say?"

"Nothing much. He wanted me to give him my side of the story."

He tugged on the hem of his jeans leg. "Did you?"

"Am I under some sort of gag order no one bothered to tell me about?"

"No."

"Then it's none of your business." Actually, I didn't know what was or wasn't the police's business. This was all new territory for me.

"If you're telling the media information regarding my case, then it is my business."

"Media?" I shifted in the chair. "It was one reporter for a local paper."

Muldoon held my gaze.

I yanked my hands from the pocket and slapped my knees. "I am getting screwed coming and going here. If I say something, I'm revealing too much. If I keep my mouth shut, it's assumed I'm hiding something. I don't even know what's going on. You tell me to back off your investigation. The next thing I know, you're keeping watch over me and telling me I am in potential danger. It's scaring the hell out of me."

"If scaring you keeps you vigilant, then so be it. You have to be aware."

"I'm supposed to be so vigilant that I check under my car for bombs?" I sighed and dropped my head back on the chair. "I didn't say anything to the reporter. Though he knew quite a bit all on his own. Said he had sources, whoever that may be. He wouldn't tell me who."

"You asked?"

"Of course."

Muldoon laughed. It was the second time I'd seen him laugh. "Of course you just came right out and asked a reporter who his source is. I'm half surprised he didn't tell you. Your tenacity alone is a worthy competitor."

"I'll take that as a compliment." I smiled back at him,

but I couldn't get past the worst worry that niggled at the back of my brain. "Can I ask you something?"

His eyebrow shot up. "Maybe."

"Is Colin totally off the hook? In the clear?"

The smile slid from his face. "His alibi the night of Mr. Jones's murder is solid. Why?"

I took a deep breath. "I need to know for sure that Paige will be taken care of. By him if not me."

"Why would that be an issue?"

"My car blew up today, remember? I get the feeling you don't think I'm worried enough. I promise you I am worried. Plenty. I'm scared beyond belief. But I don't know of what.

"My boss is murdered and I don't know why. Kelsey Pierce is killed and I don't know why. Someone puts a bomb under my car. My ex takes my child."

"Ah, Celeste…" Muldoon leaned forward.

"Don't give me your pity. While I don't like it, he's right. Whatever is going on is not worth risking her life."

"Still, I'm sorry. I know how much you adore her."

I wanted to ask if he had a significant other, or kids, but since it was none of my business I kept that query to myself. However, if he was married, the woman must be one patient lady. I'd run into Muldoon at all times of the day since Wednesday. "What time is it?"

"Five 'til ten."

"News is about to start. Do you think they got my good side?" I huffed. "Not sure which is the good side after a blast. Too bad they didn't catch it when it blew. I bet it was a sight." I snagged the remote from the coffee table and switched the TV on. "Do you want to watch with me or do you need to be going?"

"Celeste?" Muldoon grabbed my hand as I turned the channel to the local news. "Look at me."

Breath shuddered in my lungs as I lifted my gaze to his.

"Are you okay? Really?" His crystal-blue gaze held mine. The warmth of his hand seeped into mine. "No joking, smart-aleck reply or changing the subject. How are you feeling?"

"Petrified." I hadn't known how badly I needed that human connection until he touched me. The shudder increased and I began to shake. I dropped the remote and latched onto his hand with both of mine. "Worse than you can imagine. And that pisses me off, if that makes any sense at all."

Muldoon stood and pulled me to my feet. He wrapped his arms tightly around me and hugged me to his firm chest. I welcomed his strength and was glad not to be alone.

"...at Peytonville Prep." The blurb of the school name on the news caught my attention. I pushed back from Muldoon's grip and snagged the remote to turn up the volume.

"The lead detective on the Jones murder case declined to comment on the connection between that murder and the recent death of another school employee. He did say they have a person of interest for both cases and they have been keeping her under surveillance."

"*Her*?" I narrowed my eyes. "Am *I* the person of interest?"

"Celeste..."

"You were watching me when Kelsey was killed. You know I couldn't have anything to do with it." I shoved him farther away from me. "Why are you here?"

"I came to check on you."

"Because I'm *in danger.* That's what you said. Did you leave off *in danger of fleeing and getting away with murder*?"

"It's not like that." He ducked his head and broke eye contact.

"Isn't it?" I stalked away from him as the temptation to smack the hell out of him overwhelmed me—when did I get so violent? I wanted to hit just about everyone these days. And all I needed was for him to toss my ass in jail for assaulting a police officer—again. "You were awful quick to get to me in the parking lot this morning."

"I was there."

"Watching me." Not a question. "You said you heard it on the scanner." I shook my head. I'd suspected he was there. "I want you to leave. The next time you have something to say to me, go through my lawyer."

"Celeste…" His cell phone chirped. He held my gaze for a long moment, then dug it from his pocket and answered. He gave me one last look, then spoke to the caller and headed out the door.

THE NEXT MORNING was a Monday, but so not typical. I had little to do. School was still out one more day. Paige was at Colin's, and Levi was God knew where. I was housebound with no vehicle. And of course I'd woken with a horrible hangover—I might have opened another bottle of wine after I kicked Muldoon out and I might have drunk most of it—and way too early to make some of the phone calls I needed to. I was still wearing my jeans and KU hoodie, having fallen asleep in bed with a book—I don't know that I actually read any of it before I'd dozed off.

The underwire of the bra was poking me in the boob

as I lumbered down the hall to the kitchen to at least get some coffee brewing. I shoved my cold hands inside the hoodie and adjusted the undergarment so I could move without getting stabbed. Once I had a pot of hazelnut going, I walked to the front windows and peered through a little gap I made in the curtains. The sun hadn't even popped up over the tops of the houses yet. Streetlights illuminated the front of every third house. There was no movement for as far as I could see. I was, however, not interested in my neighbors. I was curious to see if anyone was watching my house.

Had Muldoon come back after whatever call sent him running out of here the night before? Had he put some rookie on my house? As much as I wanted to gripe and moan, if watching me 24/7 kept someone away from me, then I'd keep my mouth shut. For now.

I didn't see any unusual vehicles. Nothing stood out as obviously out of place, but I hadn't memorized the cars my neighbors drove. Other than Mr. Grant's bright orange Corvette, I don't think I could tell you who drove what. Still, nothing struck me as off.

A hazelnut aroma wafted around me and I made my way back into the kitchen. By my second cup I felt almost human. I buttered a piece of toast and picked through my mail from Saturday. So much had happened over the weekend, I'd lost two whole days. By the time I'd finished eating and pawing through bills and junk, I went to grab the newspaper.

A very unflattering, grainy photo of me stood out. I was front page news. It was below the crease, which meant it wasn't as important as the story about the warehouse fire on the edge of town, but still on the front page. I groaned and my headache came back with a vengeance. I poured one more cup of coffee before I could even read the article.

Coffee in one hand, article in the other, I cozied up in my chair. I took one long sip, sat down the cup and opened the paper. The article highlighted the car bombing, with speculations tying it to Kelsey's and Chad's deaths. Again, this time a direct quote from one Detective Shaw Muldoon, I was mentioned as a person of interest. I actually had little-to-no reaction to the news. I think the numbness of it all finally kicked in.

However numb I was, though, practicality seeped in. I made a game plan for my morning. I cleaned what little of the house had managed to get dirty again since the break-in. I even went through my closet and made a pile of clothes to take to the women's shelter, all to keep busy, so I didn't think too much about what had happened. At nine, I ran up to the bank. I had to dig up an old driver's license to get a new debit card issued and pull out some cash. That killed just enough time for a certain office to open at ten.

"I WANT TO retain your services." Between Muldoon's visit the night before and the newspaper article, I probably needed to cover my bases.

"Tell me what's been said up to this point."

I could hear Coz scribbling as I gave him a rundown of the past few days and the various interviews I'd had with the different departments and detectives. I neglected to include the bath escapades portion of the previous evening. He didn't need to know the detective in charge saw me naked.

Censure filled his voice when he said, "You should have called me sooner."

"I didn't think I needed to." I paced behind my sofa.

"Before you agree, is this going to be a problem for you? With your aunt?" Colin's mother had never outright banned the other members of her family from talking to me—at least not as far as I knew—but I didn't want Coz to get excommunicated in the event she got wind of his new client.

"Nah." He chuckled. "She and my mom never did see eye to eye on much. This is no different. You know I love Colin like a brother, but the man lost a good thing when he let you slip through his fingers."

I scoffed but didn't say anything to contradict him. I happened to agree. I wasn't even surprised to hear him say it. We'd always gotten along from the moment we met at Thanksgiving when Colin and I started dating. Years later, he'd been the first—of not very many—of Colin's family to call on me and make sure I was okay when they learned of the divorce. Once or twice, I entertained the idea of asking Coz out. But after so many years of knowing him, it felt a little weird. He was a good friend to have, though, and not just because his lawyerly advice had gotten me out of a jam or two.

"The next time you have any kind of run-in, with any police, you call me immediately."

"I will. How much do you charge for a retainer?" I wasn't familiar with the fees associated with being "person of interest," but I didn't think it would come cheap.

"Tell you what, send me a check for…" He rattled off a ridiculously small fee. I promised to pop that in the mail first thing so we'd be squared away.

My other line was beeping at me. The caller ID was listed as unknown. "Can you hang on one second?" I couldn't imagine who'd be calling on a Monday morning when school was out.

I clicked over. "Speak of the devil," I said to Muldoon when he identified himself. "What is it now?"

Without any preamble he said, "Will you come down to the station for a follow-up interview?"

I picked up a pen and tapped it in rhythm with my suddenly erratic heart rate. "If I say no?"

"I will be at your house with an officer to speak with you."

The tension that had built behind my right eye throbbed harder than ever. "Name the time and I'll be there."

Muldoon offered a couple of blocks of time and abruptly said goodbye.

My fingers shook when I clicked the phone back over to Coz. "So, how about I give you the check in person?"

ELEVEN

"WHY IS COOTER'S lawyer with you?" Muldoon whispered as he scooted a chair out for me once we all entered the interview room.

I sat without comment. It was a different part of the jail than I had previously seen. I had seen plenty of it to date. Working backward, when Detective Bush had interviewed me after the bomb, we'd merely sat at his desk. When I'd come in with Coz to bail out Colin, it was the front reception area. And of course, I'd seen the holding cells.

The formal interview area had much more of an ominous feel with its beige walls and beige chairs. There was no large two-way mirror like I'd seen in just about every cop show. The only thing on the wall was a lone clock. I was staring at it as the men got settled. Right under the twelve was a little black dot. Strange. Stranger still was that that was where my mind wandered. I'd had a couple of hours at home to pace and think as I awaited my interview time. I'd been almost calm on the ride over. I'd like to think I'd managed to find a Zen moment, but I think the numbness I'd felt so many times this week was becoming my new norm.

Although the moment Muldoon situated his notebook and a stack of papers in front of him and grabbed a pen, the lack of any and all sensation was replaced with every fear and anxiety all at once. My knee bounced frantically under the table. Coz gave me a quick look of concern, then folded his hands atop the table. "Why has my client been called in yet again?"

"Client?" A mask came over Muldoon's face as he sat across the table from us. "Mrs. Eagan, what was your relationship with Chad Jones?" His clipped cop-tone was as frustrating as it was a tad scary.

I glanced at Coz—he'd told me not to answer any questions unless he gave me the go-ahead. When he nodded, I said, "He was my boss."

Muldoon raised his hand up in question. "And?"

"And nothing. He was my boss." I tucked my hands into my lap. I didn't want Muldoon to see my clinched fists.

"Were you two friends?" He scribbled a note on some papers in front of him.

"I wouldn't call us friends." I shook my head. "We spoke to each other if we passed in the hall."

"You didn't spend time alone with him?"

"Not on purpose."

Coz nudged me under the table.

Muldoon's gaze shot up from the paper he was looking at. "Why? Did you have something against the man?"

Chad's unwanted and unreciprocated flirting a year after my divorce flashed through my mind. Once or twice he'd brush up against me, but I could never tell if it was deliberate or not. Regardless, I hadn't been about to invite any of his advances. I hadn't necessarily been avoiding him, but I hadn't gone out of my way to seek him out. For anything. Not until Colin asked me to intercede on Naomi's behalf. Damn it.

"I didn't wish him any ill will, if that's what you're getting at." My fists clenched tighter.

"Did you see him outside of school?"

I frowned. Didn't we already establish we weren't friends? "Absolutely not." My knee stopped bouncing and every nerve cell in my body stilled. What was with the line of questions?

Muldoon looked at me, then to Coz and back to me. He took a deep breath. "We have a video of you and Mr. Jones."

I blinked several times. "And?" The school had a surveillance system set on the perimeter to watch for people lurking around. I couldn't recall a specific time coming in contact with Chad outside the school. He was typically the first person to arrive at school and the last to leave at night. Were it not for his empty parking space from time to time, I'd wondered if the man ever actually left the school. But that wasn't what Muldoon was getting at. There was something more to it.

"Your line of questioning is fishing for something specific, Detective." While Coz echoed my thoughts, his cool demeanor contradicted the screaming demands for answers in my head. "Either cut to the chase or we're leaving."

Muldoon shifted through the papers. I'd say he was nervous, if I knew him well enough. What, in those papers, could possibly make him so nervous? I didn't have anything to hide. As I'd said all along, I'd done nothing, so why was he so hesitant to move forward with his questions?

Coz huffed and grabbed his briefcase. I wasn't sure if it was a tactic or if we were really leaving. I settled my hands on the arm of the chair as if to stand when Muldoon glanced down at the papers one final time, then returned his gaze to mine. "Chad Jones had video equipment set up in his office."

I leaned forward with my elbows on the edge of the

table. "I beg your pardon. Where? I've never seen any before."

"It was hidden."

The lump that had been in my chest since the day Chad died tightened. I wondered if I should set up an appointment with my doctor to check it out. I'd bet I was prime candidate for angina. "Whatever for?"

Muldoon cleared his throat. "Was Jones blackmailing you?"

"What?" I half stood from my chair.

Coz settled his hand on my arm. "I think we're done here, Detective."

"I can't help you if you don't talk to me, Celeste." Muldoon dropped his pen and folded his hands together over the papers.

"What do you mean, blackmailing me?" I shoved Coz's hand from my arm. "Why would he do that?"

"We have reason to believe Mr. Jones was blackmailing you. And possibly a few other members of the Peytonville Prep staff."

My throat tightened. "Me?"

"Can you explain this email?" Muldoon unlinked his fingers then slid a piece of paper across the table.

Coz snatched it up, glanced over it and handed it to me. He leaned into me and whispered, "We need to talk."

I took the paper from him. It was a copy of the email I'd sent Chad the night that he died. I frowned. "This is nothing."

Muldoon picked up the pen in front of him and started tapping wildly on the table. "We'd like you to explain this."

Coz shook his head. "Celeste, don't say anything."

"About what?" Confusion and fear swarmed through

me. None of Muldoon's lines of questioning made one lick of sense. Especially when he threw the email into the matter. "This has nothing to do with…"

"Celeste." Coz shifted in his chair. "What do you have that would make you think Celeste is being blackmailed?"

Muldoon's gaze never wavered from mine. He didn't answer for a long moment and I started to think he wouldn't. But finally he said, "Chad Jones had 'relationships' with staff members."

Members? More than one? "I already told you, I didn't have anything going on with him."

"We have video evidence that Mr. Jones lured several staff members into compromising positions."

And DVDs were taken from my home. But they weren't anything, they were home movies. Kelsey had been killed and he'd asked about the DVDs. "Kelsey and Chad?" At Grind Effects, she'd told Muldoon she and Chad were dating.

"Yes."

Why'd she tell him they were dating? "He was blackmailing her?"

"Yes." He had become monosyllabic.

"What does this have to do with me? He and I never did *anything*. You have to believe me." I didn't mean for the desperate whine to eke out of my voice, but I had to make Muldoon understand there was nothing—never had been—going on with Chad.

"Jones had a pattern. He'd pick a target—"

Target? What the hell? Chad was a school principal, not some criminal mastermind.

"—assemble the situation and entrap the prey."

Prey? I shook my head. "I don't understand."

Muldoon looked down at the papers. "Jones picks a

woman to target. He then starts a process. He would flirt. Make passes. Eventually he would force the woman into a compromising position and he'd blackmail her."

He'd flirted with me, but nothing that could lead to blackmail. Hell, until I'd sent him the email, we'd barely had contact lately. "To?" I waved my hands. "Do what?"

"Have a sexual relationship with him."

When my eyes widened, Muldoon looked away. What had Chad done? Why would he think he could get away with it? Worse, why would Muldoon think I'd been one of his victims? Chad had never even come close to getting me into anything remotely compromising. But something made Muldoon think I had been. The only evidence that related to me were the DVDs stolen from my house. It was the only thing that clicked into place. So I asked. "And you learned this from the DVDs?"

Muldoon's gaze came up. His eyebrow rose. Like I'd admitted something.

"Detective, I'm not stupid. Your line of questions points the way. I just don't know how this has anything to do with me. I have never—ever—had any kind of relationship with Chad. Sexual or otherwise. If you have DVDs as proof, then you should know. You won't find me on any."

Muldoon made a fist and released it, flexing his fingers. "He was grooming you. We just aren't sure how far along his plans were with you."

I blinked. His words weren't making any sense. "What?"

"Jones had a pattern, a very elaborate pattern when he picked a woman. All of which he documented."

It doesn't explain how my email tied into anything. On the surface.

Chad, I'm appealing to you to be fair. The last few weeks have been really uncomfortable and I think if you'd just adjust your stance, things would flow much more smoothly.

Holy crap. Considering the allegations, the email could be misconstrued. It even sounded…dirty. "Let me explain the email." The day I'd sent the email, the teachers had been discussing Chad's decision to ban the book Naomi had assigned. He'd walked in to the teachers' lounge and jumped in on the tail end of it all. He would know what I was talking about, but out of context… It sounded worse for me and my noninvolvement. "It's not at all what you think."

"No, Celeste." Coz slammed his briefcase on the table and stood. "This interview is over. Let's go. Now."

I stood and followed Coz out of the interview room. He didn't slow down his pace until we'd walked out of the building and into the lot. "Explain the email. To me," he said as we weaved through the rows to his parked car.

A chill whooshed over me, but it wasn't from the breeze messing my hair. "You don't think…"

"Of course not." We stopped at his Beemer. "But obviously it's pretty damning considering the circumstance."

I sighed. "Naomi."

"What does she have to do with it?"

"Colin came to me the night Chad died. Naomi and Chad were butting heads over a book she'd assigned to her class. One of the school donors has a child in her class. Took exception to the assignment. The woman told Chad to make Naomi pull it. Naomi said no. The two had been arguing about it for a couple of weeks."

"That doesn't explain the email."

"Colin asked me to talk to Chad on her behalf. Ask

him to back off." I ran my hand through my hair. "She has every right to assign what she wants. It's on the approved list. But one donor gets a bug up her butt…" I shook my head. "All I was doing was pointing out how stupid it was for him to demand she pull the book."

"It could be misconstrued as a plea."

I frowned. "For what?"

"It's just you and me here." He leaned forward and set his hand on my arm. "Whatever you say to me is protected under privilege. Have you ever had relations of a sexual nature—" he scrunched up his face like he'd just tasted spoiled food "—with Chad Jones?"

I knocked his hand away. "Hell, no."

He held his hand aloft in surrender. "Has anything happened recently that would make you think he was 'grooming' you, as the detective suggested?"

I bit my lower lip and looked up at the police station. Muldoon stood in the farthest window on the second floor. He had his hands shoved on his hips and he was watching us. "I've stayed away from him."

"Because?"

I shifted my gaze back to Coz. "He'd been a little… too much. He'd always flirted. With all the females. When Colin and I got divorced, he took it as open season on me. He was relentless for a while." But it had tamped down. "Kelsey started working there and he backed off. Geez, Coz. What the hell is going on?"

"We'll figure it out."

"You know I didn't do anything to Chad, right?"

He looked at me, head tilted to the side, eyes rolled up heavenward, mouth hung open just so—so similar to Colin's give-me-a-break look. "You're entitled to fair representation one way or the other. But if I thought you'd had anything to do with this, I'd pass you off to someone else in my firm."

"Why, because you don't like to lose?"

He took a step back and held his briefcase up in front of him like a shield. "No, because I'd be afraid of pissing you off."

A little tension eased from my shoulders. But only a little. The more we learned of Chad's death, the more questions that popped up. "If Kelsey was being blackmailed, she could have killed him, right?"

"It's possible."

"But then who killed her? His ex-wife wouldn't have cared." *Julia.* She'd acted all cold and distant at the funeral, not that we were bosom buddies, but we'd always been pleasant to one another. Did she know what Chad had been up to? If he'd been "grooming" me and she knew, then it could explain her reaction. But that still didn't give me motive to kill the man when I knew nothing of it. "Muldoon knows I couldn't have killed Kelsey. Not that I have motive."

"But your dressing up and approaching her calls into question what you were doing."

Was that going to come back and bite me on the ass? I'd meant well. "At first I was trying to prove Colin didn't do anything wrong. Then I found out she lied about me to the police."

"And I applaud you for the very misguided sense of loyalty. But he had a good alibi."

I thrust my hands in the air. "I didn't know that at the time."

"Relax." Coz opened the back passenger car door and tossed his briefcase inside, then opened the front passenger door for me. "Let's go grab some coffee and go over what we know."

Coz AND I laid out a chronological list of what had happened since Colin came over and asked me to talk to Chad on Naomi's behalf—which Coz thought was awful ballsy of him. We knew I didn't have anything to do with Chad's death, but still hadn't found which item was the "see, right here we can prove it..." I didn't have all the details of the crime itself. I knew what I saw when I found him and what was reported in the media. I'd discerned a tad more from being questioned. All that did was give me more pointed accusations and questions.

It also failed to shed a single light on who *would* kill him—or Kelsey. If Kelsey had become one of his targets, it gave her motive, but then who murdered her? Given that Muldoon questioned me about DVDs, and Kelsey's apartment turned up DVDs, they were the key—but who else would be looking for the DVDs?

It was so damn confusing.

I tried to put myself in Kelsey's shoes. A little shudder ran down my spine. If Chad had blackmailed me, I didn't think I could kill him. That's not to say I wouldn't want to. At the same time, I couldn't imagine him threatening me in any way that would let him run roughshod over me. However, he'd done just that to other staff members apparently.

I didn't think Kelsey killed Chad, though. If Muldoon was questioning me, he must not think so either. But how did it play into everything? If Chad had been blackmailing her, it would explain why she'd broken into the office—and then lied about it—to recover the DVDs once he was dead. Her taking advantage of the situation. That I could see.

It didn't explain *her* death.

Coz called with an update. After dropping me off at home, he'd headed back to the police station, where he'd managed to get my detail removed, threatening a lawsuit against the department for harassment. He wanted to come over and go over a couple more items but he had another appointment and would call later. He warned me to stay out of trouble while the police worked through what they knew.

I wasn't even sure I could stay out of trouble, because I didn't know which direction it was coming from. I certainly didn't know the penalty for disobeying my attorney, but I couldn't just sit back and do nothing though.

I got online and looked up Julia Jones's new phone number. I'd go right to someone who knew the man well.

Julia answered on the third ring. "Yes?"

"Julia, it's Celeste Eagan,"

She sighed. "What do you want?"

No point in playing any silly little guessing games. I decided to lay the cards on the table. "I don't know what you've heard. But I've been questioned about Chad's death."

"Huh." She didn't sound surprised.

I planted my toes on the floor and swiveled in my chair, back and forth. "I honestly don't know why. I've barely spoken to the man the last few months."

"And you expect me to believe you?" I could all but hear her frosty frown.

"I don't expect you to believe anything. I'm just trying to figure out why people seem to think something more was going on. Did Chad tell you there was something between us?"

"He didn't have to tell me anything. I saw it with my own eyes."

I stopped swiveling. "What are you talking about?"

There was silence on the end of the phone. I thought

maybe she'd hung up, but then I could hear her breathing. Finally she said, "Chad's little trophy videos."

Again with the DVDs. "He showed them to you?"

"No." For the first time, she sounded shocked rather than just plain angry. "I found them. On his computer."

"Julia, I don't know what you saw, but Chad and I never—"

"Maybe not yet, but you would have."

I couldn't think of anything to say to that. It didn't really matter. She plowed right on.

"You're all the same. Act all innocent and shy but then you perform such lewd acts on video. It's disgusting."

"Who 'all' are you talking about?" I snagged my pen and held it over the pad next to me. Julia named off several teachers and staff, all of whom—with the exception of Kelsey—were no longer on staff at Peytonville Prep. A couple surprised me. They'd left abruptly and we never knew why. It explained a lot.

"I guess I should thank you though."

I tapped my pen on the pad as I thought over the timeframe for all the teachers' resignations. "For?"

"If I hadn't found the videos I'd never have been able to divorce him. Well, I could have, but it would have cost me half of my family estate. No prenup. With the video evidence my lawyer proved he'd violated the marriage vows. I didn't have to pay him one red cent." With that she hung up.

Now I knew why Julia finally divorced Chad, and what had taken her so long to do so.

I glanced over the list. It was disgusting to think he'd used his position to force women to do anything, much less have sex with him. I knew very little about him. Only what he showed me at school.

The phone rang while I was still holding it, and I nearly jumped out of my chair. Annabelle's cheery voice met my hello.

"I just wanted to thank you. Dinner was a complete success."

"That's great." I smiled. I think it was the first time so far that day. "When's the next date?"

Annabelle giggled. "Later in the week. Hey, he has a friend. Would you like to go on a double date?"

"Oh no, no, thanks. I will not be good company." I gave her a brief rundown of my morning.

"Do you have a good lawyer?" she asked, all mirth gone from her voice.

"Absolutely." I was doodling on the corner of the notepad. "I just wish I had more answers. I don't know how to combat the questions."

"Like what?"

"Like how a seemingly mild-mannered principal could be so depraved."

"Google."

I frowned. "Pardon?"

"Google him. You would not believe what you can find out online nowadays. Most newspapers are archived and searchable." She went on to give me a few tips when searching, key words to type in—her former job paying off. "If you get stuck, call me and I can come over and help you."

"Thanks, but I don't want to bog you down in this any more than you already are." We spoke for a minute or two more, then said our goodbyes.

I grabbed a cup of decaf—I was already a little jittery, didn't need any help—settled at my desk and opened the laptop. I brought up Google and typed in Chad's name. I didn't expect it to be easy, but I sure

as hell wasn't expecting fourteen million hits for Chad
Jones. Damn. I put in our hometown and it narrowed it
down to a little over a hundred thousand. Who knew?

After an hour of using Annabelle's tips, going
through page after page and clicking on links here and
there that looked related to the man, I'd almost given
up. Then I saw a link for a Houston newspaper article
that was twenty-one years old. I clicked into the link
and looked over the first little bit, but to view the entire article, the paper wanted me to pay a nominal fee.

I drummed my fingers on the desktop. I wasn't even
one-little-percent sure it was the Chad Jones I knew,
though it listed a college that *was* his alma mater.

"Might as well." I popped in my credit card number,
and the rest of the article opened up.

To say I was surprised was an understatement. The
article itself was a report of a female college professor,
Eileen Patts, found hanged in her apartment. Her young
son had found her body and reported it to the police.
The original speculation was homicide but it was later
determined she'd hanged herself.

My palms itched as I kept reading.

It was believed she'd committed suicide after being
videotaped having sex with three of her college students: sophomores Joseph Carpenter, Beau Henderson and last but not least junior Chad Jones. Professor
Patts was so disgraced she couldn't take the scrutiny
and subsequent suspension from the college and ended
her own life.

Initially, it looked like she'd been murdered, and all
three men had been questioned at length, but a suicide
note had been found under the desk in her office.

I leaned back in my chair and stared at the ceiling.
Chad was a piece of work. It was scary to think you

could work alongside someone for so many years and never know what lurked behind their smiles.

Anger spiked when I thought of the times Paige lingered after school and waited for me or Colin in the teachers' lounge. With Chad. I'd like to think I couldn't kill someone, but you mess with my child and all bets were off. If I only learned one thing from my mom, it was definitely how to protect my child.

It didn't exactly explain what was going on now. The professor had died well over twenty years ago. By her own hand.

A little voice niggled the back of my head. *Just like Chad was staged to look.*

"That can't be a coincidence." I sat up straighter and printed off the article. Then I unlocked my cell phone, let it go into standby then unlocked it again. Before I could change my mind, I dialed a number.

After a quick hello, I dispensed with any chitchat. "It's Celeste, I need to see you. Can you come over?"

TWELVE

ON THE SECOND ringing of the bell, I ran down the hall to the front door. "Sorry, sorry," I said when it swung open. "I got hung up in my closet literally." I lifted the ruined sweater off my waist. A gaping hole formed where I'd caught it on a hanger that had come off the rack and stuck between several shirts. "I appreciate you not busting the door down."

Muldoon's cheeks tinted red for a moment. He didn't speak or move as he waited on the porch.

I opened the door wider. "Are you coming in?"

He stared at me for a long moment, then nodded and followed me into the house. I walked us back to my office and motioned him to a chair. "Sit."

He stood in the doorway in his cop pose; hands on hips with ready access to the gun or the handcuffs that poked out from the edge of his jacket.

"Please."

Muldoon took a deep breath, relented and sat.

"What's with the attitude?"

"You're going to talk to me without your lawyer?"

"Can you honestly tell me you'd go into a police interview without a lawyer present?" I turned and looked down at him. I rather liked the height advantage with him in the chair. Before he could answer my question, though, I said, "Never mind. Look what I found." I handed him the article and sat in the other chair. I scooted it until we were knee to knee.

"Where'd you get this?" He kept his eyes trained on the paper.

"Google."

He read through the article.

"More specifically the *Houston Monitor*. Chad went to school in Houston." I pointed to the name of the college. "He had mega school pride. Like their bookstore vomited all over his office."

"I remember."

I tilted my head and looked at him. "How did you not already have this info?"

He lowered his hands to his lap, still gripping the printed sheets. "What makes you think we didn't?"

I fought back a smug smile. "For one, the surprised-as-hell look on your face."

"There was no crime committed by anyone other than the professor. Jones wasn't charged with anything involving this so he wouldn't be in the system related to it. We checked him out for records of any kind. There weren't any. Didn't even have a parking ticket. The man was squeaky clean."

"On the surface." I took a deep breath. I looked him in the eye. "I didn't know what he was up to."

Muldoon squirmed. "I will ask again, shouldn't you wait for your lawyer?"

I shook my head. "I'm telling you. Shaw Muldoon. Not Detective Muldoon." I didn't know why the distinction made a difference, but I wanted to make him believe me. "I never once encouraged Chad to flirt with me. I never got the feeling it was anything other than some guy being a jerk and hitting on anything with a pulse. All the teachers knew he was like that—the flirting—but I don't remember anything that would have made me think he was capable of blackmailing women for sex."

I leaned back in my chair. "I can't imagine anything he could have said or done that would put me in that same position. I guarantee you, he wouldn't have been able to do that to me."

"Even if he used something you cherished to make you?"

"There was only one thing I would risk anything for…" My heart beat heavily. "What aren't you telling me?"

"He had pictures of Paige."

"What kind of pictures?" I asked slowly through gritted teeth.

Muldoon leaned forward, shaking his head as he grabbed my hand. "Nothing like that. I didn't mean to imply anything. They were just regular pictures from school. He also had a file on her. When did she jump up two grades?"

I frowned. "About two years ago."

Muldoon nodded. "It looks like he tampered with some tests to make it look like she'd cheated."

My grip tightened on his. "What?"

"With him gone, we don't really have proof one way or the other, but I'd bet money he was going to use that against you. To make you…" He trailed off and lowered his gaze.

"My baby." It came out on a whisper because my throat had tightened.

Muldoon gathered me up. How many times had I had to lean on him in the past week? Hell, it hadn't even been a whole week. But in that short time, I trusted him.

I pulled back and looked at him. His gaze froze me

in my spot. He eyed my mouth for a long moment, then let go of me. "You okay?"

"Uh, yeah." I blinked and tried to shake off whatever weird heat that had zipped through me. The man was sex on a stick and turned me on with a simple touch— which I totally didn't need at the moment, considering I kept finding more and more to make me look guilty of killing Chad. If I didn't know me better, *I'd* think I'd killed him. The last thing in the world I needed to do was tear up the sheets with the überhot detective.

"Can I?"

I choked. "Can you what?" Toast some marshmallows on the flames you've ignited? Turn up the heat to a five-alarm blaze? Hell yeah.

He waved the printed pages at me. "Can I keep these?"

How could he keep doing that to me? My overinflated ego and sex drive shriveled up as my shoulders slumped on a sigh.

"If you don't want me to—"

"No, no that's fine. Take them." I waved at him. It had been so long since I'd gone out with the opposite sex I was latching onto the first guy to come within proximity. And dating a man—even if we reached way out on a limb and assumed he'd even consider me dating material—who wanted to lock you up for one crime or another was probably not the best relationship to jump into. Maybe I needed to call Annabelle back and go out with her friend's friend. Or I could just give in and let Levi sign me up for that dating service he'd been threatening me with.

Muldoon folded the sheets and tucked them into a pocket inside his sports coat. He looked at me for a long moment, then asked, "How have we not met before?"

"Up 'til now?" I waved my hand at him as I worked out a dating bio in my mind. "I have pretty much been a law-abiding citizen. I wouldn't have been on your radar." I could add that to the bio, my law abidingness up to last week. I'd have to broaden my scope to the outlying areas as well as home. Peytonville was fairly small compared to Fort Worth or Dallas. Actually, home might be too close for comfort as my notoriety had made the papers a few too many times over the course of the Muldoon's investigation.

I glanced up at him. Did you need references for online dating? He didn't strike me as someone who would give me a glowing recommendation so I wouldn't broach the subject. Who could I get, though? I was mentally ticking off acquaintances.

Muldoon looked down at his feet. "Have you eaten?"

I was in full online-dating mode. Thinking of which picture I'd need to post and what my profile could reveal that wasn't too desperate, and yet not too aloof. I was vaguely cognizant of Muldoon asking me a question. "Eaten what?" We locked gazes for a moment, then Muldoon shifted his chair away from me, putting a little space between us.

"Dinner? The meal that is usually partaken in the evening." The corner of his mouth kicked up.

"Naw." I sighed and swiveled in my chair. "It's too depressing to make anything without Paige being here. Just reminds me how lonely the house is." I tapped my finger to my chin as I wondered if I should mention on the profile whether I have kids. Was that a deal breaker?

"Would you like to eat something?"

I shook myself. "What? Get something to eat as in go out? Together? You and I?"

He shrugged. "Sure."

I straightened in my chair and frowned at him. "Is this a new interrogation technique? Wining and dining a suspect? If you get me relaxed I might reveal something you have otherwise yet to get from me. Yeah, I think I'll pass." I didn't mean to sound so snippy—actually, I probably did. The man could go from interrogation to dinner for two without batting an eye. I didn't get it. And the fact that he didn't even try to deny anything only validated my case.

I stood. "It's getting late. I have school in the morning."

Muldoon rose and headed for the front door without so much as looking back. What right did *he* have to get pissy?

"You're welcome, by the way," I said as the front door slid shut. "Whatever."

I walked back to my office, sat back at my computer and dug around on the internet a little more to see what other info I could glean on Chad and the professor. I put in all the names involved in the college case and got very little information. Beau Henderson had a successful business in Dallas, but other than that, all the links associated with his name were typical. Joseph Carpenter died a few years back and had very little info out there.

I tried looking up Professor Patts but the case was so old that the links that popped up were newspaper archives.

Hmm, newspaper.

I hurried to the kitchen and looked in my junk drawer. I'd shoved Kellen Schaeffer's card between Paige's eye doctor reminders and the Chinese restaurant menus.

The man answered on the first ring. "I just had a feeling I'd be hearing from you."

"Mr. Schaeffer—"

"Kellen please." His voice purred on the other end of the line. It was probably perfected to get unwilling interviewees to open up. Damn if it didn't make me want to talk.

"Kellen." I cleared my throat. "Can we meet?"

"Absolutely. When and where?"

"Are you busy now?" I did need to eat. "We could meet up at Barney's." Since I was still without wheels, I mentioned a local hamburger joint about a mile from my house.

"Half an hour good?" he asked.

"See you there."

I'D FINISHED HALF my bacon cheeseburger before Kellen sauntered in and joined me. He was wearing a faded pair of jeans and a striped button-down shirt untucked with the sleeves rolled up to his elbows. He looked like a college student rather than a reporter—though really until he'd knocked on my door, I'd never really thought of what a reporter might look like.

"Am I late?" He motioned to the plate in front of me.

"No. I was starving." Despite what I'd told Muldoon about eating alone, the wonderful aroma from Barney's was too much to withstand once I'd been seated. "Sorry."

He waved away the comment and took up the seat across the table. "What would you like to get off your chest?"

I took a long drink of water and set the glass down with a loud clank. "What makes you think I have something to get off my chest?"

One sandy-colored eyebrow rose. "Why else would you be calling me?"

"Maybe I'd just wanted some company for dinner."

Kellen took several fries from my plate, dipped them in the ketchup and shoved it all in his mouth. He chewed slowly then smiled. A boyish dimple winked from just below his cheekbone. "If that's the case then even better."

The waitress came over and took his order before I could respond—thankfully. I was already regretting the call. This man could charm the chocolate coating from an M&M and I was feeling particularly vulnerable. But I only had means to dig so far into things. And while I knew Muldoon would check into everything I would bet my last drink of coffee he wouldn't share anything he found with me.

"While my boyishly handsome looks and charming character do win me many dates—" his smile broadened "—I don't think that's why you called." He leaned back in his chair. "Care to clue me in before my burger gets here?"

"Off the record?" I didn't know if that really worked. I'd seen it in many movies over the years, and while I did want to speak with him and get some info, I didn't want to be quoted in any way that would foster more suspicion.

The smile that tilted his full sexy lips was more amused than flirty now. "Sure."

I laid out all the info I'd gotten off the internet. I gave him the extra copies I'd made and he leaned closer and closer with each word. When I finally finished, he glanced over the printed sheets and shuffled through them. The waitress brought his food and set it in front of him.

I asked her to bring me a chocolate shake. My nerves were too shot to forgo a craving while I waited for Kellen to answer me. She brought it back to the table with two straws—as if. I slid one straw into the tall chilled glass and shoved the other under the edge of my plate. "Well? Is that all crazy or what?"

He eyed me for a moment, then took a bite of his own burger. "I'm impressed. You did a lot of work," he said after he swallowed. "Give me a sec, let me think." He ate some more. Actually finished the entire burger in just a few bites and started in on his fries.

I intermittently nibbled at my food and sipped the creamy chocolate shake while he thought over everything—whatever the hell that entailed.

He took a drink from his soda and swiped at his mouth with a napkin. "What would you like me to do?"

"I was hoping you could dig a little deeper into this…" I motioned to the papers he'd set beside his plate. "This scandal happened years ago. I'm assuming you have access to some newspapery things I can't get in to."

"Newspapery?" He chuckled. "Assuming I can, what do I get out of this?"

"A story of what's what." I frowned and fought off a "duh."

"From you." He steepled his fingers over his plate. "What do I get from you?"

I wadded the napkin in my lap as I said, "Dude, I am so not for sale."

His bark of laughter was loud and a wee bit insulting. "Like I said, charm and all, I am not in need of forcing, bribing or otherwise bartering myself off for dates. I mean, what kind of *story* can I get from you? If I do this digging around, I need to have something else waiting on the other end. If your info doesn't pan out, I'm left with squat."

Oh. I gave myself a mental *duh*. "I suppose that's fair enough."

Kellen smiled. "Care to start now?"

"I uh…" I sucked down half my shake and immediately regretted it. "Gaw, brain freeze." I pinched the bridge of my nose.

"Oh, I can so see how you're the mastermind behind a man's death and the subsequent cover-up to make it look like suicide."

I frowned at him. "Rude much?"

His smile widened. "What? You'd like to be thought of in that light?"

"I guess not. But don't underestimate me."

"Or you'll what? Blow up my car?"

I twirled the straw around in the leftover shake. "Real funny."

"Sorry, trying to lighten the mood." Kellen flagged the waitress down. "But at least they can't shove you in the suspect pool for that one."

"What do you mean? Detective Bush all but asked me to confess."

The smile slid from Kellen's face. "They pulled some guy in for questioning this morning. Last I heard, he hadn't lawyered up but was keeping mum. They didn't tell you?"

I shook my head. "Who is he?"

"It's in my notebook." He shifted his gaze away while he thought. "Some guy named Jerry. Something with a P."

Did I know a Jerry? The only one was from years before. "Pullman?"

He nodded and the glass nearly slid from my hand. "Jerry Pullman? Are you sure?"

Kellen's eyes twinkled and he leaned forward. "That's the name I got. How do you know him?"

"We used to have lunch together, him, Colin, and I with a few other teachers. Years ago. He worked up at the school. Taught science." I gnawed on my bottom lip. "Are you sure it was him?"

He held his hands aloft for a moment. "How would I know his name if I hadn't heard it?"

"I don't get it. Why would he target me?" My palms started sweating and my brain raced to remember the last time we'd seen each other. Maybe at the faculty Christmas party three years earlier? I didn't think I'd seen him at Chad's funeral. Then again, I had a few other things on my mind at the time. "He and I were always friendly to one another," I said more to myself than to Kellen.

The waitress brought the check over and Kellen handed her his credit card before she even came to a completely stop. "My treat." He waited until she left before he asked, "Are you sure it was you he was after?"

"Are you saying it's just a huge *coincidence* that he blew up my car at the funeral?"

"Not exactly." Kellen scrunched up his forehead and rubbed at his ear. "Why did he leave Peytonville Prep?"

"I don't know. They didn't give us a reason for his termination."

"Hmm." He scooted his plate over and leaned into the table. "Did he have any kind of beef with your ex?"

"Not that I'm aware of." I shook my head. "Why would he come after me? He'd get more mileage going after Naomi." Though I didn't wish any of this on her— believe it or not.

"How long have you been divorced?" Kellen pulled

a pen out from his breast pocket and took notes on the back of the papers I'd given him.

"For about two years."

"Did Jerry Pullman know that?

"I have no clue." I tried to think back on the last time I'd seen the man. Not a single thing stood out that would give him any reason to come after me or Colin. "I didn't stay in touch with him once he left the school. I don't know about Colin."

Kellen finished scribbling something and tucked the pen back in his pocket. "Y'all were both at the cemetery yesterday. You and your ex."

I narrowed my eyes at him. "How'd you know?"

"Celeste, it's my job to know. Aside from the sensational story by itself, Jones's admin gets killed shortly thereafter. Folks are going to show up to see if anything else happens." He grabbed a couple more fries and dabbed them in ketchup. "Did you see Jerry there?"

"I don't know. Only about half the current staff was there. Granted, I did leave a little early and was sidetracked, so maybe more came later. Actually, I don't know if the funeral even happened after I left the cemetery."

"It did and it was only half the staff. Minus you, Colin and his girlfriend. They left shortly after you. I didn't realize that woman and Colin were together-together. She doesn't really look his type."

"And I did?" I shook my head. "Don't answer that. Do you mind if I tell you how creepy it is how well acquainted you are with the staff at my school?" Not one but two stalkers if I counted Muldoon, three if I included Jerry Pullman and four with Chad's killer, but I'd like to not think about him, her, whoever it was.

"What are the chances that Jerry killed Chad?" Kellen tapped the stack of papers in front of him. "It's not without reason since Chad was the one who fired him."

"There's always a possibility. But as far as I know Jerry and Kelsey never crossed paths. She joined the staff after he was already gone." I swiped my finger through the condensation on the side of the milkshake. She was tied to Chad with the growing sex scandal. What would that have to do with Jerry?

The waitress returned and Kellen stayed quiet. He took his credit card back and signed the receipt. When she walked off with a little wink and a shimmy, he didn't even seem to notice.

Points to him for that.

"Back to the funeral, how do you know the players?"

He tucked the receipt in his wallet with his credit card. "I had a yearbook and marked people off. How do you think I knew who you were?"

"The way things have been going—" I waved my hand in the air "—I might wonder if the police put out a most wanted poster with my face on it."

Kellen chuckled. "It's not as bad as all that."

"Isn't it? What's your take on Detective Muldoon?" Did I sound as teenyboppery intrigued to him as I did to my own ears?

Judging by the way his dimple winked, I'd guess so. "He's a good guy. A good cop. Very by the book." He stood and slid his chair back to the table then came around and held out his arm.

How very charming. He wasn't kidding on the ability to get dates. Half the female population of the restaurant were all but drooling over him, the other half were batting their eyelashes. Even a couple of men perked up as we headed toward the door.

A little flutter of what-ifs palpated through my heart.

I gave a mental headshake; definitely needed to get on that dating-service thing before I did something stupid, like throw myself at Kellen. Or worse, Muldoon.

We walked out through the front door and Kellen released my arm. The evening had cooled substantially and I tucked my hands into the pouch on the front of my hoodie.

"Which car's yours?" He dug in his pocket and grabbed a set of keys.

"None."

His step faltered a tad. "What?"

"It's not that far from my house." I shrugged. "Little car, big explosion. Did you forget? I'm still without wheels."

"That's... Hmm, kinda far, isn't it?"

"Maybe a mile. Not that you need it, but exercise is a good thing." I lightly punched his arm.

"If you say so, but I'm not going to break a sweat. Unless I have great motivation."

How did the man make everything sound naughty? "Yeah. Thanks for dinner, Kellen. Call me when you get some info?"

We stopped at his shiny new Dodge Charger. I'd seen it when he'd come by before. I guess I needed to start thinking about a replacement vehicle. The insurance company wouldn't give me a final assessment until the police filed their report. As long as they didn't pin it on me, I'd be okay.

I'd have to call Muldoon again and ask for an explanation on my car bombing. I'd done that far too many times as of late. And it wasn't like he was forthcoming. He'd been over and hadn't bothered to tell me about Jerry. How could he do that? Shouldn't he have interviewed me to find out what was what?

"Want a ride back to your house?" Kellen broke into my mental rehashing.

I'd love to. But the thought of being confined with him any longer… A walk in the brisk evening air would do me some good. "No thanks."

He got in his car, though he looked like he wasn't sure if he should leave me.

"Kellen, it's a mile. If that. It's Peytonville. What could happen?"

THIRTEEN

"FORTY-TWO CUPS OF mocha-lattes on the wall, forty-two cups of lattes…" I yawned and shivered. I was only a few blocks away from my house and was regretting not taking Kellen up on his offer. I'd be warm in my hot pink robe and bunny slippers and I'd plop myself in front of the TV until I found the perfect movie—I'd probably end up watching *Breakfast at Tiffany's*. I hurried up my step.

I hadn't gone too many feet when I heard the distinctive whine of a car engine getting closer and closer. I was surprised because I hadn't seen any headlights coming up the street in either direction. I glanced over my shoulder. The streetlights in that part of the neighborhood were all out, thanks to budget cuts and teens with rocks. Normally it wasn't a problem. Paige and I had walked around the neighborhood many a time when she got a wild hair that we—meaning me—needed to exercise. But with the lack of lighting, I didn't see anyone—but I could hear them.

I patted my hip pocket for my cell, then remembered it had been blown to smithereens and I hadn't gotten a new one yet.

Crap.

I walked a little faster. Not scared, no, not me. I just wanted to get home to my TV and slippers.

Someone was probably picking up their date. Yeah, because Monday evening was the primo date night.

"Gaw." Every wild thought ran though my head. Between Muldoon and Kellen, I was getting myself worked up into a full-blown case of paranoia.

I wanted to cut through the houses, but the way the neighborhood was laid out, the garages sat in the front of the houses, and the fences in the back touched the neighbors' on the sides and the back. So unless I wanted to do a little parkour and dog dodging, I was going to have to keep hoofing it down the sidewalk.

When my house was one block up and one block over, I looked back and still couldn't see anyone.

Maybe my imagination had finally taken its own adventure. "Get over yourself, Celeste."

I stepped off the curb. Immediately headlights whipped on and shined directly on me. Like the proverbial deer in headlights, I froze midstride. Couldn't say why, but I did. The car came right up to me and stopped. I could feel the heat rolling off the engine.

I stifled a scream when the driver's door came open. It wasn't until Kellen stepped out that I breathed again. "What the hell are you doing? You scared the ever-loving crap out of me."

"You just walked away at the restaurant. Very rude."

"Uh, no." I took a step back. "Why are you following me? With your headlights off."

He walked up to me, threw his arm over my shoulder in an awkward side-hug. "I'm sorry. The fight was entirely my fault."

What? My head spun a little. Especially when he whispered, "Get in the car." Had he yelled or even used his normal voice I might have balked. But the whisper held an edge that made his sneaking up on me pale in scary comparison.

I slid into the passenger seat and closed the door. Kellen got in and drove off.

"You were being followed," he said with no pre-amble.

"Yeah, I know, you."

"Not me." He adjusted his rearview mirror. "When we left Barney's, I was stopped at the next light. I checked the mirror to make sure you were headed out and I saw someone tailing you on foot."

I looked out the windows of the car, tried to see if anyone was on the street around us.

"I turned around but I'd lost you. I don't know this area so I had to guess which way you might have gone." Kellen turned on the next street, away from my street. "If I hadn't found you when I did... I was ready to call the police." He turned on yet another street. He was doubling back the way I'd just come.

"Why did you intervene when you did?"

"Your shadower was closing in on you."

We both scanned the area but the streets were free of foot traffic.

"If Jerry weren't locked up, I'd assume it was him following you."

"I told you, he has no reason to harm me."

"Yet he blew up your car." Kellen shook his head. "Like I said, he's locked up. Who else would be after you?"

I blinked and stared at him. How in the world had I set myself up to be targeted by not one but at least two people? Just last week I was a theater teacher bemoaning the fact that life had gotten a little staid and I was lacking excitement. The scariest thing I had to do was decide on changing jobs.

I'd hoped for a new hairstyle or finding a killer pair

of shoes. Not a plain killer. Not double-homicide. Attempted murder—attempted on me. Lockups and interrogations. Last week the only person I'd say would harm me was Naomi Michaels.

"Celeste?"

"Sorry. I have no idea. It's not like this is commonplace for me."

Kellen pulled into my driveway. "Would you like me to come in and take a look around?"

I started to say yes when a dark shadow detached itself from the front porch. "I don't think that will be necessary."

Kellen stiffened. "I'm calling the police."

I sighed. "He is the police. It's Detective Muldoon." I'd recognize those broad shoulders anywhere. Even in the dark. "Is that who was following me?"

"Uh-uh. Don't think so." He tapped his fingers on the steering wheel. "Whoever it was, they were smaller. I couldn't tell if they were male or female." He glanced over at Muldoon, still hidden in the darkness of my porch, then back to me. "Would you like me to come up with you? The way you've been questioned…"

Did I? Did I want a reporter to hear whatever Muldoon had to say—this time? Did I need a bodyguard or go-between for Muldoon? I wasn't ready for lies of omission or even a veiled "Did you do it?" It would be nice to have someone there on my side.

The need for privacy, though, outweighed anything else. I was afraid of what Kellen could glean and then use in his newspaper. "Thanks, but no. I think I'll be fine." I opened the door and started to get out. "Thanks for…well, everything. Call me when you learn anything?"

He nodded.

I walked slowly to my front porch. I don't know why I felt like I'd been caught doing something I shouldn't have. I owed Muldoon no explanations. On anything.

"We have to stop meeting like this." I decided to go for flippant rather than irate and annoyed as I stuck my key into the lock.

Muldoon shoved his hands in his pockets. "New friend?"

"You could say that." I opened the door a hair but didn't go in. I turned and leaned against the doorjamb. "Did you need something, Detective? Or do you just like to skulk around suspects' houses late at night?"

"I'm not skulking, I'm just standing." A smile tinted his voice. "Perfectly normal."

"In the dark?"

His shoulders rose and fell in a quick shrug. "There was no light on." He stepped a little closer. "And I've never said you're a suspect."

"Not in so many words, but it's there."

Muldoon crowded closer and closer. "Celeste."

"What, Detective?"

His breath feathered over my face as he said, "Shaw."

"Pardon?" A chill ran down my spine.

"It's my name."

"I know what it is. Why'd you say it?"

"Every time you talk to me, you call me *Muldoon* or *Detective*." He settled his hand on the doorframe and leaned in close. "I just wanted to hear you say it. Shaw."

I was damn glad there was no light on when my cheeks heated. "I uh…" I racked my brain. What did one say to a statement like that? "Actually, I did say it. Several times in fact."

"When?"

"Remember a little matter of my ass holding down

a bomb. I believe I said it three or four times." I could easily open the door and walk right on into my house. But some stirring deep inside me kept me rooted to the front porch.

"Under duress." He nodded.

"Why does it mean that much to you?"

"I uh…" It was his turn to be at a loss for words. Tongue-tied. "Never mind." His hand slid from the doorframe and he stepped back. "I came to apologize for earlier. And to thank you for the research you did." He turned to go.

I shoved off the frame and grabbed his hand. "Don't leave. Shaw."

A slow smile crawled across his mouth. "See, that wasn't so difficult."

"I figured I'd throw you a bone since it seemed so important to you." I winked but I doubted he could even see the small gesture.

"So."

"So."

He leaned in and I closed my eyes awaiting…something, then I heard an odd buzzing noise followed by wood splitting. The next thing I knew he was shoving me to the ground. Face-first.

"What the hell?" I tried to push up from the porch, but he was stronger and kept me pinned.

"Stay down," he hissed in my ear.

I blinked rapid-fire as my head spun at the sudden change. "What're you…"

"Someone's shooting."

"A gun?" Surely, I'd misheard him.

"Shh." Moonlight glinted off his gun as he slid it from his holster.

I groped at his hand to try and stop him, but he was too quick. "Shaw, come back."

"Shh." He nimbly ran in the direction of the gunfire.

Another round busted a pot a few feet to my left. I scrambled backward, still prone—not an easy feat when you're tense and scared, let me tell you—and in through the front door. Once inside the confines of the house I got to my feet—sort of—and duck-walked through the living room, then grabbed for the phone on the end table. I dialed 911 and told the dispatcher what was what.

"Ma'am, stay on the line."

"I need to go see if Muldoon is okay."

"Ma'am, he's a trained police officer."

For a moment I stared at the phone and all but said "duh" aloud. I knew that, I told *her* when I called.

"Ma'am?"

"I'm still here." I eased to the front window and peeked through the curtains.

No sounds came from the front or even down the street as far as I could tell. A few porch lights lit, but none of the neighbors ventured out with the sounds of gunfire—a first for our subdivision as far as I knew. I didn't see Muldoon. Or whoever may have been taking shots. Off in the distance, the wail of sirens was discernible. "I hear the police."

"They will be there shortly. Is there anyone else in your home with you?"

"Not that I'm aware of." I glanced over my shoulder and looked through the darkened house. No shadows moved, nothing looked out of place.

Barely a week ago, I couldn't have imagined my life being in such turmoil.

I nearly jumped when the 911 operator asked, "Where are you in the house?"

"In the front room by the window."

"Do you see anyone moving about?"

"No. The street is quiet now." For the past week, though, the police had been on my block for one reason or another. I wondered what my neighbors thought of me. And after tonight's incident, I'd given them something to talk about for the rest of the month for sure. Assuming it was tied to me.

I'd like to think one of Muldoon's other cases had followed him, but given the "shadowy figure" tailing me earlier and the overabundance of crap heaped on me, it was more wishful thinking. A gal could dream, though.

It seemed like an eternity before I saw the flash of lights coming down the street.

"Celeste?" Muldoon called from the front yard. "Are you okay?"

"Detective Muldoon is calling me," I told the operator. "Thanks for…thanks." I hung up quickly and stood from my crouch at the window and eased toward the front door. "Yes."

Two squad cars pulled up right in front of my house. The neighbors ventured out of their houses. After only a couple of minutes, the yard was awash with lights and uniformed officers.

On shaky knees, I moved over to the sofa, sat and waited. I'd be questioned yet again.

Muldoon came in and sat in the chair across from me. "You sure you're okay?"

"Do you know how often you've asked me that in the last few days?" I tried to smile but it fell flat.

He didn't smile in the slightest, just knotted his hands

in front of him. "Do you have any idea who would be shooting at you?"

I frowned at him. "Why couldn't they have been shooting at you?"

Muldoon ran a hand through his hair.

"I don't know." I tossed my hand upward. "Someone was following me earlier when I was walking home from Barney's. That's why Kellen picked me up."

"What?" Muldoon sat up straighter. "Why didn't you tell me?"

"When would I have had the time? We'd just started talking. The next thing I know, you're shoving me to the ground."

"I didn't hurt you, did I?" When I shook my head, he leaned forward as if to check for himself, but he eased back into his seat. "Tell me about Barney's." He pulled out his notebook. "Please," he added when my shoulders stiffened.

I sank back into the cushions. "Kellen met me up at Barney's for a bite to eat. He offered to drive me home." Muldoon looked up from his notes and frowned. Was he was miffed I'd turned down his dinner offer for another? Was he jealous? Oh, silly me. Of course not.

He tapped his pen on the pad. "Why were you walking?"

"I still don't have a car. I'd walked up there."

"You walked. To the restaurant?"

"It's only like a mile." Why was walking such a foreign concept? "It's not like I walked to Dallas."

He wrote something down. "Go on."

"I was walking home. At some point I could hear this car. I couldn't tell exactly where it was, but I could still hear it. As I was crossing the street the lights came on and I about peed myself." I grimaced. "Sorry. TMI."

He kept scribbling and didn't look up.

"Turns out it was Kellen. He followed me from the restaurant to make sure I got home safe. He said someone was lurking in the shadows behind me and was moving in."

"I knew better than to pull that damn detail…" He made a fist around the pen as he spoke more to himself, then he scribbled something else. He didn't look up and asked, "Did you see anyone?"

"No." I picked at a loose string on my sleeve. "I had a weird feeling like I was being followed."

Muldoon finally met my gaze. "You were. He even admitted it to you."

"Yeah, but…you don't think Kellen was the one shooting at me? That's ridiculous."

"Why? Because he's a reporter? Babe, I hate to tell you that any and every profession has its share of bad guys."

I didn't comment on him calling me *babe*. He'd done it once before—when my car went kablooey. That whole under-duress bit worked both ways, I guess. "Do you know Kellen?"

"The entire police department knows him." Muldoon tipped his head to the side slightly. "His dad is the chief."

Kellen was the son of the chief. That explained some of his sources. "I didn't know that."

Muldoon's eyebrow rose.

"Please. That gives him even less reason to shoot at me. Right?"

He shrugged. "I'm just saying, don't assume someone is or isn't guilty of something just because they have a particular job. People are people. They all have eccentricities."

Was he kidding me with the "eccentricities"? "I'll keep that in mind."

"Why were you meeting with Kellen?"

I frowned. "Does it matter?"

"You tell me. You were meeting with a reporter. You were followed home, if he can be believed. And you were shot at."

"Why do you *assume*—" I threw the word at him "—that I was meeting with the reporter Kellen and not the man Kellen?"

Muldoon's cheeks reddened. "I guess I don't know for sure."

"Damn straight you don't." I huffed. Then it was my turn for red cheeks. "Sorry. I'm a little edgy, I guess."

He snorted. "Only a little?" He sat back in his seat. "You don't have to tell me why you were meeting with him." He said the words, yet poised his hand over his notepad.

"I gave Kellen the, uh…" I mumbled, "The same info as you."

"Come again."

"I gave him the same info as you. The printouts."

Muldoon didn't say a word. The muscle in his jaw twitched, matching the tic in his eye. He thrummed the fingers of his left hand on his knee. The right hand clenched the pen.

"Are you going to say anything?"

He shook his head.

I laced my fingers in my lap. "You never said that that was confidential information. I gave it to you. I had every right to share that with whomever I wanted. I could post the damn thing on the internet. Oh wait." I snapped my fingers. "It *is* posted on the internet. That's how *I* found it. You don't get it, if I want to look into it all by myself, I can. You can't tell me what to do."

Okay so I'd gone over the edge there. He hadn't said a single word and I'd worked myself up a full head of steam. So what if I sounded like a recalcitrant child rather than a grown-ass woman.

"Are you done?"

"For now." I pursed my lips and sniffed.

He stood, tucked the notebook in his breast pocket. "Please come to the station sometime tomorrow to sign an official statement. 'Night." He turned and headed to the door.

"Hey." I jumped up from the sofa. "Wait. That's it? You're just going to leave?"

He took a deep breath. "There's a reason why it's against department policy for us to get involved with people we deal with on a case."

"What the hell is that supposed to mean? You came to me, Shaw. You came here."

"I did. Now I'm going back to work." Muldoon shut the door behind him.

A few minutes later the street cleared of all Peyton-ville police. I sank down on the club chair, then immediately got up and moved to the sofa—I could smell Muldoon on the chair. I'd just closed my eyes when a knock came at the door.

Maybe Muldoon had come back to say he was sorry for being such a typical male, all closed off and grumbly.

Nope. It was Kellen. "What brings you by?"

He clucked his tongue at me. "You're kidding me. You get shot at not five minutes after I leave, and you ask what brings me by?"

"You mean that doesn't happen to *you* every day?" I

waved my hand at him like he was some kind of slacker. "Look, Kellen, it's been a long day. Off the record, I'm fine. I appreciate you stopping by, checking on me. On the record, no comment. I hope you don't take this the wrong way, but I hope I don't see you again for a while. Good night."

For a moment, he stood with his hand on the door so I couldn't shut it. The harsh frown pulling down his eyebrows and mouth softened. "Are you sure you're okay?"

A shuddered breath escaped before I could control it. "Yeah." I gave him a crooked smile, about all I could muster after the evening I'd had.

"Call me if you need anything. On or off the record." He winked, then turned and left.

I shut the door and slunk to my bedroom. Still wearing my jeans and sweater, even my sneakers, I climbed into bed. The second night in a row I'd gone to bed fully clothed. Tired did not begin to describe the weariness that seeped into my bones. This day would go down as one of the worst days in a long string of worst days. At least with school resuming, I had something to look forward to.

FOURTEEN

THE NEXT MORNING came screaming in with a headache-vengeance. No amount of coffee improved my mood. I was angry and frustrated with the situation, scared I would make a wrong decision, and just plain exhausted. Despite all but falling into bed, I'd lain awake for hours. When midnight rolled through, my brain was still running over and over every scenario to make sense of what had happened so far. And nothing jibed. Then I tried to figure out what the hell was going on between me and Muldoon. That was an enigma that couldn't be solved. I was weighing the pros and cons of turning up the flirt with the man when sleep finally came crashing in. I didn't dream, which was unusual for me. Judging by the crick in my shoulder and neck, I'd barely moved once I slept. Then overslept by almost forty-five minutes.

The only good thing I could say about Tuesday morning was I'd get to see Paige. That was one of the best perks of teaching at Peytonville Prep—the one I'd miss the most when I started full-time at the playhouse. In light of the past few days, seeing my precious daughter was well worth starting the day.

Levi dropped me off at the edge of the school parking lot. I had no car for the foreseeable future if the insurance company had any say. They were being relentless about not issuing me a replacement, saying they weren't sure of all the facts. Meaning they were waiting to see if I was going to be charged with blowing up my own car.

Apparently they hadn't gotten the notice that someone else was being questioned in the incident.

My car notwithstanding, I was surprised to see how empty the lot was, especially with me running a little late.

Rachel was at her desk frantically typing away when I walked in.

"Morning." I dropped my briefcase on top of the desk.

She jumped up and hugged me. "Oh my gosh. How are you? I heard about your car. You could have been killed. Was it as terrifying as it sounded? What do the police think?"

Before I could answer any one of her questions, there was a knock on the door. It flew open and Paige ran in. "Mom."

I smiled so hard my cheeks hurt. "Sweet pea. Oh, I've missed you so much." I hugged her so tight she squirmed and moaned.

"I've missed you too. Naomi is insufferable. *Me, me, me*. It's all about her. She is so self-absorbed it's nauseating."

"Well, be patient and you'll be home in no time." Over Paige's shoulder I saw Rachel's perfectly sculpted eyebrow float up into her bangs. I rolled my eyes in a "it's a long story" motion. She nodded and went back to her typing.

Paige held onto me, but leaned back and asked, "How many more times did that detective come over?"

Chills ran down my spine. "Wh-what?"

"Colin said the detective was clearly sniffing around you." She frowned. "He said the man was probably making excuses to come and see you."

"Your dad is quite chatty with you."

"No." Paige gave me one more, quick squeeze then let go. "I was hiding under the dining room table when he and Naomi were talking after the funeral." She balled her little fists and shoved them on her hips. "Do you know that woman had the nerve to call you a drama queen? As if you asked for your car to be blown up. Doesn't she know that your insurance rates will sky-rocket?"

I laughed. "I doubt she does. You'd better get going. You don't want to be late for Mr. Colgate's class."

"I love you." She grabbed me around the waist and hugged me once more, then rushed out as fast as she'd come barreling in.

"I love you, too," I called after her. I plopped down onto my chair.

Rachel rounded her desk. "Why exactly is Paige staying with your ex?"

"Too many policemen to contend with." I dropped my chin to my chest and rubbed the back of my neck. "We want to keep her safe."

"So it's true?" Rachel leaned a hip against the desk.

My gaze darted up.

"It's all over the school. That you've been questioned in Chad's death. Some say you might be involved in Kelsey's death, too."

"I had nothing to do with either death. I don't even know what's going on with Kelsey." For the most part, that was true. "What else are they saying?"

Rachel shook her head. "All sorts of things. But you're just part of it. About a quarter of the staff have made noises about tendering their resignations." She shrugged a shoulder at the empty desk. "Holly came in this morning, packed up her things and left. The gardener quit and two of the lunch staff. There's a half-dozen kids already pulled from the class lists and another ten or so whose parents threatened to pull them. It's crazy."

Man oh man. The twinge in my neck tightened.

"Has that detective really been sniffing around?" She fanned herself. "I flirted with that man and he acted all oblivious. He had his eye on you, though."

I shook my head in a slow sweeping motion at first and picked up enough speed the ends of my hair slapped my chin. "Nope. The man has a strict policy never to get involved with women on cases he's working."

"Ho, ho. You sound a little disgruntled."

"Not disgruntled. I am perfectly fine with the fact that he can be so dedicated to his job. Yep, I sure am." My headshaking morphed to nodding.

"You've got it bad." She giggled and went back to her desk.

"I've got nothing." The first bell rang. "Nothing but class. I'll talk to you later." I shoved myself up from the chair.

Rachel snagged her grade book and tucked it under her arm. "See ya."

I dug through my briefcase and pulled out my own grade book and the kids' projects. When I got to the classroom I couldn't believe how many empty seats there were. Vice Principal—*acting Principal*, I had to get used to that—Hardin was waiting at the desk. "Oh, good. You're here."

"Mark?" I frowned. "Did you need something? Actually, there's something I'd like to talk to you about." I needed to tell him about the playhouse. Annabelle was generous enough to let me work out the remainder of the school year—between weekends and holidays, I'd still be able to put in many hours at the playhouse before school got out.

He swallowed heavily. "Let's take this in the hall."

I followed him to a set of lockers. He was treating me like a kid caught cheating in class.

"I'd meant to catch you at home, but people were calling all morning." He ran his hands through his graying hair. He took a few steps away then came back. "I—we—I need you to take a few days off."

"What? Why? For how long?"

"Let's not worry about that right now." He let out a long breath. "We've had several parents concerned. In light of all the news…"

"The news hasn't said a thing that could give them reason to be afraid of me."

"I don't think it's so much them afraid of you, they're afraid of what might happen to their kids with you around."

"But—"

"To be fair, Celeste, your own daughter has been removed from your home for her protection."

"She was not *removed*. She's staying with her dad." For the very reasons Mark stated. "Are you firing me?"

"No. You have a strict contract." His cheeks pinkened.

That sure didn't sound like, "We love you and can't afford to lose you as a teacher." I bit my lip to keep from saying something that might go on my permanent record, like *bite me* or *suck it*.

"I know this is not your fault. But the school has a board we have to report to. And benefactors who have been all up in arms since Chad died. Think of it as a sabbatical. While everything gets put to rights again." He shrugged. "I'm sure it will be fine. Things will get sorted out." He patted me on the arm, then set his hand on the doorknob. "Take what you need from your office and consider this a long overdue vacation."

I didn't want to know the answer, but had to ask, "Am I getting paid on this unexpected vacation?"

The red in his cheeks darkened. "I'm afraid that a leave like this isn't covered under the protected pay."

"I see."

"Thanks for understanding, Celeste."

I understood nothing. I was fuming too much to have a coherent verbalization of the nasty words rolling around in my head. One thing for sure, the school would be hearing from my lawyer. As soon as I could get to a phone. "Mark," I said as he turned.

He paused.

"Here." I handed him my grade book and the thick file folder for the class. I hated to acknowledge it, but the man flinched slightly as if he thought I'd hit him or something. Had shock not already burrowed its way into me I might have been offended. Instead, I simply said, "The kids' projects. They're all graded and ready to be handed back. They're all doing superb work so you shouldn't have any problems." My throat constricted.

He nodded and headed into *my* classroom. To teach *my* kids. While, yes, I was taking another job at the end of the year, that was supposed to be after the classes were done, and on my own terms.

Thankfully Rachel was off in her class and I had the small office to myself to pack up my belongings. If Mark was to be believed, I'd be back. But who knew when Chad's case would be solved? I personally doubted I'd ever be back in the office again. I jotted a note to Rachel so she wasn't left wondering if I'd bolted of my own accord. I set it on her desk with the jar of candy she was always snatching from—she didn't realize it, but I stocked it for her. She was the only person I knew who liked the little licorice chunks.

I gathered up my things. It was sad, really, that I fit most of my meager trappings into my school bag. The two sweaters from the back of my chair I tossed over my arm. I locked the door and started to slide my school card key, as well as the office key, under the door, but I had just a wee bit of optimism that it would work out and I'd be able to finish out the year. Or at the very least, it was a bargaining chip for Coz—the school almost never changed locks when someone left. They'd deactivate the card key, but the inside door keys had been around for years. The board was too cheap to replace them.

Numb legs carried me across the school grounds. I wasn't sure if I'd be bodily escorted off if the campus security found me, so I hurried to my destination. At the boys' locker room, I knocked and yelled, "Female coming through." I counted to ten and heard a flurry of movement. Then I entered the locker room and went straight to Colin's office.

He was sitting behind his desk looking through game photos. His head snapped up when I knocked. "Celeste? Shouldn't you be in class?"

"I was asked to leave." I shifted the heavy bag on my shoulder. "By Mark."

"What?" He stood so fast his chair shot back into the wall. "He can't do that."

"Yes, he can. It's what the board wants. It's not permanent. Supposedly." I kept my hands fisted at my side. "I just wanted to come in and tell you before I left. You have stuff to do." I motioned to the boys suited up for practice, who weren't even trying to hide the fact that they were listening in. "I'll call you later."

I squared my shoulders—okay, so I hunched over and covered my eyes just in case any of the boys were still in varied states of dress, but when I escaped the locker room, they squared—and I walked solemnly to the parking lot. It was only then that I realized I had no car.

How had I gone from everything was fine—if a little dull—to being put on an indefinite, unpaid "vacation" and murder suspect with no car or phone. Had I woken up in an alternate reality? Had someone put a curse on me? On the upside, I could tell Annabelle I was free to start sooner.

I half sobbed and half laughed as I started out on the trek toward my house even though the subdivision was clear across town. Peytonville was just small enough there was no form of public transportation—lucky me, I got to walk again. The good thing about walking, I got to work off the anger and fear at losing my job. The bad thing, it gave my mind much more time to wander. And wander it did. I thought over all my well-constructed plans and how one death at school sent them tail-spinning. It seemed like all I did lately was think and I was damn tired of it.

Worse, and most telling, I knew I was in a bad way when calling my mother niggled the back of my head as a possibility. Asking her for help was as close to the bottom of my to-do list in life as I'd ever come. I must have skipped anxious altogether, screamed past fearful and was pulling up on desperate fast with next to no brakes. All of this was with the school still in sight if I looked back over my shoulder.

At the strip mall halfway home, I got a small coffee

and a very large brownie—I deserved a treat. I stopped at the cell phone store and splurged on a new smart-phone. A little therapeutic shopping never hurt. I called Levi—it was the only phone number I had memorized besides my mom's, and I wasn't ready to give in to that niggle just yet. He agreed to meet me for lunch and I formulated a plan of attack on getting my life back—a new plan as my other one had been shot to hell.

"JUST LIKE THAT he asked you to leave?" Levi forked a huge bite of his Caesar salad and shoved it in his mouth. "That's just wrong."

"So is talking with your mouth full." I moved the lettuce around on my plate. My appetite for good and healthy had flown out the window when I'd eaten a tri-ple scoop of mint chocolate chip ice cream—after the brownie—while waiting for Levi to join me for lunch. I totally blame him for being late.

Thick, heavy clouds rolled eastward as the morning turned to afternoon. The humidity was almost oppressive even for an eighty-five-degree November day. My hair stuck out every which way with the frizzies. If I could have blamed that on Levi, too, I would have. Actually, I could. We'd had to take a table on the patio since the inside had already filled with the regular lunch crowd.

I dropped my fork to the plate and pushed the un-touched salad away. "Where are you at work-wise? Do you have any more time to do some more snooping?"

His eyes lit up as he picked up his club soda. "Oh, absolutely. What do you have in mind?"

"I need to delve a little more into Chad's college days." I'd told Levi about the death of Professor Patts and the scandal that had surrounded everything. "I won-der if Kellen found anything."

Levi frowned. "Aren't you worried you're playing both ends of the field here?"

I was reaching for my glass and paused. "What?"

"You've got the detective checking out information for you and you have that reporter looking into it. You've got them both doing your bidding."

"My bidding? I'm not some Victorian damsel. And they have jobs to do." I eyed Levi over the top of my glass as I took a long sip. "I gave them some info neither seemed to find on their own. Is it too much to ask what they've found in return?"

"Too much from you, no. But as they do have jobs to do, returning the favor may not even be in their realm of ability whether they want to or not." He shrugged.

"Since when did you get all waxing professional?" I tore apart the little paper ring that had held together the napkin and flatware. "I guess the wording I should use is I *hope* they will be forthcoming. But...in the event they're not, I need to find some more useful info that maybe I can barter with them." I needed to have ammo for a little tit for tat, as Kellen called it.

"You, my friend, are a scary woman." Levi finished his lunch and pushed the empty dish to the side. He leaned his elbows on the table. "Devious and a little too wired to be turned loose on an unsuspecting community."

I ignored Levi and kept going with my ideas. "I was thinking we need more Google searches. There's something we're missing. I can feel it."

"Even the World Wide Web should fear you. Nonetheless, my workload is slowing down with Thanksgiving coming up next week. I'd be happy to assist." Levi scrunched his eyes and tapped his finger to his lips. "Let's go over to my place first."

"For?" I dropped the tattered paper. I was a little afraid of what was coming next.

"You need some wheels."

I sat up straighter. I'd expected his offer much sooner. How could I delicately say thanks, but no thanks? "Um, no thanks. I'd rather wait out the insurance company."

"Don't be silly. You need a vehicle. And I happen to have an extra."

I wouldn't call Harriet—yes, he named everything from his hairbrush to his vehicles—an "extra." Harriet was in a class all her own. One of the original consumer Hummers, the vehicle in question was massive. I could see all my energy-conscious, Prius-driving neighbors shaking their heads as I thundered down the streets.

"It will keep you safe and get you from point A to point B, which is more than you currently have. No arguments. Let's go get her, then we'll work on what's next."

IF I HAD my druthers, I'd have taken the Lexus, but Levi said something about a date he had later and wanted to impress... I let it go. I wouldn't win that argument no matter what.

I could admit—to myself, I'd never tell Levi—that I did feel a little safer in the luxury tank. Especially when the rain came pouring down. Little cars were getting stuck in the deeper puddles and I zipped through. I think I even scared a person or two when they saw me coming up behind them in Harriet. She had her advantages.

They ended at home, however. Harriet didn't even come close to fitting in my garage—had I had the opener with me, which had gone to heaven with my car. With the massive vehicle taking up almost my entire driveway, I jumped down, made a mad dash for the front door and beat Levi by only a minute or so.

"Okay, what's next?" he asked as he settled in at the kitchen table. Lightning lit up the windows. A minute or two later a clap of thunder shook the house.

I tried to shake the creepy tingle that ran up my spine as I took a seat next to him. My laptop sat between us and we each had paper and pen. "I'm going to get some info on the two other men involved."

"Isn't one dead? Why look him up? You know he couldn't have committed any of these crimes."

"Yes, but every little link helps." I fired up the computer and then made some coffee. "The info I got on him was from links off of Chad's search. You never know what we can turn up if we search him outright."

Levi shook his head. "Does any of that—the scandal, I mean—sound like something your boss would do?"

"If you'd asked me a week ago, I'd say no way. But in light of everything that's come out..." I shrugged. "I guess you never really know someone." I poised my hands over the laptop then pulled them back and turned toward Levi.

"What?" He leaned away from me.

"Would you do me a huge favor while I'm on the internet?" I batted my eyelashes at him. Levi only smiled and waited for me to hit him with my request. "Would you pretty please program my new phone?"

Levi let out a sigh. "Is that all? I thought you were going to ask for a kidney or something." He winked and held out his hand.

"All the stuff is up in the cloud." I handed him my brand spanking new cell phone. "My password is—"

"I know what it is." He was tapping away on the phone in an instant.

The coffee finished brewing and I poured us both cups. I doctored mine up with enough sugar to send a diabetic into a coma. I'd picked up some chocolate, chocolate chip biscotti earlier—I'd had way too much time to kill at the shopping center—and set them out on the table and took my seat.

"Okay, let's see." I typed in the deceased coconspirator's name, Joseph Carpenter. It was amazing how many people shared names. But with a little extra info like the year he died and the college he attended, I was on the right man's path in no time.

Another streak of lightning zipped across the sky. I jumped when the thunder clapped through the house. It distracted me from the laptop momentarily and I lost my place on the page. I used my index finger to speed-read through the text. I was finding a whole lot of nothing, and started to wonder if the internet was going to be a dead end.

I clicked through several links as Levi refilled the coffee cups. Nothing was of any help whatsoever, though I did find a mention of Carpenter's wife. I jotted down her info and picked up a biscotti. I'd just bitten down on it when the link I clicked on popped up and the loudest, longest clap of thunder rattled the widows. "Oh my *gawd*." The little treat fell from my mouth and hit the table with a thud.

"Still afraid of storms?"

I shook my head and pointed to the laptop.

"What did you find?"

I shifted my gaze from the computer to Levi as I turned the computer where he could read it better.

Levi read the article aloud. *"Mr. Joseph Carpenter was pronounced dead at the scene. The coroner eventually ruled the hanging a suicide—"* His breath caught and his gaze darted to mine, then he continued *"—despite the man's wife insisting he would never have taken his own life."*

"Oh, no no no no no. This can't be a coincidence." I held onto my coffee mug with both hands, let the warmth seep into my suddenly chilled hands. "Chad is found hanging, to look like suicide but is actually murder. This man's death is ruled a suicide."

"By hanging."

I nodded. "You have a professor both men had in college—whom they videotaped having sex with. Who hung herself, and it first looked like murder but turned out to be suicide." Even the warm coffee mug did little to ward off the chills.

"I don't know what's going on." Levi toyed with his snack. "But do you think you should call Beau Henderson?"

The third man in the scandal had an office in Dallas. "And what? Warn him he could be in danger? From whom? We don't know who could be doing this."

Levi straightened in his seat. "I know, but still."

"How would you take this phone conversation? 'Hi, Mr. Henderson, you don't know me but I promise I'm telling you the truth.'" I sent three copies of the article to the printer—one for me, Muldoon and Kellen. "The man would hang up before I could tell him what's going on."

"Do it in person then? Make an appointment. Take him all the evidence you've racked up to this point." Levi waved at the growing stack of articles and news blurbs. "If you tell him and he doesn't heed your warning, there's not a whole lot else you can do. But at least you tried, right?"

"You're right, but you have to come with me."

FIFTEEN

"Excuse me, but you're doing what?" Kellen all but yelled through the phone.

I rolled my eyes even though no one could see me. "I made an appointment to meet with the man day after tomorrow."

"You have some pretty compelling information, but nothing more than a lot of coincidence."

"Just coincidence? Give me a break. When was the last time you saw a case that had so many similar deaths?" He started to interrupt me so I hurried on. "But even if it is a major coincidence doesn't mean it's not all related. All you have to do is find the thread that holds it together then—"

"Celeste, listen to yourself."

"Kellen, listen to *yourself*. Aren't your reporter senses tingling up a storm? The chances of it not being related have to be astronomical. I can't just sit on this info. I have to give it to Henderson."

"And make the man paranoid." He scoffed through the phone.

"Hey, better paranoid and wary than oblivious and the next statistic on the crime blotter."

Kellen laughed. "You're a scary woman."

"I've been told that." I twisted around in my desk chair and checked the clock on the far wall. I had about half an hour before I was due at the police station to sign the official report for the shooting. The thunder and lightning had long since stopped, but the rain kept on. Several of the streets would be impassable—with or without Harriet—by the time I needed to get to the police station.

Muldoon had called an hour after Levi had left for his date. I'd debated not answering when I saw the number on the caller ID, worried what the police wanted from me now. But temptation and curiosity won out. He'd asked me to come up to sign off on the incident from the night before. While I was there, I could pass along the new information. If he wanted it. "Who knows, maybe Henderson has an idea of who's doing all this."

"Did you ever stop to think he could be the one doing it?"

My foot slipped off the edge of the desk as I tried to push myself around. "No, not really."

"Why not? You have to consider all the possibilities. I mean, why couldn't he? He was involved in the original crime, even if only on the periphery. He stands as good of a chance as anyone to be the culprit."

I could only come up with one argument. "He's a businessman."

"And Chad Jones was a principal, who blackmailed staff for sexual favors."

I shuddered. "You have a point. I'll give you that. But why then would he agree to see me?"

"To find out what you know? To see if you're a threat to him? Hell, Celeste, someone has been doing their best to get you out of the picture. You could be walking right up to the killer and saying, 'hey, have at me.'"

"The car bomb was not part of this case." I was making excuses that in the grand scheme were still pretty scary.

"So far the shooting and your house being broken

into haven't been tied to Jerry Pullman so unless there's someone else out there floating around…"

"Okay, that's enough." If he kept throwing up reasons why I shouldn't go, he might just talk me out of my plans. I was pretty sure everything would be fine. And it wasn't like I was going to meet the man in a dark alley. "It's just an appointment. At his place of business. In the middle of the day. And besides, I'm not going alone. I'll have Levi to protect me."

The phone beeped in my ear. "Kellen, I tell you what, when I get back you will be the first person I call. I'll even go on the record. How's that sound?"

"Like you're going to do what you want whether it's a good idea or not. As I said before, if you need help…"

"And you're offering out of the kindness of your heart?" I didn't mean to sound skeptical. But he was a reporter, whom I didn't know well.

"Take it for what it's worth. And yes I'll be keeping notes."

The phone beeped again. "Gotta go." I clicked the button to take the other call. Coz started talking before I could even say hello.

"Why didn't you call me as soon as the school terminated you?"

"Coz. Ugh. I totally forgot." I'd been so busy searching for clues into Chad's death I'd neglected taking care of myself. "I guess you spoke with Colin?" I pushed myself around in the chair again. "I'm not terminated. Just on leave. When it happened this morning I didn't have your number on me. My phone got incinerated, remember? Kablooey."

"Celeste, this is no joke. We're talking about your livelihood. What if they decide to fire you outright?"

"I'm already not getting paid, so—"

"What?" He harrumphed. "They did what exactly?"

"They gave me leave without pay." I leaned my head back against the chair but with the spinning it was making me nauseous. I sat up straighter. "Said my presence was a danger to the student body."

"You sound a little blasé about it all."

"Don't get me wrong, I'm upset. But at the time, I was too stunned to think. By the time I got home, I got a little sidetracked." I didn't think it was prudent to tell Coz about all the internet findings. Really, as my lawyer, he'd be better not knowing *beforehand* if I was going to get into any more trouble. There were things I did need to talk to him about. "Since you're representing me, if I tell you something in confidence you can't tell, right?"

"Right."

"I've actually had a job offer. That I'm taking, have taken." I rubbed my hand over my face. "I hadn't told the school yet. Colin either for that matter. You remember the playhouse I've been involved in for years." He grumbled a yes and I went on. "The owner of the playhouse offered me a full-time position with the understanding that I would start when the school year's over."

"Congratulations." Warmth fill his voice and eased a little of the tension from my chest. "Okay. Well at least you have something. Not to mention that takes away motive. Still, the school can't suspend you without pay. They're in violation of your contract."

"Really?"

"I read over Colin's most recent contract when they changed a few items. Assuming yours is the same, then no, they can't just suspend you without pay. And if they fire you they have to offer severance. Granted it depends on the circumstances, but as you haven't been charged with anything... Get me a copy of your contract and I will look it over and we'll start by sending out a letter to the school." He was silent for a moment. "Let me ask you a couple of questions."

"Okay." I grabbed a pen and tapped it on the desktop.

"Can you start sooner at the theater?"

"I suppose. Annabelle's only waiting because of my contract with the school."

"If I could get you a severance package and you're done with Peytonville Prep, as of today, are you okay with that?"

Was I? When I'd left with my things, I didn't think I'd be back—on the school's terms. I could ask for Coz to fight so I could finish out the year. Even though I didn't know how long that fight could take. And there was still the matter of me being a danger. As much as I'd love to finish out the year with my kids, I would be devastated if anything followed me to Peytonville Prep. Their year was already tainted with two unexpected deaths.

"I think that would be okay." I wasn't lying down and letting the school railroad me. Even if I didn't get a severance package at all I'd be standing up for myself. "Yeah, if you don't mind, go ahead and do that."

I was about to hang up after he asked a few more questions but remembered my appointment at the police station. "So you've looked over the statement they want me to sign, right?"

"Yes, they faxed it to me." He cleared his throat. "With any luck you'll be done with them once you sign it."

"SIGN HERE AND HERE." The young officer pointed to the bottom of the page on the counter.

I did as instructed and set the pen down. "Is that all?"

The officer read through some papers on a clipboard. "Um, yes. Thank you, Mrs. Eagan." She turned and walked away. I'd been dismissed.

I wondered why Muldoon hadn't come out and spoken with me. He'd called the meeting after all. And I knew he was there. At least, a car was in the lot in his assigned space, but no one came out from the back.

"Time to move along." I shouldered my bag and made my way down the short hall to the glass double doors at the front of the building. The rain hadn't lessened one iota since it'd rolled in. I looked where I'd left my umbrella in the corner, not wanting to dribble water all over the floor. But it was gone. "Stolen. In a police station of all places."

"Looking for this?"

My rain boots squeaked as I pivoted around. The pink-and-blue polka-dotted umbrella looked comical in Muldoon's large hand. "Yes, thank you." I reached for it but he tucked it behind him. I tapped the toe of my boot. "Do you have a social life? I've never seen you when you're not on duty. Hell, do you even go off duty? Maybe have a girlfriend or a wife waiting at home to occupy your time when you're not harassing people on your cases?" I'd waited as long as I could before I'd asked what I was dying to know. Unfortunately, it came out snippy and mean instead of inquisitive.

It was also the wrong time/place for it. The little crooked smile on the corner of his mouth fell and he shoved the umbrella at me.

"What did I say?" I said with mock innocence. I sighed and shook my head. I was tired of this game he was playing, though I couldn't decide if it was a personal or professional pastime. As he tried to pass me I snagged a hold of his sleeve. "Look, Detective." I lowered my voice. "I don't get what's going on with you. And me. The two of us. I feel like there's a spark of… something. You sometimes act like there's a spark—and I don't think I am imagining that. Am I?"

He sucked in a slow, deep breath and pulled his arm away from my grasp.

"One minute you're basically telling me to get lost. And then the very next you're teasing again." I stepped closer to him, could smell the warm musky scent that just oozed from him. "I'm confused. There's so much going on I can barely keep my head above water and you—" I waved my hand at him "—you confuse the hell outta me."

Muldoon held my gaze. Just stood there giving me a serious case of "why'd I have to go and open my big fat mouth" as my brain tried to whip up a quick apology. Not that I owed him one. Still, I hated the hinky sensation that tweaked my conscience. I didn't want to hurt his feelings, but I couldn't get a handle on my own when he was there all dark, sexy and silent.

Not that I had a chance anyway. He left me standing there.

"Do I know how to clear a room or what?" I pushed through the glass doors and popped open the umbrella. The wind was whipping it all around as I trudged through the parking lot puddles to the Hummer. I was just about to open the door when I heard my name called.

I turned to see Muldoon running across the lot toward me with a jacket held over his head. When he reached me he stooped under the umbrella, his nose a breath away from mine. He had little navy flecks in his ice-blue irises that matched the dark band around the edge. His sooty eyelashes made them so bright and vibrant, even on an overcast, gloomy day. Up close the color was amazingly breathtaking.

"Your car?"

His question shook me from being mesmerized by his eyes. "Levi's. It's a loaner. The insurance company is still hesitating to act on a potentially self-planted bomb."

The line of his lips thinned. "Hmm."

"You didn't dash out here in the rain to inquire about my wheels, did you?" I don't know why I couldn't keep the snippy out of my voice. "Checking to see if I've planted more explosives?"

Muldoon blinked slowly. "We know who tampered with your car."

"Yet you never shared any of that info despite how many times I've seen you lately. I learned it from Kellen."

His gaze never wavered from mine. "I should have informed you myself. I'll have questions."

"Questions." So cold and impersonal. If he was going to keep his icy demeanor, why didn't he just stay in the damn building? "Do you need something? Right now."

"For you to understand."

I leaned against the Hummer's door, to put as much distance from the man as the confines of the umbrella would allow. "Understand what?"

Muldoon reached up and touched my cheek. "I am just as confused as you are."

I think my chin hit the collar of my raincoat. I can't be sure as my brain slowed at that precise moment.

"My gut tells me you were just in the wrong place at the wrong time, but the evidence puts you in it up to your ass." One black eyebrow shot up to the fall of hair on his forehead. "Which means I have no choice but to back off until this case is solved. And I have to let go of the urge to kiss you every time you come within arm's reach, but God I want to so bad it hurts."

I swallowed hard. I was at a loss for what to say—which almost never happened to me.

"If I'm not careful, I could lose my job or, worse, jeopardize the case."

Typical Muldoon—funny I knew what was typical of the man having known him barely a week. I didn't point out the "worse" was not about him at all. How many men would worry about protecting their case over themselves?

"I'm not trying to be an ass to you. But the more I try to do right by all…" He shrugged. It drew him up closer. "The end result is I feel like crap and I make you feel like crap. And I'm sorry."

"O-okay." What else could I say to that?

He held my gaze. Even over the rain pelting the umbrella I could hear his cell phone on his hip.

"You should get that."

Muldoon nodded, pulled the phone from his pocket and answered it as he dashed back to the police station. He stopped just outside the door and called back to me. "Will you be home tonight?"

"Yes."

I PACED THE living room. That seemed to be my new pastime—pacing and waiting for Muldoon to show up, invited or not. Not that he'd *actually* said he was coming over. For all I knew, he was checking to see where to start a new tail on me.

I'd turned off the television. Either a bunch of singing and dancing high school kids were performing at a naval shipyard or even my regular short attention span had run its course. I put on the Michael Bublé CD and tried to let his dulcet tones relax me.

Unfortunately, as much as I loved old Mikey, it wasn't working. My nerves were all twitchy. I missed my child. I missed my students. Hell, I even missed growling at Naomi in the halls. I was not the kind of woman to sit idle. Oh sure, I could veg out on the sofa with my box set of BBC's *Pride and Prejudice* and a pint of double mocha fudge, but that was a planned vegging out. The forced sit-on-my-ass-and-do-nothing was a little harder to wrap my head around.

Since the school's impromptu hiatus, I'd tried to stay active, if in a somewhat furtive sort of way. And even then, my failed attempts at getting to the bottom of what was going on only managed to embed me into further trouble.

The more I thought about it, if I were Muldoon, I'd stay away from me too. I was nothing but trouble. And clearly I didn't know boundaries, though it wasn't as if I'd gone out there looking for all the trouble I was in. Shoot, I didn't even *know* the extent of the trouble I was in. Every other moment something deadly or dangerous popped up.

I was wandering in my head and lost track of the route I was taking in my living room. I smacked my leg on the table next to the sofa. "Dang it." I rubbed the sore spot on my thigh.

Since I started limping, I shifted my pacing into the kitchen to start a pot of coffee. "Might as well do something useful." Once I got it going, I grabbed a Ben and Jerry's pint and scanned the pantry. I hadn't eaten since lunch with Levi. I frowned and put the lid back on the pint—after I took two quick bites. I'd had ice cream for lunch.

Between sleeping in my clothes and eating ice cream morning, noon and night, my personal habits were reverting from single mom to college freshman. If I wasn't careful, I'd put on the freshman fifteen and I'd graduated fourteen years earlier. I shoved the ice cream back into the freezer and perused the fridge. There was a bag of carrots, green tops and all. Levi must have left them, because I sure didn't buy them. I took one carrot from the bag just as the coffeemaker finished brewing. I stuck the root veggie in my mouth as I poured the fragrant brew into my favorite mug. I was just raising the coffee to my lips when the front bell chimed. My nerves did a quick shimmy through my system. Why should I be anxious? Was it the man? Or the potential for why he'd come to my house—again?

Muldoon smiled when I opened the door. He was shaking out his umbrella and set it on the corner of the porch. It took me a minute to realize he stood sans his sports coat. He was out of his regular uniform altogether. He wore a dark blue sweater with a white tee barely peeking from beneath and a pair of well-worn jeans topping a dark brown pair of square-toed boots.

"Hey," he said and shifted a thick manila folder from one hand to the other.

"Hey." The immediate need to fidget engulfed me. You'd think I was fourteen again. This was not a date; still, I know I stood and gawked at him for way too long. "Manners. Sorry. Come in." I opened the door wider and let him enter. "I have coffee." I motioned toward the kitchen. He'd been in my house enough to know the way.

I made quick work of fixing him up a cup and we

sat at the table. I took a long sip of mine. "So. What brings you here?"

Muldoon pushed the manila folder to me. "This is a copy of the police report for your car. If you have any further hassles from the insurance company, have them call me and I'll make sure they pay out on the claim."

I glanced down at the folder, tapped my name written in tight, precise letters. "You could have mailed this."

"I could have. But I wouldn't get to see you then." He wrapped his hands around his mug and held my gaze. He had such a straightforward way—about some things. Other things, I didn't know where I stood. I broke eye contact and ran my finger around the handle of the coffee mug. I sucked at small talk when I was nervous. My brain would seize up and I couldn't think of anything witty or charming, or even casual, to say. I ended up just blurting out, "The school suspended me today. They don't want my presence to harm the students."

"Man." His mouth pulled down at the corners. "Are you okay?"

I shrugged. "I get it. Between my car being blown up and being shot at—" I didn't think they even knew about that yet "—they can't take any chances. If I was one of the parents... Hell, I am one of the parents."

He reached across the table and squeezed my hand. The warmth from the mug transferred from his hand to mine. Just as quickly he let go again.

I tried to pretend he hadn't affected me. It was getting harder to stay immune with each touch. I shook myself from the thoughts. "I do have another job lined up actually." I told him about Annabelle's offer. "Plus Coz is looking over my contract to see if they've violated it. I'll be okay." I said that as much for me as for an answer to his earlier question. But I didn't want to talk about my future. That wasn't why he'd come over. "Can you tell me about my car?" I pulled the folder in front of me and opened it. "What directed you to Jerry?"

"We followed fingerprints. Which led us to him. He was in the system. Pullman claims he had nothing to do with it, but his prints were all over pieces of the device we recovered at the scene. Including the tape he used to hold it into place."

I looked up from the folder. "He was in the system? For what? He always seemed so…" I shrugged. "Mild mannered."

"Drug possession with the intent to sell."

"Seriously?" I blew out a low whistle.

Muldoon gave a quick nod. "His trial is coming up soon."

"Did you—" I tapped the folder again "—check him out to see if he could have had anything to do with Chad's death? He did work for him for many years."

He nodded again. "Once we got forensics back on your car, we ran his alibis for the dates in question regarding Mr. Jones. The night Jones was killed, Pullman was in the emergency room for a bad burn."

When I frowned, he continued, "We think he burned his arm constructing the explosive device."

A shudder ran through me. "What about when Kelsey died?"

"Says he was at home. No one to verify one way or the other." He took a sip of his coffee. "We don't think he's connected to her. Or Jones for that matter."

I closed the folder and looked out the back window. The rain had slowed to a heavy drizzle. A chill ran up my spine—like when you're being watched. I chocked it up to Muldoon watching me as we spoke. I shook my head. "I don't get it. Why go after me?"

"Or Colin."

"Or Colin?" I frowned and waved my hand. "Why would he go after either of us?"

"You don't know?"

"I haven't the foggiest clue." I started to sip my coffee. I stopped so quickly some of the hot liquid sloshed out and onto the folder. "Dang it." I snapped up some napkins and dried the widening stain. "You know something more about this than I do?"

Muldoon grabbed a napkin and dabbed at a spot I'd missed. "Why do you think Pullman got fired?"

I narrowed my eyes. "No clue. They just said he was let go." I crumpled up the wet napkins and tossed them into the sink.

Muldoon held my gaze and said, "Jerry was dealing—"

"Drugs?" I blinked as if the word didn't register in my brain.

"Yes." Muldoon finished off his coffee, dropped the soiled napkin inside and pushed the mug away from him. "From what I understand, Pullman had a little racket going at the school—"

"At the *school*?"

"—for a while. No one told or found out until one of the boys on the football team came to practice high. The kid finally admitted to Colin where he'd gotten the drugs."

Colin knew? It was all so incredulous. How did that not get around the school? "Why didn't Colin tell me?" We were still married when Pullman left. What other secrets had he kept? I rubbed my forehead. I didn't think I actually wanted to know the answer to that. "Why would Jerry come after me?"

Muldoon shook his head. "Don't know yet. We're still trying to get to the bottom of it."

"Colin took Paige because he said it was too dangerous for her with me. If Jerry was after Colin, then she isn't safe. With either of us."

"Jerry Pullman is behind bars now. We found his lab. It looks like he'd started to dismantle it after the car bombing. There were enough materials in his garage to add more charges on top of the original drug charges. Between that and the links to your bombing, he more than likely won't get out before he goes to trial. And hopefully not for a very long time after."

The usual calming effects of coffee did little to put me at ease, even with Muldoon's assurance Jerry Pullman was locked away keeping me and mine safe and secure.

Muldoon leaned his elbows on the table. "You don't need to worry about Pullman. He won't be bothering you ever again," he said as if reading my thoughts.

"I know I should be relieved, but…" My eyes widened. "The shooting?"

"Wasn't him. He was in lockup by then."

I guess that was too much to hope for. "Are there any leads on the shooting?"

"No." His gruff answer told me he wasn't any happier about it than I was.

At least one person gunning for me was gone, though. I slid the folder to the other side of the table, like having the information farther away from me would somehow scare me less. "So many things in my life are not what they seemed."

"Very few are."

I'd give anything to go back a week, back to sedate and settled. When I didn't know the evil things people did, didn't know the depths of deception people were willing to go. "I think I liked being oblivious. I don't know how you stay sane having to delve into people's lives like you do. Trying to ferret out when they're lying and why."

He shrugged. "It's what I do."

"I guess you had to question Colin again?"

"Yes. Through his lawyer."

"You talked to Coz again?"

"Mmm-hmm." He rose and deposited his mug in the sink, then turned and leaned a hip against the counter. "He didn't want us to use the explosion and Pullman's drug case as a reason to ask Colin about the Jones case." He chuckled. "He hasn't changed, has he?"

"Coz?" I smiled. It felt almost foreign after all the talk of Pullman. "No, he's the one constant in the Eagan family. Always the same. He's a good guy." I stood, cradling my mug. I drained off the remainder. "I'm surprised you remember him from school. He and Colin didn't exactly hang out in the same social or extracurricular circles, from what I understand."

"There was more to me than just football."

My cheeks heated. "I didn't mean to imply…"

"I'm just giving you a hard time." He chuckled. "I didn't know Coz well since he was a few grades ahead. But he was legendary in the school for challenging the teachers. If he thought they were on the wrong side of an issue, he'd take them to task on it."

"Sounds like Coz. He's quiet as a church mouse unless he gets worked up over something. Then all you can do is get out of his way."

"He rub off on you a little bit?"

"I guess, maybe. Not bad qualities to have."

"As long as you can keep from getting locked up in the process."

"There is that." I reached around him and set my mug next to his. Muldoon hadn't so much as moved but the air between us thickened. His musky scent invaded my nostrils and I wanted to fall into him. Instead, I took two steps back slowly. "So…did you make any progress with the information I gave you?"

"A little." His breath hitched slightly.

I tried to pretend I didn't notice, but I noticed all the way down to my toes. "Are you going to share that with me?"

He settled his hands on either side of his hips, holding onto the counter. His gaze raked over my mouth. "Not just yet."

Goose bumps spread across my arms. I'd forgotten the question. When I expected Muldoon to lean forward, make a move, any move, he shifted his weight and actually leaned farther away. He was a mix of confusion—but at least he was consistent. My ardor cleared and I remembered the thread of the conversation. "You won't share because it's against department regulations?"

"No, because I'm afraid of what you might do with the information."

I didn't take it personally, not much anyways. "I gave you the places to start looking."

"Yes, you did. And as you have the uncanny knack for getting into trouble with what you do know, not to mention a slew of costumes at your fingertips where I might not even know it's you…"

"I am banned from the school, remember?"

He tilted his head to the side. "But you now have a job with access to even more costume choices as well as makeup. I wouldn't even know how far you could go to alter your appearance."

"I wouldn't, I haven't…" I cleared my throat. "I don't even have a key to the building yet."

"But you're pretty chummy with the leggy brunette who does. Remember, I followed you the other morning." He winked. A smile played at the corners of his mouth. "I'm not sharing for your protection as much as whoever might become the beneficiary of your disguises. As a peace officer of this fair city, it's my duty to protect its citizens."

I set my hand on my chest in true Southern belle indignation. "From me?"

His shoulders lifted upward in a shrug. "What can I say? I am precautionary."

"I don't know if I should be insulted or pleased you think I have enough moxie—and costumes—to become a nuisance to the Peytonville Police force."

He snorted. "Maybe a little bit of both."

"Can you just give me a hint? A direction to Google?" I wasn't above begging, but I preferred to hold out on that until I absolutely had no other choice.

Instead of an answer, his stomach growled. "Sorry. I worked straight through dinner and only had time to run home and change."

He'd come straight over and bypassed food. As was now the norm when I was around Muldoon, the little flutter in my tummy started kicking up her heels. "I could fix you something…" As I stepped toward the fridge, there was a quick hum, then the electricity went out and plunged us into total darkness and silence. "I guess the storm—"

"No." His warm hand grabbed my arm and pulled me over to him.

I hadn't even heard him move. "What're you—"

"Shh," he whispered against my ear. "I don't think the storm knocked out the electricity."

"Why?" I whispered back. "It's been raining like crazy all day."

"The neighbor's isn't out."

I looked through the window over the sink and he was right. The Pospieches' house was lit up like Christmas Eve.

"What do we do?"

"Is your pantry a walk-in?" I shook my head—then said no when I realized he couldn't see me. Muldoon directed me over to the kitchen table, bumping into a chair as we rounded the end to the side. "Get down under the table and stay there. Got it?"

SIXTEEN

EVERY CREAK AND groan echoed through the kitchen. I couldn't tell what was actual ambient noise and what was Muldoon—or anyone else—moving through the house. I'd like to think I'd just blown a fuse. The house being less than ten years old, however—and the fact that my father had checked out everything from the water to the electricity last time he was here—I couldn't ignore the coincidence of everything.

There was a loud thump followed by a crash. I covered my head with my hands and just prayed no one started shooting again. I stayed hunched over and wasn't sure how much time passed, but the hum of the electricity kicked on a second before the lights all came back on. When I finally opened my eyes, all I could do was stare down at the floor, a little surprised to see dirt in the linoleum crevices. My mopping skills were clearly lacking. I shifted and leaned my head against the padded seat in front of me. I was cowering under a table from some unknown assailant and my love/hate relationship with Mr. Clean should not be called to my attention.

Muldoon's boots appeared at the edge of the table a moment before he called my name. "Celeste." A chair moved and his large hand snaked under the table. "You can come out now."

I ignored the little tinge that zipped through me when

I let him guide me out. "What happened? Did you find anyone?"

"Did you leave your garage door open?"

I frowned. "No. I haven't opened it in days. Levi's Hummer won't exactly fit inside. Besides, my controller bit it with the car."

"Come here." The flirty, easygoing guy was replaced with super cop.

He set his hand at the small of my back and guided me into the garage. Boxes with all sorts of decorations and Paige's too-small clothes lined the slot where Colin used to park. My spot was barren with my car not yet replaced with a human-size vehicle.

"The garage door was open." He pointed at the closed bay door. "Someone came in and flipped the main breaker on the fuse box. A wet trail from outside led straight to the box. The door into the house was unlocked." He tapped the deadbolt with his index finger.

"I always leave it unlocked. You can't get in without the remote."

His lips disappeared with the disappointed purse of his mouth. "Someone did."

I closed my eyes and ran my hands down my face. Yet again, I'd screwed up. How many times had my dad told me to keep that interior door locked? I'd always felt safe, though, because the big garage door was locked up tight and now without a remote… "How could someone get the garage door open?"

Muldoon shook his head and looked down. "You gather up a couple and try different frequencies and wham, there ya go. Thieves will troll alleys or streets pushing buttons until they get a hit. It's an easy score, especially if the interior door is easily accessed to them."

"Did someone get in the house?" I pointed to the last remnants of the wet trail.

"Not far. They'd just opened the interior door when I heard them. I almost had my hands on them but I tripped over some little table. They took off and I couldn't see where they went."

I stuffed my hands in my jeans pockets. "That was awful brazen of someone to do this when a cop was in my house."

"They may not have known I was here." He guided me back into the house and into the living room. "There was a good-size puddle in front of your house so I parked a house over. But whoever it was may not have cared either. I'm going to put a guard back on you." He was reaching for his phone.

"I don't want that." I sank onto the sofa. I didn't want to be watched all the time again. We—well *I*, who knows what Muldoon uncovered from the leads I gave him—had no idea who to be wary of. "Please, no cops watching me."

"Celeste…" He sighed and sat across from me.

"I don't get it. I just don't." I kicked my heels up on the coffee table. "Chad and Kelsey are murdered. I didn't do it. I don't know who did it. So why are they coming after me? Do they think I know something? 'Cause I swear to you, I don't."

"There must be something. Anything."

I hadn't told him about my appointment with Beau Henderson. But if he was the bad guy and I was coming *to him*, why would he continue to come after me?

"Let's start at the beginning and go over this again."

"Fine." I ran through everything I knew up to that point. All the leads I'd followed and everything I'd printed. Well, all except the info on Mr. Henderson.

Other than Levi, no one knew we had that info. Okay, Kellen knew we knew *something*. But I never elaborated or told him details. Honestly, I was afraid he'd try to get an interview and anything candid the man might say would be tainted. So other than Levi… I trusted Levi with my life. He was not involved. No one would be the wiser about my appointment, so it couldn't be a threat. And that's assuming it was even relevant. I didn't have proof it had anything to do with anything. I was going to see him to tell him what *I* knew.

"You never spoke to the gardener after you got picked up by the Fort Worth Police?"

"Danny?" I shook my head. "Nope. Not since the night I ran into him getting my grade book. Why?"

Muldoon leaned his elbows on his knees and laced his fingers together. "The night the office was broken into." He tilted his head back and closed his eyes tight. "He got your sweater all greasy."

"Yes. My pink cardigan." I was getting beyond fidgety. I thrummed my fingers on my thighs and bounced my knees. "When you examined Chad's office after the break-in, did you find grease on anything?"

He straightened his head and looked at me. But didn't speak.

"Aw, come on, Muldoon. I get that whole confidentiality part. I really do. But at this point what difference does it make if you give me an itty bitty detail here and there." He still didn't speak. "Unless you really think I'm in on it."

"I don't." He sighed. "Fine. Yes, we did find a couple of spots with grease. But only on a light switch and one spot on the corner of the desk. No viable prints."

"See. There ya go."

"The place was trashed. If he had enough grease on

him to ruin your sweater you'd think we'd have found more. Yes, I think he was definitely there, but maybe he was just curious and went to see what was up."

"Maybe? You say it like you're not sure. Didn't you question him?"

"At the time of the school break-in, yes. In regards to you. He didn't admit to being there."

"But I told you…"

"Yes, you did. We've had a little trouble tracking him back down. He hasn't been questioned again." He sat up straight. "And there was nothing to tie him to the office."

"The grease."

"Which you had on you, too. As well as the fact that you were the only person to log in that night. When we tracked down Kelsey to speak to her again…"

I shivered. "That's when your guys found her body?" Muldoon nodded.

"And you found the DVDs."

"Yes. She also had a small handheld DVD recorder. We think it came from Jones's office. After watching a couple of the DVDs, we knew the entrapments were mostly filmed there."

"You confiscated his computer, didn't you? And your techie guys found videos uploaded on it too?"

"Yes." He had that wary, "uh-oh why's she asking" look.

"His ex-wife said something to me at the funeral, couldn't believe I'd had the nerve to show up. At the time I thought she considered me a potential killer, but later when we spoke on the phone…" His dark eyebrow shot up—damn, those things moved around a lot, it was sexy as hell. I gave myself a mental smack to the back of the head. *Mind off the sexy detective and focus.* "I called her to find out what that whole cold shoulder was about. She told me about the videos and about being able to divorce him because of it. Said she should have thanked me and the others. How many others?" I waved away the question. "Even if you could tell me, I don't think that I want to know."

"'Kay."

"Was his office the only place he, um, shot footage?"

"No. There was a hotel room. We checked it out. He rented it as needed so there was nothing he kept there."

I tugged on the end of my sleeve, pulled at a piece of lint. "Was his house scavenged like someone was looking for the DVDs too?"

Muldoon shifted in his seat. "Why do you ask?"

"If I, whoever the 'bad guy'—" I did air quotes with my fingers "—might be, were to look for something, I'd check any place Chad could potentially leave it. If I was going to go to all the trouble to kill the man and make it look like suicide, I'd want to find it. I wouldn't want to take chances that it was found by the police."

"No, his house wasn't trashed."

Really? That was strange. "Why would mine and Kelsey's be trashed but not Chad's? Did they find what they were looking for at Kelsey's?"

Muldoon shrugged. If he had a theory, he wasn't sharing.

"Do you think it was a former victim?" I couldn't wrap my head around any of the women who left the school killing him. Once they were gone, what was the point?

"It would be hard for a woman to do it by herself. But it's not unheard of. And if she had help…"

"Do *you* think it's a woman?"

"I have a few ideas."

And with that, the open-answer portion of the night closed down again. "Which you won't share with me." It was a statement. Muldoon'd started to put the wall back up.

"You ask pretty good questions," he said by way of redirecting the conversation.

"*Veronica Mars*."

"What?"

"I've watched every episode of *Veronica Mars*. The TV show—well, and movie. Teenage super sleuth. Never mind. What made you become a cop?" Not the best segue, but I was curious.

"My dad was a cop."

"Was?" I gulped. I didn't want to open a whole can of "remember when" for Muldoon and his dad. As much as my mother annoys me, I'd never wish her gone—gone over state lines, yes, but not gone, gone.

"He retired about ten years ago."

"Oh good. I mean not good that's he retired good that's he's not dead, which was my first thought when you said *was*. I'm sorry. I get diarrhea of the mouth from time to time."

"I've noticed that." He chuckled. "I don't mind. It's kind of cute."

"Cute. Gaw." I leaned my head back on the sofa cushion. "That's like being friends. No girl wants to be cute. Especially someone sneaking up on forty."

"I happen to like cute."

I lifted my head slowly. This game between us was a little too much for my brain to process along with everything else. "We should focus on our case."

He cleared his throat. It almost sounded like he was trying to smother a laugh. "*Our* case?"

I shrugged with one shoulder. "Chad used the DVDs as blackmail of sorts. Kelsey was the current victim?"

"She was the only recent one as far as we could tell."

"Do you think she killed him?" I was holding my breath a little, wondering if he'd actually answer the question.

He took a long breath himself, then said, "She had a pretty good alibi for the night Jones died."

"Did you talk to her boyfriend?"

"Yeah, but he was alibied even tighter for that night. He was in jail on a DUI stop. And when she was killed, he was at a court-mandated AA meeting."

"That quickly?"

"From a previous DUI stop."

I tapped my lips. More people were ruled out than in. "So it could have been a previous mark."

"Mark?"

"His victims."

"I know what a mark is. But coming from you…" He shook his head. "You're a teacher. You shouldn't be worrying about marks or victims."

"I'm a *theater* teacher. Former teacher." The words caught in my throat. It was going to be hard to get used to that. "Drama is right up my alley."

"Pretend drama, not car explosions, shootings and dead bodies."

"Tomayto, tomahto. I'm in it now, so the best thing is to get to the bottom of it to get out from under it. Don't you think?"

"Where you're concerned I don't know what I think." He slapped his hands on his knees and stood up. "There weren't any recent *marks* as far as we could find."

I stood as well to keep from having to crane my neck

at an alarmingly uncomfortable angle. "So why go to the trouble to kill him now if he'd moved on."

"Exactly."

"I still think the scandal with the professor when he was in college has to be the key." I reached out and set my hand on his arm. "It can't be a coincidence that he just so happens to be videoing people and dies eerily similar to the way she did."

He didn't move or shy away from my touch. "I agree. That was an excellent find." He patted my hand, let his fingers linger a moment before he dropped his hand to his side. "And we're talking to the police involved back then. Going over old case files. But it's been over twenty years. Some of the key witnesses have moved on. Sources have forgotten the details."

"What about the professor's son?" I stepped back and let my own hand fall away. "Do you think he knows anything?"

"He was a kid at the time. I doubt she'd conduct any of her affairs in front of the boy. But no, we haven't gotten a hold of him. He was a minor and was put into foster care after his mother's death. There's a couple of decades of paperwork to wade through for his info."

"That poor little boy. Can you imagine? Losing your mom and then having to be sent to live with people you didn't know." My mind flashed to Paige. No matter what happened to Colin or me, Paige had enough family that she would never have to worry.

Muldoon started to comment when the doorbell rang. He immediately stiffened. His hand crept to his side and he lifted his sweater to reveal a gun handle.

I was halfway to the door when the bell rang again followed by a key in the lock. "Sweets, you home?" Levi called when he got it open.

"It's my friend." I patted Muldoon's arm. "You can re-cover your cannon."

He snorted and adjusted his sweater back over the weapon.

"Do you always pack heat?" I arched an eyebrow over my shoulder at him as I went to greet Levi.

Muldoon shook his head and smiled broadly but didn't answer.

Levi walked in and I shut the door. "How'd you get the key in the lock by yourself?" His arms were loaded down with bags. An umbrella was wedged between his neck and the side of his head. It took some doing but I pried it loose and set it to dry next to Muldoon's umbrella. Then he pushed past me and stopped so quickly I smacked into his back.

"You have company."

"Levi, you remember Detective Muldoon, don't you?" I leaned closer in the guise of kissing his cheek and whispered, "Ixnay on the plans for Thursday."

"Got it." He shifted the bags in his arms. "How are you this blustery evening, Detective?"

"What's in the bags?" I interrupted any conversation the two might get into. "What did ya bring me?" I stood up on my tiptoes and tried to peek inside but Levi shifted the bags.

"Have you eaten?" he asked instead of answering me.

"I—"

"Something other than ice cream?"

He knew me too well. "Nope." I turned so I could see both Levi and Muldoon. "I was just about to offer to fix the good detective something."

"Gracious." Levi twisted his mouth up in a grimace and squeezed his eyes tightly closed. "Then I got here in the nick of time." He looked at me. "Are you trying to get thrown back in jail with your cooking?" He shifted his gaze to Muldoon. "Assaulting an officer?" He tsked.

"I am not a bad cook." Did I or did I not save Annabelle's date with my pot roast recipe? Granted she'd set her food on fire, so mine was definitely a step up."

"No, you just lack inspiration." Levi scurried down the short hall to the kitchen. "I have mu shu pork, kung pao beef and broccoli beef. Regular and fried rice. Oh and some egg rolls and wonton soup."

"You got takeout." Lack inspiration? I could have called for takeout.

"I also stopped at the grocers and got you some bread, milk, coffee and cereal. Your pantry was bare the last time I peeked in."

Which was earlier that morning. "Thanks, hon," I yelled after my friend. I waved Muldoon to follow me back.

He set his hand at the small of my back and leaned in to whisper, "Did you call him and ask him to pick up food?"

"Sadly, no. That's often how he arrives—loaded with food." I smiled up at him and was rewarded with a rare flash of his pearly whites. "Can you stay and eat?"

"Sure. Why not?"

Levi had already gotten down plates and set the table for three. He was filling glasses with ice when Muldoon and I walked into the kitchen. He glanced over his shoulder as he set the first glass in the water slot on the fridge. "So, Detective, where are we at in our case?"

"*Our*?" Muldoon moaned as he eased into a seat at the table. "Him too?"

"He's coming around, Levi." I popped open the kung pao beef and scooped some onto my plate. "But he still has that silly old code of ethics the police department makes him go by." I nudged Muldoon's shoulder and winked at him.

The three of us ate and chatted. But we didn't discuss the case. Turned out Levi and Muldoon had a mutual friend of sorts. One of Levi's first house sales was to a buddy of Muldoon's. Small world. Okay, maybe living in Peytonville, Texas, it wasn't all that small. If you have a job, shop for your own groceries and go to church, you're bound to run into at least a quarter of the residents.

Levi, like myself, was a non-Texas transplant—seldom did he let on he was born and raised smack-dab in the middle of New Jersey. He and I had to start building up those connections of who knows who from scratch. Since I'd married into a Peytonville family, my degrees of separation lessened considerably. It was hard to believe I'd never seen Muldoon before. He would stand out just about anywhere he went. Those broad shoulders alone would draw your eyes. If you were close enough to see his strong jaw and gorgeous eyes…he was not a man easily forgotten or missed.

I shook myself and grabbed another egg roll as they continued to talk. The two men conversed easily. I can admit, I was a little jealous at how effortlessly Levi meshed with people. Very few people weren't charmed by Levi after only a few minutes. I think I'd married one of the only people he hadn't won over. I sat back and enjoyed the instant camaraderie between Levi and Muldoon, for once not the center of the conversation.

My hip started vibrating. I plucked my new phone from my pocket. The screen showed an unknown caller. I pushed the talk button. For a long moment I didn't think anyone was there and said hello again. Finally the person on the other end whispered something that had my heart pounding, but they hung up before I could ask who was calling. My shaking fingers dropped the phone down to my lap.

"What is it, sweets?" Levi patted his mouth with his napkin and leaned forward. "Is everything okay?"

"The caller said, 'You won't always have protection.'"

SEVENTEEN

SITTING ON MULDOON'S SOFA, I hugged my overnight bag to my chest. After he'd called the station and started whatever it was he'd had to do to get a trace on my cell phone, he'd ordered me to pack a bag. He was taking me into protective custody. With him and only him. Ugh.

I'd argued that I could just go stay with Levi. Whoever was playing these sick games couldn't know where my friend lived. But the last thing I wanted was for whoever was after me to get to Levi. I figured he'd be safer without me so I begrudgingly agreed to let Muldoon call the shots. Once that was settled, he barked out instructions and less than an hour later we were headed out. To his house. Which was only seven minutes and thirty-four seconds away—yes, I watched the clock that closely.

Originally, I thought I'd end up locked up rather than on a beautiful leather sofa. On the one hand, I think I'd much prefer the six-by-eight jail cell to the intimacy of a manly decorated space ten times the size. Especially given the strange dance the two of us were in. On the other hand, I didn't have a choice so it was all moot.

I was mentally drained but strangely wide awake. When I crashed—and there would most definitely be a crash—I knew that even as anxious as I was at Muldoon's house, I'd sleep well with him nearby.

Muldoon had been on the phone since we'd pulled into his garage several hours earlier. I'd parked myself

on his sofa, making myself into the smallest ball of a
person as I could and sat with my mouth zipped and my
ears open. I couldn't remember the last time I'd stayed
so still or quiet. Try as I might, though, I hadn't been
able to glean a single thing that made sense as he spoke
to this person or that. He'd finished the most recent call
and tapped endlessly on his phone. It was approaching
midnight and my eyelids were drooping.

"Can I show you to your room now?"

"No, thanks, Warden. I'm good." And apparently a
little snippy to boot.

The detective eyed me for a long moment, punched
a few more buttons, then returned the cell phone to his
ear. He paced in front of a huge natural rock hearth. It
was gorgeous. Well, the man and the hearth, but the
hearth was extraordinary. Built with varying shades of
gray and black rocks, it expanded from the hardwood
floors up to the ceiling. There was a plasma TV where
one might expect a deer's head hanging over the mantel. Two black leather sofas took up the center of the
room. A man's living room.

I didn't realize he'd stopped talking until he took
a seat on the sofa across from me. "They're running
traces on your cell phone. I called in a couple of favors.
There's an officer watching your house in case anyone
shows up. We'll catch this guy, Celeste."

I nodded. Too tired to do much of anything else. I
shivered as one chill after another whipped through
me. I even tapped my foot wildly on the floor to keep
from leaning back into the soft leather and closing my
eyes. The crash began.

"Off to bed with you. You're wiped."

I didn't argue when he grabbed my elbows and lifted
me to my feet. We stood for a moment, face to face,

breath to breath, neither offering anything to the other. I wondered what he'd do if I leaned up on my tiptoes and planted a wet one right on him. To be honest, I don't think I could handle either reaction he might have. Indifference would probably be the last straw my delicate psyche could take. And if he returned my kiss…as much as I'd relish his attentions, until I was out from under whatever had gotten a hold of me, I didn't want to try and start something. Not to mention, there would be a niggle in the back of my mind that he'd be "humoring" me, not knowing another way to comfort someone in my predicament.

At midnight, though, on another rollercoaster of a day in a string of amusement park days, was probably not the best time to try to reason out the dos and don'ts of jumping into a relationship. I yawned so hard I nearly toppled back onto the sofa. Muldoon took it as an opportunity to head me off in the right direction. He guided me down a long dark hallway to the last room on the right.

"I'm just across the hall if you need anything." His eyes locked with mine and he waited. For what I couldn't say.

I doubted he had the same mental struggles I did. He wasn't in jeopardy or putting anyone else in jeopardy. He sure as hell shouldn't be lonely. He was the type of man who had women falling all over themselves to be near him. He'd have his pick of the litter.

Finally, with a quick shake of his head, he walked back down the hall.

His scent lingered as I let myself into the bedroom. I was tempted to follow after him and say to hell with all the problems of the world. Which was when I knew I was in desperate need of sleep. I didn't bother to flip the switch. I didn't think my grainy eyes could take the brightness. Luckily, outside light filtered in from behind the window curtain. It gave enough illumination for me to maneuver around the room without bumping into anything. I set my bag next to me on the bed and leaned up against the pillows.

It was hard to think one phone call was enough to knock down whatever bravado I'd been waving around. I just wanted to curl up in a ball and sleep. Sleep for days if I could. I had no job to go to in the morning. Some asshole was hell-bent on making me a statistic and I was fantasizing nonstop about a man who was so dedicated to his job he couldn't loosen up enough to throw caution to the wind and ravage me.

I scoffed. Which turned into a quiet laugh. It built and built until I was laughing so hard my side hurt. Laughed until I could barely breathe. I needed that, needed the outlet, the release. It zapped what remaining energy I had left and I took a deep, cleansing breath before lying down. I should have gotten up to change out of my jeans and sweatshirt—sleeping fully clothed was my new norm apparently—but frankly I was a goner with the warm pillow squooshed under my head.

One thing I'd decided, I definitely needed to tell Muldoon about my meeting with Beau Henderson. If he disapproved, he could take my place and ask all the questions he wanted to. *First thing in the morning, I'm telling him.*

I'M SO NOT telling him anything. The light of day helped me ratchet up my bravado to self-deluded again. I did have a day and half before I had to confess my plans. With Muldoon sitting across the little dinette table with the heaviest scowl I'd ever seen on a man, it wasn't prudent to add to it just yet. And yes, I was making excuses. I could rationalize with the best of them and, in my rational mind, he had enough on his plate to not worry about a man who might not be connected to any of this at all.

"It was a throwaway phone," he said finally in lieu of normal breakfast conversation.

"That just means it was probably someone over twelve. Anyone with half a brain and cable TV knows to use a burner phone." I sipped my coffee. Not bad. Not a special blend of my favorite brands, but as I didn't have to make it and it wasn't instant, it was downright lovely. "That's what I'd do anyway."

I could practically hear his teeth grinding. I'd bet by lunchtime he had a killer headache if he didn't relax. How and why I could be so blasé I wasn't sure. Maybe having him so worked up—he had enough steam for the both of us, and then some—left little room for me to be any more anxious.

"Don't you find it a little strange that this guy, who-ever he is, would bother to take the time to warn me? I mean, do you think he warned Chad? Or Kelsey?"

Muldoon ran his hand through his hair and dropped his fist to the table. "We've gone all over their phone records and nothing jumped out as unusual."

"I was thinking, why don't I walk around out there with a big old sign saying here I am." I was only half-kidding. I was tired of hiding, and anything that might draw the guy out in the open was starting to look better than holing up with Muldoon, both of us taking turns being tense. "You guys can catch him when he makes his move on me."

He slammed to his feet. "That's not funny." He

walked over to the sink. His knuckles whitened as he gripped the edge.

"Relax. Gaw. I didn't mean it." I did, actually, but he was ready to explode so I backtracked a little. I got up and moved behind him. I clasped his shoulders. "Did you get any sleep at all? You're so tense." I tried my best to massage out the knots but he was a tad too tall and so damn tense. It would take some powerful muscle relaxers and probably a big-ass hammer to conk him out completely before he could actually rest.

I settled my forehead against his back—his firm oh-my-gawd-did-he-work-out back—and sighed. I let his warmth seep into me. Tried to absorb some of his strength. "I know you think I should hide away." Maybe if I handled the idea more calmly, and less flippantly, he'd consider it. Something had to give. "What good does that do if I have to stay a prisoner here, or at my house? He wins that way too, don't you think? But if we can figure a way to draw him out..."

"The risk is not worth it, Celeste." The words rumbled through him. "I wish you could understand." He sighed. "Let's go over this. Who has your cell number?"

"My family. Colin's family. Levi. Everyone at school. It's in the school directory. I put it in there instead of my home phone."

"Who else?"

"Isn't that enough to make it easily accessible?" It wasn't like I posted it on every social network, but with so many people privy to it, it wasn't like my number was private. "That's pretty much it. I don't have this huge social life. Levi's about the only person I talk to besides family." I straightened away from him.

He turned and faced me.

I craned my neck to meet his gaze. "I can guarantee

that none of my or Colin's families would be involved
in this at all. His mother is scary as hell, but she'd just
as soon kill you with disapproval."

"So we're back to the school then."

"Haven't you checked everyone out? You got all the
names and whatnot the first day you came out. You
could compare the info to the employee files." When he
frowned, I went on to say, "Before any of us were hired,
we all had to undergo an extensive background check.
Did you get those from the administrative offices?"

"No."

"Mark should have given you those." I reached for
my cell to call Mark, but Muldoon still had it.

"I need my phone."

Muldoon shook his head. "I'd rather hold onto it in
case another call comes in."

"And what if my mom calls. Or Paige. You've got the
tracer thingy on it. What more do you need?"

He tilted his head back. "I need you to stay out of
trouble while we figure out what the hell is going on."

"And me not having my phone prevents that somehow? Come on, Muldoon. I'll let you know the second
a call comes in, assuming this guy is dumb enough to
keep at it." I stuck my lip out in a pitiful pout.

Muldoon didn't budge.

"It's not like the phone's wired to blow."

He didn't crack a smile at my attempt at humor. He
didn't tense up either, which was progress.

I went round after round all but begging before Muldoon finally agreed to let me have it back—though he
did punch a few buttons into the phone once he re-
trieved it from his room. I didn't bother to ask what he
was doing as long as I got it back.

He stayed right by my side as I dialed the school.

Mark wasn't too happy to get a request for the police from me, I could tell from his tone, but he agreed. "You can go up to the school and he'll have it ready in an hour," I said after I ended the call.

"Thanks."

"You're not used to getting help, are you? Do you ever work with a partner?"

"That's different." One dark eyebrow arched upward.

"Why, because I'm a woman?"

The hint of a smile hung on his mouth.

At least he'd finally lightened up a little. "Is it because I'm not a police officer?"

He rolled his shoulders. "I guess. Maybe. Maybe I don't want *you* to get in any deeper than you already are."

"So this is about you protecting me?" Little ripples of warmth filled me like every time Muldoon spoke to me in that he-man sort of way, or when he got all proprietary. The goose bumps shimmied from head to toe. I couldn't remember Colin ever being protective. Sure, he was a little jealous from time to time, but that was more like a little boy not wanting to share a toy. It was a different and wonderful feeling to think someone put me, Celeste, first.

It was probably a cop thing. That whole protect and serve was ingrained in every fiber of this man.

"Is that bad? Wanting you to stay alive?" He said it sarcastically but there was a little hitch in his voice.

"No, I am completely in favor of the idea." I set my hand on his chest and gently rubbed.

"What are you doing?"

"Trying to see if I can feel your costume. See if I can find the emblem plastered to your chest. Don't all superheroes have some sort of emblem?"

Muldoon captured my hand and pinned it in place. "Funny." His thumb skimmed over my knuckles lightly. "Are you content staying holed up here for today? Otherwise, I can get one of the off-duty officers to come by and keep you company."

Was that meant to sound like a threat? "No, no babysitter." I scrunched up my face. "As long as you have more than basic cable, I'm good. I just can't abide by so few channels."

"There's any channel you want." He released my hands and slid out from between me and the counter. "The fridge and pantry aren't that well stocked, but there's stuff in there when you get hungry. Stay out of the liquor cabinet. I'm a little afraid of what you might be like fully loaded."

"Buzzkill." I smiled.

Muldoon slid his own cell phone from his pocket. "I have an hour before going up to the school. If I leave now, it should give me time for a couple of interviews," he said more as an aside than to me. He started for the door that separated the kitchen from the living room.

I rocked up on the balls of my feet. "Who are your interviews with?"

"Like I'm gonna tell you," he called over his shoulder.

"It was worth a try." I shrugged. "So if the home phone rings or anyone comes to the door?"

He paused between the two rooms. "I have voice mail and no one should stop by, so you shouldn't be bothered."

"Any of your sibs or your parents know that I'm here?"

His shoulders straightened.

"Sorry, I looked through some of Colin's old yearbooks. I wasn't trying to pry necessarily. But Muldoon's not that common of a name." I linked my hands behind my back. "And y'all all look just alike."

He gave a quick laugh. "If you think that we looked alike in school, you should see us now." He turned back into the kitchen and pulled open a drawer. He shuffled through for a minute, then produced a photo and handed it to me.

"Holy cow. You weren't kidding." If I hadn't known he and his brother were at the opposite ends of the sibs chart I'd have sworn they were twins. And his sisters, other than the varying hairstyles they were dead ringers for each other. "I can't even imagine. I'm an only child and kind of look like my parents. Paige looks like me, but she's still just a baby to me. Is it freaky? To look at your brother and see your face?"

"Naw. I'm much prettier than he'll ever hope to be." Muldoon joked. It was a good sign that he could relax a little.

"Are any of the rest of them on a police force?"

"My sisters own a catering business. My sister Darcy went through the academy, but…" He shook his head. "She decided not to pursue it. My brother, yep. He works for the Dallas PD. SWAT."

"Wow. The testosterone you two must emit. I would hate to be in a room with you both."

"You should be so lucky."

"Really now. Bold talk from someone holding a woman hostage."

All humor left him.

"Sorry. I went too far." I released a heavy breath and left the kitchen for my nicely furnished and coordinated jail cell. I leaned back on the made bed—I'd never even untucked the blankets the night before when I'd lain down.

I'd expected Muldoon to find me and say something. But all I heard was the front door slam a few minutes later.

I stayed immobile for about five minutes before the restlessness set in. With my phone in hand I roamed the small three-bedroom home. It was nice for a bachelor. Probably more room than one man needed. As much time as he'd spent on Chad's case, he couldn't possibly be home much. Unless that was not the norm. But seeing how torn he was just at the idea of impropriety, I didn't think he was much of a slacker.

Around lunchtime, Muldoon came home for half an hour. I think it was just to make sure I was still tucked away as he didn't have time to spare. He didn't even have time to sit with me for a sandwich, said he would grab something on the way back to the station. That didn't seem healthy, but since I'd been eyeing an old tub of ice cream in his freezer just before he'd come in, I didn't think I was the best one to try to judge.

I watched TV for all of an hour, not able to concentrate. Leaving me alone might have kept me safe of body but not of mind. I was stir-crazy. I called Levi every twenty minutes or so, but he was busy with one work issue or another. It was half past two before he and I spoke long enough to firm up the plans for our meeting with Beau Henderson the next day.

And that created a whole new host of problems—mostly with my conscience. I dithered, torn between telling Muldoon or not.

"Not" was winning.

He finally came in that night around eight. "Rough day at the office, dear?" I teased.

Muldoon chuckled. "Nothing like getting nowhere fast."

"I know the feeling." I set a casserole of baked ziti on the table. It'd been in the oven keeping warm for a couple of hours. It felt weird to eat dinner in his house without him.

He glanced over at his pantry. "You cooked?"

"If I say yes, can I go home for good behavior?" I laced my fingers together in front of me like a five-year-old begging for a new toy.

"No." A smile tilted the corner of his mouth.

I set napkins beside the plates. "Well then, I called and ordered it."

Just like that, the smile fled. "You had food delivered here? Did you not listen about staying out of sight?"

"I'm not a nincompoop. Levi went and picked it up for me. He even practiced his evasive maneuvers—his words not mine—making sure no one followed him over here. Sheesh, Muldoon. Give a girl some credit."

His cheeks reddened slightly. "Sorry." He shucked his jacket and set it on the back of his chair.

"Can I get you some beer or wine? I saw an open bottle of Shiraz tucked in the back of your fridge. Not that I was snooping." At least not in the fridge. I'd gone through a couple of his drawers. I'd drawn the line at his underwear drawer, though I was mighty tempted. It'd seemed a little too intimate to see the man's jockeys whether they were on his firm body or wadded up next to his socks.

"No, thanks. Water's fine." He sat and ate in silence for a bit. When he'd scooped seconds onto his plate, he said, "Jerry Pullman lawyered up today."

"Did you get any indication of why he blew up my

car? Not that I want him to blow up some other poor unsuspecting person's car."

"No. I did talk to the prosecutor, though, and he's confident that he'll be denied bail." He took a bite and chewed. When he swallowed, he asked, "How bad was it being cooped up here all day?"

It would have been completely bearable with you, I wanted to say, but didn't. "I'm still here and in once piece so I guess it went okay." I pulled out the chair and sat across from him. "How goes Chad's case?"

"We're at a standstill. We went through the background checks for the employees. So far, nothing has jumped out. The school was pretty thorough."

"For what they charge the parents to place their kids there, they'd have to be." It was all too easy to get comfortable sitting at Muldoon's kitchen table, going over his day and watching him eat his dinner. Since my divorce, that was probably the only thing I could say I missed of Colin.

"What's the matter?"

I shook myself. "What?"

He reached across the table and tapped the corner of my mouth. "You're frowning."

"Nothing. Sorry." I stood and pushed the chair back under the table. And just like that, comfort could morph into a longing that I had no business feeling.

THE RAIN HAD cleared up overnight, letting sunlight stream into the bedroom the next morning. I stretched and looked at the clock on the nightstand. "Oh, crap." It was half past nine. It was the longest, most restful sleep I'd had in days. I picked a fine time to catch up, though.

I jumped out of the bed and made a half-assed attempt to straighten the sheets and comforter, then hurried to shower. Still wrapped in a towel, I pawed through my bag and realized I didn't have an outfit appropriate to visit an office complex—I didn't think I'd still be a guest at *chez* Muldoon and hadn't packed accordingly. I slipped on a pair of jeans and a T-shirt and went in search of coffee.

Muldoon had left me a note right next to the coffeepot—was he getting to know me or what—letting me know that he'd be home for lunch again.

Guilt ate at me for not telling him about my meeting with Beau Henderson. I flipped his note over and gave him the time and address with a quick message why we were headed over there. When he came home for lunch, he'd see it and have plenty of time to meet Levi and me. Guilty conscience abated, I poured myself a cup of coffee and sat at the table.

Once caffeinated, I called Levi to pick me up so I could run to the house and get a change of clothes.

By ten forty-five he was dropping me off at the house. He ran in, did a closet check for any boogeyman who could be hiding, thankfully to no avail. "I'll meet you at the office ten minutes before the meeting. I have to run over to the bank and sign a couple of papers on a new property." He gave me a quick kiss on the cheek and rushed back out of the house.

"Okeydoke, hon." I waved as he shut the door behind him. To say I was a little nervous was a vast understatement. The house was so quiet. Despite Levi's search, I stood in the foyer for a full five minutes. I listened for any creak or groan that was out of place. I finally tossed my bag onto the sofa and went about the business I needed to do to get ready. I was in a little bit of a huff, too.

I was pissed that Chad's killer made me afraid to be

alone in my home. I half wished he—she, whoever—would show up and let me kick him square in the ass. Still, I kept my cell close just in case as I slipped into a pair of black slacks and a parent-meeting china-blue silk top. I went with my black ballet flats instead of my usual wedge loafers—übercomfy rather than übercute.

By the time I was done primping, it was time to head to the office building. My cell rang as I was settling in behind the Hummer's steering wheel. Muldoon's name came across the screen. "You programmed your name and number into my phone?" I said as a way of a greeting.

"To keep you on your toes." All sorts of noise and clanking echoed through the phone.

"Where are you?"

"There was a freight train derailment on the far side of town. We have six cars off the tracks."

"Geez." I started up the SUV. I thought about backing out of the driveway, but I didn't think I could maneuver Harriet with one hand. "Is everyone okay?"

"No injuries, but it's screwing up traffic all over town. A couple of intersections are closed." Another series of metal banging came through the line. "I'm not going to be able to make it to the house for lunch. I'll be tied up here for a while."

"Oh. Okay. What part of town?" If it was between me and the highway, it would take an extra half hour to drive out and around and double back.

He named off an intersection on the far west corner of town nowhere near my subdivision, but one of the largest strip malls was surrounded by the tracks. "Before I forget, the gardener, the one who got grease all over your sweater—"

"Danny Something-or-other?" I couldn't remember his danged last name.

"Eems. Danny Eems. Turns out he was employed with Joe Carpenter for a short while."

"Are you serious?"

"He worked at his office."

"As?"

"Office manager. There's something hinky about this. Please stay put until I can get with you and we can go over a couple more things. It's coming to a head, I can feel it." Muldoon cursed. "I gotta go." He hung up.

I tapped my fingers on the Hummer's steering wheel. Stay or go? I *was* armed with even more info than before I made the appointment. A little voice in the back of my head—that sounded remarkably like Muldoon—said to do nothing and let Muldoon do his job. In my gut, though, something was pushing me to go talk to Beau Henderson. Today.

Don't be mad at me, Muldoon. I plugged in the address into the GPS and pulled out of the driveway. I made a beeline through the neighborhood for the highway. I was half an hour away from Henderson's office building—if I went a teensy weensy bit over the speed limit most of the way.

Danny the gardener? He had access to Chad, but why would he kill the man? Or Kelsey for that matter? And what could he possibly have against me? I'd barely crossed paths with him at school, didn't think I ever said more than a few words to him. What did I even know of him? He was in his mid-twenties I'd guess. He'd come in as an assistant to the gardener at the end of the term the year before. Over the summer, the head gardener retired and Danny took over.

How could he be involved in Chad and Joe's pasts?

He'd have been a kid at the time. A kid. Hmm… Could he be…? My mind drifted for a moment but was quickly brought back by a loud honk.

"Whoa." I swerved and nearly hit the car in the next lane. Professor Patts had a son at the time of her death.

I groped for my cell on the seat next to me. It took several tries to drive and dial—I know I should have pulled over, but the urgency of talking to Mr. Henderson grew exponentially so I didn't want to stop—but it finally connected. Muldoon's phone went straight to voice mail. I wasn't sure if I was relieved or anxious that he hadn't answered. "I know you said Danny's last name is Eems, but could he be related to the professor? Her son'd been put in foster care after his mother's death. They could have changed his name, right?" I took a deep breath. "I'm going to meet with Beau Henderson right now. The other man involved with Chad and Joe Carpenter." I went on to give him the details in case he didn't get back to the house to find the note. "I know you're probably mad, but the man needs to know. Don't worry, Levi's going to meet me there."

EIGHTEEN

"I'M STUCK IN TOWN," Levi said the moment I answered the phone.

"You haven't even left Peytonville?" I stood in the lobby of the Henderson building—the man had his own building, for goodness' sake.

"No, sweets. There's a freight train off its track."

"Yeah, so?"

"I was running late and now I'm stuck in traffic. It's gridlock."

I tucked the folder of articles for Beau Henderson under my arm and looked at the board listing the different offices and floors. Mr. Henderson's business occupied the top three floors. When I made the appointment, his assistant had given me instructions for which floor to get off, but I'd left the paper sitting on the front seat of Harriet. "Do you remember what floor his office is on?"

"You're not going it alone, are you?"

"I'm already here. I have the stuff to give him. Plus, what Muldoon told me." I gave Levi a quick recap on Danny Eems as I pushed the button for the elevator. When the car came to the first floor and the doors opened, I stepped in. "At this point, don't worry about heading out this way. No point now, it'll be done before you can even get to town."

The doors hissed shut and I pushed the first of the three floors that were listed under Henderson's company name.

"Don't think...idea...be..." Levi cut out. The cell service in the elevator disappeared and the call dropped.

I shoved the phone in my pocket and gnawed my lip on the ride up to the eighteenth floor. I could still turn around and leave. No one knew who I was or why I was there. But I'd come all that way. I was simply going to give the man some information. And then I could leave.

The doors eased open to a carpeted bullpen with wall-to-wall cubicles. I walked over to the first desk and asked where I could find Beau Henderson.

"You need to go up to the twentieth floor. Mr. Henderson's offices are to the right."

"Thanks." I shifted the folder under my arm and eased my cell out of my pocket. Three missed calls from Levi. I stepped back into the elevator and pressed twenty. As the doors shut, I thought I saw someone running toward it. I pushed the door open button but it was too late.

Two more floors up, I gave my name to Mr. Henderson's assistant and was waved to a set of cushy seats. I didn't even have time to get comfortable before the office door opened.

"Mrs. Eagan?" A man in his late forties with salt-and-pepper hair stood in the doorway. He was dressed like every other businessman in his dark suit, white shirt and green striped tie. "This way."

His office was huge—a little bigger than my living room—and gorgeous. All dark woods and leather chairs with bookshelves lining two full walls. A huge wall of windows overlooked downtown Dallas. I had no idea what his business entailed, but apparently he was very good at it.

He sat behind the large desk and motioned for me to sit in the leather chair across from him. He intertwined his fingers on the blotter in front of him and frowned. "I was a little hesitant to take this appointment with you today. But I must admit, you piqued my curiosity." He took a deep breath. "You worked for Chad?"

"Yes." I ran my finger around the edge of the folder but held his gaze. "I am going to apologize now as there's no easy way to say this. I think you're in danger." I just blurted it out.

The man blanched.

"I think whoever killed Chad—" I handed him the folder with all the articles "—may have killed your friend Joe Carpenter a few years ago, too."

"Joe's dead?" He set the folder down, never taking his eyes off mine.

My hip was vibrating. Someone was calling me, but I couldn't answer the phone. "Didn't you keep in touch with your friends since college?"

Henderson shook his head. "I'm guessing since you connected the three of us together, you know what we were accused of." His composure fell and he leaned back in his chair.

"Are you saying you didn't do it?"

He loosened his tie. "The video was not one of my finest moments. But we had nothing to do with Professor Patts taking her own life."

I scoffed before I could help myself.

"We had no intention of sharing that video with anyone. We were all a little…high. There, I said it."

I know I gawked, but how could I not? Nothing that I'd read indicated they were high. "Even the professor?"

"Yes." Henderson ran his hand over his face. "Chad left the tape sitting on the desk in his apartment and his girlfriend found it. She was so furious he'd cheated on her she took it to the dean without thinking of what it would do to the rest of our reputations. No one expected the woman to kill herself."

"Y'all were questioned, though, right?"

"At first they thought it was a homicide. But eventually they found the suicide note and they checked our alibis for that night she…died." He stood and walked over to a floor-to-ceiling window. "From what I understand the police are no closer to finding Chad's killer. How did Joe die?"

I cleared my throat. "It was ruled a suicide. By hanging. But in light of the ties to Chad and Professor Patts's deaths, I think the police are reopening the case to see if there might be a connection." I actually had no idea if that was true. But that was what the police did in the movies, right?

"Anyway, that's why I came to talk to you. I found out this morning that there was a young man working at both Mr. Carpenter's office as well as at the school where I teach. His name is Danny Eems. I don't know what the connection is yet, but it—"

"Come again. The name?"

"Danny Eems."

Henderson's hands shook as he turned and pushed a button on the front of the phone. "Liz, call Security up here immediately." He tugged more at his tie. "Liz?" He frowned harder. "Always leaving her damn desk."

"What's the problem, Mr. Henderson?" I stood and waved my hand and tried to get him to focus. I worried that he was in the throes of a heart attack or something as sweat beaded on his forehead.

"Liz? Where is she?" He slammed the phone down and paced behind his desk. "Danny Eems? You're sure?"

I nodded. "He was the gardener at the school."

"Was." It was more of a statement than a question.

My hip vibrated again. I reached for the phone. "He quit a couple of days after the murder. But so did several other teachers."

"I hired him a few days ago."

My hand froze. I had to swallow before I could speak. "He works here?" My mind flipped over to the person running to the elevator when I ended up on the wrong floor. I hadn't gotten a good look at the person, but it was definitely a guy. Could it have been Danny? "Are you sure it's the same guy?"

Henderson sat at his desk and started tapping away on his computer. He pulled up Danny's personnel file complete with a picture for a badge.

"That's him." Ohmygawd, ohmygawd. I was breathing entirely too fast. "Is he here today?" I turned in a circle not sure what to do before I finally hurried over to the double doors I'd come in through. "Is there a deadbolt? Does this lock? Mr. Henderson?"

Henderson dug through his drawer and produced a gun. "Up at the top of the door."

I found the latch at the top. The left door was engaged already. I shoved the lock of the other door into place as I groped in my pocket for my cell. I was dialing Muldoon's cell number as I hurried back to the desk and picked up the office phone and dialed 911.

Muldoon answered on the first ring. "Celeste, where in the hell are you?"

"In Dallas, hang on." The 911 operator answered on the office line. I shoved the handset at Henderson. He took it but only stared. I snapped my fingers in front of his face. "Mr. Henderson. Give her the address here," I said when he came out of his daze. "Tell her the floor and everything."

I set my cell phone on the desk and took the gun

from him while he was distracted with the phone. He didn't even seem to notice when I shoved the gun into the bottom drawer.

With a shaky hand, I picked up my cell phone. "Muldoon, I think I'm in trouble." I ran my hand through my hair and paced the space between the desk and the door. "Danny Eems works here."

"What?"

I cringed when he shouted through the phone.

Slower he repeated, "Where the hell are you?"

"Didn't you get my message?"

"Yes, but I could barely understand you."

"I drove to Dallas to meet with Mr. Henderson. The last guy in the article I gave you."

A string of curse words echoed through the phone.

"It was no big deal, I thought. I just wanted to talk to him. Give him a heads-up. Levi was supposed to come with me but that stupid freight train jumped the tracks. He got stuck in traffic. You're stuck there helping. And Danny's here." My voice rose with every word. "We're locked in Henderson's office."

"Calm down, babe." Muldoon's smooth, even voice broke through my near hysteria.

I took several deep breaths.

"Call 911. Lock the door."

"I did. We did." I turned and found…nothing. "Mr. Henderson?" I rushed to the other side of the desk and looked under it and the chair. "He's gone. Where'd he go? Muldoon, he's gone."

"Who's gone?"

"Mr. Henderson. He was just here. But…how does someone just disappear from a locked office?"

"Celeste. Babe. Take a breath."

I did and saw one of the bookcases off-kilter. "Secret door. There's a secret door."

"Shut it and stay put. Wait for the police to come in and get you."

"What about Mr. Henderson?"

"He should have stayed. Did you shut the door?"

I had my hand on the edge to shut it. I peeked around the corner and found a narrow hallway. I didn't want to be that girl in a scary movie who didn't listen to the hero and ended up naked and running from the masked killer. I shoved the bookcase back into place. "Hang on."

I set the phone down, flipped the speaker on, then shoved the desk. Or rather *at* the desk. It didn't want to move, but still I pushed. By the third try, I was huffing and puffing and blowing hair off my face. "Move, you goddamned desk." I swore aloud and growled as I managed to get it to scooch only the slightest. I was one level beneath full-blown panic. I braced my feet and gave it another shove, and it slid toward the door. I was sweating like crazy by the time I got the damn thing up against the fake door. "Desk's covering the opening," I huffed.

"Good. Good."

"What now?" I leaned my hip against the wooden bastard and caught my breath. I'd never barricaded myself in an office before with a potential murderer running loose. "Do you think he took off if he knew I was here? I mean if I was trying to kill someone over and over and they showed up right at my feet... The man shot at me. With a cop on my front porch, no less."

A quick knock came at door—the regular door, not the sneaky disguised-as-the-classics door. "Wh-who is it?"

"It's Liz. I'm looking for Mr. Henderson. He has another appointment."

"I'm afraid he stepped out."

"I beg your…" Liz's voice sounded muffled through the door. "I'm calling Security."

"Good. Do that, please." I ran over to the window. Were the police coming? I looked down on the streets in Dallas. There was so much traffic and I was so high up that I couldn't discern one car from another. "Where are the police?"

"They're not there yet?" Muldoon's tiny voice came from the desk. "What did you say to them?"

"I didn't. Mr. Henderson talked to them."

"Call them back. Right now."

I scooped up the phone but got no dial tone. "It's not working." I pressed the switch hook several times but never did get a dial tone; I even tried the intercom button. "The phone's dead." I ran over to the door. "Liz, did you call Security?" She didn't answer. "Liz, is your phone dead, too?" She still didn't answer. I swallowed hard. I was trapped in a room. On the twentieth floor. "Should I hang up with you and call 911?"

"Do not hang up with me. Understand? I've got one of my officers on the squad car radio with the Dallas PD as we speak. You got them, Bradford?" There was a muffled conversation. "Tell me where you are exactly. The address."

My brain was frazzled. "I'm not exactly sure. It's the Henderson building downtown. I asked Mr. Henderson to tell the police where we were." I gave him the details I could remember when I drove up to the building using Harriet's GPS and parked in the garage. "Why would he take off?"

"I don't know, babe. Chickenshit maybe."

Another knock sounded at the door.

"Yes?"

"Police, ma'am. Open up," a deep voice called from the other side of the door.

"Muldoon, the police are at the door." I reached up for the lock.

"Don't open up yet," he shouted through the phone.

"Why not?" I could hear him speaking with someone on his end of the phone.

"Ask the officer his name," he said finally.

I pressed my hand onto the wooden door. "What's your name?"

There was some slight rustling around. "What?"

"Can I have your name, Officer?" I heard a loud thud. "Officer?" I picked up the cell phone and took it off speaker. "He's not answering me."

"Bradford's on the radio with them now. They're just now getting to the building."

My heart sped up and I stepped slowly away from the door. "Who is that then?"

"I don't know." The big, bad detective's voice shook a little. "Are you okay?"

"Scared spitless but otherwise just peachy." A scratching sound came from the bookcase. The desk was heavy as all get-out so I wasn't too worried about it moving, but still I eased over in front of the window. I had no idea if there were other secret passages into the room but I was pretty sure the flat drop, twenty floors down, would prevent anyone getting to me through the window.

The scratching increased. A book or two rattled but the desk didn't budge. "I think he's at the secret panel," I whispered into the phone.

"I can't hear you, Celeste."

"Someone's at the other door." I tried to whisper louder.

"I can't tell what you're saying. Just stay put. The Dallas police are at the building. Security has it locked down. They're looking for Danny and Henderson."

I pressed my back against the cool glass window. The scratching increased and the books rocked on the shelves. One small book fell from an upper shelf. My breath raced in and out. And my knuckles hurt as I gripped the cell to my ear. Muldoon was still talking to someone on the other end of the phone.

Just being able to hear his voice kept me calm(ish). The only thing that would have been better was if he were standing next to me. Actually, if I'd listened to him in the first place I'd be sitting comfortably at his home while he conducted his case…that would have been so much better.

A hard knock came at the front door. "Ahhh," I screamed and almost dropped the phone.

"Celeste?" Muldoon called at the same time as a man's voice from the door called, "Ma'am? Dallas Police Department."

I was hesitant to move away from the window. "What's your name?"

A muted voice came through the door. "Officer Reed, ma'am."

"Muldoon, Officer Reed?"

"That's him. You can unlock the door."

My knees shook as I crossed the room to the door, but I hurried and flipped down the lock. I ripped the door open. "I heard someone at the other door."

The uniformed officer, a good ten inches taller than me and just about as wide as the door, stepped in. "Where, ma'am?"

I pointed to the desk. "That bookcase swings out. It was shaking just a second ago."

He shoved the desk back just as four other officers came into the room. Two helped Officer Reed with the desk—they lifted it with ease. One stood at the door and the last one took hold of my arm. "Come with me." I dropped the phone to my side but didn't hang up with Muldoon. I paused in the doorway. "Oh, and Mr. Henderson had a gun, I tucked it in the bottom desk drawer."

The officer standing guard at the door asked, "Why?"

Was he insane? "I wasn't taking any chances of him shooting me by accident." I left off the "duh."

The officer led me from the office into the lobby area next to the elevators. There were a couple of EMTs hunched over a mass on the floor. It took me a minute to realize it was Liz, Henderson's assistant.

"What happened to her? Is she okay?"

"I don't know just yet, ma'am." The officer guided me away and across the room to the other side of the bank of elevators.

"Did you find Mr. Henderson?"

"The building's security locked down every exit." He was good at non-answers. He clicked the little microphone on his shoulder. "This is Officer Scott. I have Mrs. Eagan at the elevators on twenty."

"Copy," came a squeak from the microphone. "Someone's on the way up to get her."

That sounded way more ominous than it should.

I couldn't see around the corner to where Liz and the EMTs were or into Henderson's office. The officer at my side had me blocked up against a wall, hadn't even let go of my arm. Was I in trouble? I decided to keep my mouth shut just in case. I wanted to pace—instead I stood as still as fidgety possible and worked on how many ways I would have to apologize to Muldoon. The hum of the elevators was about the only sound on the floor. They hissed open and Muldoon stepped out.

"Oh, thank God, Shaw." Before I had time to think, I broke free from the officer and flung myself at *my* detective. I planted a big kiss square on the man's lips. The long searing kiss ended with his lips trailing across my cheek to my ear.

His breath shuddered, then he wrapped me tightly in his arms and smooshed my face to the clean white shirt covering his firm chest. His heart beat heavily against my ear—almost as fast as mine. I did nothing but soak up his warmth.

Then all I could think of was, *I kissed Muldoon.* I wanted to revel in the moment of glorious lip-lock, but my surroundings came crashing back around me. "Why didn't you tell me you were coming?" I said against his chest. "How'd you get here so fast?"

Muldoon pushed me to arm's length and gave me a quick once-over. He turned to the Dallas PD officer. "I've got this, Scott. Thanks."

The man nodded at Muldoon and left us standing alone.

"Are you insane, coming out here?" His hands tightened. "Alone."

My well-constructed apology flew out the window. "I wasn't supposed to be alone." I should be pissed he was talking to me that way, but I was so damn happy to see him I didn't care. "I really thought I was doing the right thing, telling Mr. Henderson my suspicions."

"Ever heard of the phone?" His words were still harsh, but his hands gentled and shook just a wee bit.

"You're right. Not one of my best ideas. But I thought it might be a little harder for him to take over the phone.

I swear it seemed like a good idea at the time. Hindsight and all…" I shook my head. "What's the deal with Danny Eems? Why is he here? There's no way he is innocently connected to all three men."

"His birth name is Patts."

That whole wobbly-knee thing intensified and Muldoon had to wrap an arm around my waist to keep me vertical. We walked over to a set of chairs near another office. "So I was right, he was adopted."

Muldoon nodded. "After being in foster care, he was adopted by the Eems family."

"Holy…" I was torn between sorrow for the little boy who lost his mom and anger at the grown man who'd probably killed at least two people that I knew of. Maybe even a third and was gunning for two more—myself included.

"We have someone at his apartment in Peytonville, but it looks like he cut out of there a few days ago. If he has a new place, we haven't found it yet."

There was a bustle of noise near the elevator. I stood but Muldoon snagged my hand and pulled me back down. "Sit. They're taking Henderson's assistant down."

"Is she okay?"

"Knocked unconscious."

I wondered how he could possibly know, but then I heard the squawk of a radio at his hip. All sorts of police chatter crackled through, but none of it made any sense to me.

I kept my gaze averted as they wheeled the gurney into the elevator. When the doors whisked close, I looked down at my hands. They still shook slightly. "What now?"

"We find the sonofabitch."

NINETEEN

Piece of cake. Because up 'til now no one's been looking for him? I knew I wasn't being fair. Until earlier that day, the connection between Danny and the late professor hadn't been known, so there was a piece of the puzzle missing. Now that it was a clear picture, and the man was last seen in the very building we sat, someone better be moving their ass.

What are you doing sitting with me, Detective? I wanted to shout. I had finally reached the pinnacle of suck-ass weeks by not only putting myself in the middle of Muldoon's case again, but this time actually getting within striking distance of the killer himself. Not to mention I'd reached the trifecta of police attention having been questioned by a couple of Dallas PD officers—three different departments in one week had to be a record.

The officer in charge moved the entire group of people down one floor and commandeered a conference room, while the crime scene techs went over the twentieth floor office area and the secret hallway.

Yes, I came to tell Mr. Henderson how eerily similar Chad's case was to that of Joe Carpenter's and Professor Patts's.

No, I don't know where he went.

Anything else, they'd have to ask my lawyer—who happened to be tied up in court so other than those two sentences they weren't getting squat from me.

Muldoon hadn't said a word, hadn't jumped in to confirm anything I'd told them. He stood in the corner of the room with his arms crossed. I think the only thing keeping me from getting to tour the inside of the Dallas facilities was the fact that he was there—so I gave him credit for that.

My stomach was growling by the time they'd set up an appointment with me and Coz for the next day and said I was free to go. I didn't get more than three steps, however, before Muldoon grabbed my elbow. "Not so fast."

"What now?" I didn't hide the whine in my voice. "The other detective told me I could go."

Muldoon nodded. "They're done with you, but I'm not."

"Come on. Can you yell at me later?"

"The building is still on lockdown. We haven't located Danny yet."

"He's probably in Oklahoma by now. I know I'd hightail it outta here if the jig was up." I tucked my hands over my stomach when it growled again.

"This way." Muldoon led us through several uniformed officers to a little alcove off the back of the floor, which was next to a bank of vending machines. "What's your pleasure, ma'am?"

I eyed the vast array of candy bars and chips. "One of each, please." He was already reaching his wallet. "I'm kidding." I pointed to one candy bar and one bag of chips. The salt balanced the sugar out so it was almost a healthy meal, right?

He also grabbed a couple of sodas from the other machine and we found a quiet place to sit for a minute.

We were both silent long enough for me eat the candy bar and finish half the chips. I offered him a bite.

He shook his head and sighed. "I think I lost ten years when you called and told me where you were."

You and me both. "Sorry."

"I know why you did it even though I can't pretend to understand what you're going through at all." He ran his hand over his face. "To tell you the truth, I'd probably have done the exact same thing. I'm not saying you should do it again."

"I should hope this never becomes an issue again. Being a suspect in one murder and sought after by a killer is more than enough excitement for me for a very long while." I grabbed a chip. "Why'd he do it?"

"Danny?"

I nodded.

"Revenge is a powerful motive. It makes people lose the ability to think straight. Which reminds me…" He drained the remainder of his soda and tossed the can in the trash. "Pullman's lawyer is trying to cut him a deal. He offered to give up his supplier—which he'd refused to do up to this point—if we drop the car-bombing charges. Even admitted he went after you to scare Colin off from testifying against him. Didn't know you two were divorced."

"Wow. I, uh, just wow." I dropped the chip back in the bag.

"He blamed Colin for getting him busted. Thought the funeral was a good place to set it off because people would think it was connected to Chad's death." Muldoon shook his head. "It's almost…" The radio at Muldoon's hip crackled and he sat straighter. He raised his hand when I opened my mouth to ask what was going on. He lifted the radio. "Go ahead."

"We have a suspect in custody down on the fifth

floor. We need you to come down and get a visual on him for verification."

Every relief possible raced through me. "Really? Thank God."

Muldoon stood. "Stay here." He raced toward the elevator. Before he rounded the corner he called over his shoulder, "It's almost done."

That held so many meanings. It could be that he was done with me, it could be that he was free to pursue…whatever…it was that sparked between us. It could mean simply the case was coming to a close. As long as I was out from under suspicion, I was all for it.

Several of the officers went with Muldoon. Only two still mulled about on the floor with me. I finished my chips and washed it down with the rest of the soda. I got up and headed to a trashcan. I was dusting my hands off when the door behind me opened.

"You."

I frowned and swiveled on my heel. Every ounce of me froze. Danny Eems was reaching for me before I could do much of anything. He latched onto my wrist and pulled me behind him. "Help! Hey, it's him. Hey!" I screamed and struggled to get his hand off of my arm. Other than leaving a few scratches, I made no progress as he dragged me down a short hallway with him. I'd lost sight of the officers on the floor with us.

"Shut up." He paused long enough to yank my arm. The quick jerk clanked my teeth together and took my breath. And it did just that, shut me up while I caught my breath. Despite barely being taller than me, he was stronger than I would have ever suspected.

He paused at a door and cracked it open. "How do you turn up everywhere?" He spun me and grabbed a handful of my hair, then shoved me into the stairwell.

"Danny, let me go. Please. I didn't have anything to do with your mom's death."

He pulled up short and jerked me to a stop in front of him. "Don't talk about my mother." He yanked my head back so hard spots danced across my vision.

I'd seen enough crime-prevention specials with experts stressing that the "victim" should fight as hard as they could so as not to leave the initial area of attack. I was damn determined to stick to that advice, but I wasn't even sure how long it would take the officers to notice I was missing. And the way he was holding my hair and arm, I had no leverage to wrestle away—I was forced to go where he wanted me to. I was physically at his mercy. My mouth, however, was all my own.

"I know you must have been heartbroken when your mother passed away. You were just a little boy. And to lose her like that." I panted as we took the stairs—going up. Not down, as I anticipated. The only thing above us was the roof. *Gawd.* I had to stop him, somehow, anyhow. "I have a daughter. Her name is Paige. She's ten."

"Shut up." He jerked his hand in my hair tighter, tilting my head upward. I was unable to see where I was walking.

I banged my shins against the edge of the stairwell as we rounded a landing. Pain radiated every which way up my leg. "You may have seen her around school. She's smart as a whip." I wanted him to sympathize with me, to feel guilty and let me go. "She's already in the seventh grade." I moved as slowly as possible going up the stairs. With the added limp and him propelling me up every other step, it wasn't that hard to do. "Just let me go, please. I won't tell anyone I saw you, I swear."

"If you don't shut up, I'll toss you all the way down and be done."

He shoved me into the handrail and half over the edge. Thankfully, my eyes were so blurred with tears I couldn't see what "down" looked like. "I just want to get home to my daughter."

Danny pulled me back from the handrail and pushed us up to the next landing. His hot breath feathered across the back of my neck as he leaned into me. "I don't give a damn about your brat."

Anger stirred. This man had tormented me for the better part of a week. And I didn't know why. Now he was dragging me through a stairwell. Calling my kid a brat was the last straw. I shoved back off the midway landing and stomped down square on his foot as hard as I could. He was wearing boots so my little black flats did little damage, but the momentum threw him off balance and he tripped backward. He released my arm and grappled for the handrail. He did not release his fist in my hair, though, and took me down with him.

Danny cried out in pain when we landed, his back and head taking the brunt of the fall, me landing flat on top of him. His scream quieted just as quickly as it started. In a heap the two of us rolled down to the next landing and up against the wall. His head lolled to one side, his eyelids mere slits.

I cracked my right elbow somewhere along the ride. It and the lower half of my arm went numb immediately. The stars I'd seen earlier multiplied by a billion. Despite the pain and nausea, I pulled myself to my feet and grasped the doorknob, but it was locked. "Crap."

Danny moaned.

The sound echoed off the cement walls. I tried to move faster, but I ached everywhere, except my right arm. I didn't want to think about how awkwardly it hung at my side.

I limped down the next flight of stairs and tried the door there. It was locked too. I pounded on the door. "You have got to be kidding me," I screamed with every smack of my hand. My palm stung.

I wanted to sit down and cry, but that wouldn't get me out of danger.

"Celeste!"

Something wet landed on my cheek and I looked up. Danny was one floor above me leaning over the rail.

For a moment I thought he might jump down—from the wild look in his eyes, I'd bet he was contemplating it. Instead he released the rail and disappeared from sight, but I could hear him lumbering down the stairs.

"Gawd." I twisted around so quickly I rammed my side into the wall. Something sharp bit into my hip. My cell. As I hustled my ass down to the next landing, I dug in my pocket for the phone.

"Yes!" It pulled free from my pants pocket. "No!" It slipped out from my hand. It bumped and bounced down the last six steps and crashed up against the wall.

I slowed down long enough to scoop it up and round the turn to the next section down. I didn't even stop to try the door. My heart pounded heavily. I wasn't sure if it was from fear of the pursuit or the physical exertion. Did it really matter at that point?

I'd have to stop to look at the phone. I was afraid I wouldn't be able to keep my balance and try to work it at the same time. I ran down one more flight and leaned against the wall to steady myself.

"Aw, no." The screen was cracked. The LCD lit but was blurry. Without visible icons I couldn't get into the menu and find Muldoon's number.

Danny was getting closer if the noise was anything to go by. I didn't have time to fidget with the phone.

I moved again. As I landed on the next floor down, I wondered if I could fumble my way into the calling function and dial 911. At least it would be a start to get someone aware of my problem—a problem that wasn't slowing down even though he had to be in incredible pain. I ran through the motion to unlock the phone as I descended the steps, but I wasn't one hundred percent sure if it did. What choice did I have but to try though?

I had my finger poised over the area when the little green phone icon was but remembered the last time I'd used the phone I'd called Muldoon. If I hit the area twice it might just call him back.

I tried it.

I put the phone to my ear and kept my gaze focused on my feet as I descended the stairs moving as fast as I could. I nearly dropped the phone again when his voice shot out. "Celeste?"

"Stairwell…" I slowed slightly to be able to speak, I was so winded. "Chasing me…need help."

"What floor are you on?"

"Don't…know."

"Does he have a weapon?"

"No…clue." I came up to a door. With my other arm numb it was either put down the phone to try the knob or keep going. I glanced at the little sign next to it and kept moving. "Fifteen."

He growled. "You're on fifteen? Going up or down?"

"Down."

Muldoon shouted at folks relaying the info. "Okay, okay. I'm several floors up. If you can keep going down to twelve, there should be an officer waiting for you."

I was all set to tell him I'd try when Danny tackled me. He hit me square in the back. All the breath rushed from my lungs as I hit solidly onto the wall and then tripped down the last few steps. Fiery pain radiated from every inch of my body. The phone was gone. I didn't know which way it'd fallen.

Danny was jarred as much by the attack as me and was slow getting up.

Doors slammed all up and down the stairwell, but I couldn't tell for sure how close they were. And I didn't know if Danny had a weapon or not. He hadn't showed me one but that didn't mean anything, so I struggled to my feet. Unfortunately, Danny did too. He had me in a corner and blocked both stairs.

"They know—" I sucked in a deep breath "—where we are." I held his gaze. "You can't get out of here."

His eyes were wild. He took a step closer.

"Stay back." I raised my left arm.

"Like hell. You're the only way I can get out of here."

I backed up until I hit the corner. "I won't be your hostage." There was nowhere else to go. Except through him.

I changed my stance. The past year watching Levi train Paige in karate was not for naught.

Danny laughed—actually laughed. "You can't stop me."

"Wanna bet?" I adjusted my stance more, planted my back foot and kicked. He jumped back and I missed. His laughter echoed over the thunderous clap of feet scrambling toward us.

The next kick however, square to his crotch, was dead-on. The man crumpled into a heap, screaming like a little girl. His head connected with the edge of the step. A gash opened up and blood pooled.

I tried to look away but…

"Can you hear me?"

I could. But was achy all over. Even my eyelids hurt

and didn't want to cooperate. Muldoon said my name. So much concern laced his voice that I fought harder to open my eyes and moaned.

"She's coming to."

I managed to get one eye open. Muldoon's face hovered just above mine. It took me a minute to remember where I was. "Danny?"

"In custody." Muldoon stroked the hair off my face. "Can you tell me what happened? Did he hit you?"

I started to shake my head and instantly regretted it. "Blood."

He frowned for a moment, then a huge smile slashed across his face. "You fainted. From his cut."

I opened the other eye only to glare at the man. "Not funny, Detective."

"Babe, I'm not laughing at you." He shifted his hand from my head to my shoulder. "Can you sit up?"

"I can try." The world spun, but I much preferred being somewhat upright instead of at the feet of a handful of officers. "Whoa. I'm dizzy."

Muldoon rubbed my back and gave me a moment. "Better?"

I glanced up. And did a double take. "I thought I was, but I'm seeing two of you."

The other him shifted to the side and gave a Muldoon half smile. "That's Finn."

The brother. Right. "Oh, that's good. I was starting to worry about me for a minute there." I took a deep breath. "Did you find Mr. Henderson?"

Muldoon grunted. "Yeah. The SOB was hiding in a closet several floors down." He gently rubbed my back again. "Where are you hurt?"

"I hit my elbow on one of the falls. It went numb so

I don't know how bad it is." I tried to shrug but I was already tightening up. "I'd bet I'm covered in bruises."

He called an EMT over who prodded my elbow. All the police officers standing around me left to give me a little privacy while the EMT examined me a little more thoroughly. Other than a nasty bruise on my elbow there were no open wounds or obvious broken bones. Without X-rays, though, there was little else that he could tell. He fitted me with a sling. "One of the guys is bringing a backboard down."

"Is that necessary?" We were still in the stairwell, not a whole lot of room to maneuver much of anything, much less a bunch of EMTs and a backboard. "Can I walk to the nearest floor at least?"

The young man shook his head. "You really shouldn't."

"I fainted. That's all."

"After God knows what else." Muldoon pushed up next to the EMT. He confirmed my...affliction when seeing blood.

"Most of the falling was on Danny."

"Okay." The EMT spoke into a walkie on his shoulder and told them to meet us on the fourteenth floor.

Fourteen—Wow. I couldn't believe I'd gone down so many floors. But once the chase was on, most of it had been a blur. I took a deep breath and readied myself to stand, but I still needed a little help. "Can you give me a hand?"

"Absolutely." Muldoon wrapped his arm around my waist and helped me. When my knees gave out, he scooped me up in his arms.

"Put me down." My weak protest was losing steam. "I can walk."

"Sure you can." He chuckled.

I was too sore and too tired to protest any further.

And it was nice not to have to move more than absolutely necessary. Pain radiated out of everything from my hair to my toes. "How did you guys not find Danny? He didn't seem to have any trouble finding me."

"We think he was hiding in an AC duct. Maybe even tried to gain access to Henderson's office that way when he couldn't get to you through either door."

A gurney waited by a bank of elevators for us and Muldoon set me down atop it. I felt silly but there was no telling what damage I'd done on my descent.

I lay back and chills set in. They covered me with a blanket and wheeled me into the elevator. "Muldoon?"

"Here." He moved beside the gurney and took my non-slinged hand.

"Wh-why—" my teeth chattered some as I spoke "—was he so hell-bent on getting me, do you think?"

"We haven't figured that out yet."

"Did he say anything? Wh-when you took him away."

"Other than cursing your name for unmanning him? Not really." If I wasn't mistaken, there was pride in Muldoon's voice.

Despite the man coming after me, it was unnerving to know that I'd wounded him. "He gave me no choice." I didn't get a chance to say anything else as we'd reached the first floor. There was a great hustle and bustle of noise outside the building. Muldoon didn't let go of my hand until they were ready to load me into the back of the ambulance. "Are you coming, too, Shaw?"

"Do you want me to?"

"I need you to."

TWENTY

I NEED YOU TO. Gawd, I couldn't believe I'd said that. Muldoon hadn't said a word, just climbed into the back of the ambulance, held onto me and didn't yell one single time. When we'd arrived at the hospital, I was whisked in a flurry through the halls and into a cubicle. Muldoon had let go of my hand and was nowhere to be seen—in my limited line of curtained sight.

Quite a while later, I was x-rayed, poked and prodded. And other than a severely bruised elbow and some abrasions, I was good to go.

Unfortunately, my car was at Henderson's building. My cell phone was broken and Muldoon had disappeared. I had a huge hole in my blue silk shirt. If I moved just so, most of my bra popped into view. If the painkiller they'd given me hadn't already kicked in, I might have sat down somewhere and just cried. Alas, I was a wee bit high and found it all funny. I snickered as I walked to the lobby. I needed to find a way home. "Eureka. A pay phone. I didn't know they made these anymore," I said aloud. I was bummed. There wasn't anyone around to congratulate me on my find. "Whatever." I patted my pockets. "No change."

Maybe the little lady inside the phone could help me. I pushed the zero. When the operator answered, I told her I needed to call my friend but I didn't have any change.

"You want to make a collect call?"

"Collect? Sure."

I gave her Levi's number and my name and waited. "Hey, Levi."

"Celeste." He sighed heavily on the other end of the line. "I have been so worried about you."

"Me too."

"Sweets, are you okay?"

I leaned against the wall, not entirely sure my legs were steady yet. "Depends."

"On?" So much concern laced those two little letters.

"Can you come get me?"

"Where are you? I haven't been able to get one iota of info from anyone. Your cell keeps going straight to voice mail, and the Peytonville police station refuses to patch me into your detective."

"I busted my phone."

"Where are you?" he asked slower.

"At the hospital."

"Which one?"

I frowned. "I'm not entirely sure." I stepped away from the wall and looked around the lobby to see if I could find a name. "Somewhere in Dallas, I guess." It hadn't occurred to me to ask. Maybe the doctor had said, but my brain had been a little fuzzled since they gave me the painkiller.

"Sweets, *why* are you at the hospital?"

"Danny and I fell down some stairs. Like forty thousand of them, I think."

Levi gasped.

"That was before the police arrested him. Hang on." I let the phone receiver drop to the length of the cord. My nose itched and I needed my hand to rub the tip. When it was thoroughly scratched, I snatched up the receiver. "I bumped my elbow. Arm's in a pretty blue sling. But it doesn't match my shirt." I tilted my head and examined the rip down the front. "But it's garbage now anyway so I guess it's okay."

"Did you hit your head, too?"

I took a moment to see if there was any pain from my head. Naw. "Don't think so. Why?"

"You're not making too much sense."

"Oh that's just the Percodan or cet. I'm not sure which one they gave me. It works pretty dern good, though. No pain."

"And even less sense," Levi mumbled. "Who brought you into the hospital? Is there anyone around who I can talk to?"

"The ambulance dropped me off. They released me. I didn't have anyone waiting so I called you."

"Sweets, I don't think they'd just let you up and leave without someone being there. I'm sure the police have some questions for you."

"I already answered everything."

"Where's Muldoon?"

I looked around the lobby and didn't see Muldoon anywhere. "Don't know."

"Celeste, sweets, you need to listen to me. Go up to one of the information centers and have them page Detective Muldoon. Do you understand?"

"Sure." I nodded.

"Right now. Hang up the phone and find someone who works there."

"'Kay."

I pulled the phone from my ear, but I could still hear Levi. "...let the woman just walk around without supervision." I wondered who he was talking about when I hung up the phone.

I frowned again. What was I supposed to do? Find

an info desk. I walked around the corner and saw several lab-coated men. "Can you help me? I need to page my detective."

The men all looked at me suspiciously, but the taller one in the front pulled away from the group. "Sure. Mind if I have a look at your bracelet?"

I wasn't wearing any jewelry—they'd made me take it off before the X-rays. Come to think of it, I hadn't gotten that back.

The doctor gently took hold of my non-sling wrist. "Mrs. Eagan?"

"That's me."

"How about I take you to your detective?"

I sighed. "That would be so great."

He escorted me to a desk two floors up. Muldoon was pacing back and forth. He glanced up when we neared. "Where in the hell have you been?"

"You say that a lot, you know." I smiled up at him. "They told me I could leave."

"No, they didn't."

"Ya-huh. The doc put the sling on me and said I was good to go."

"He didn't mean it literally. He meant..." Muldoon ran his hand over his face. "We need to sign you out before you can leave."

"Oh, sorry." I nodded, a little too wide-eyed I think because Muldoon narrowed his gaze. When he didn't say anything else, I snapped my fingers. "Make sure they give me back my jewelry. They're holding it hostage, I think," I said in a loud whisper.

Muldoon held my gaze for a long moment, then turned to the woman at the desk and said something.

The young woman was batting her eyes. At my detective. "Hussy."

I didn't think I'd said the word aloud, but Muldoon glanced over his shoulder at me with amusement on his face while the hussy merely went back to typing away at her computer.

It took a few more minutes with some paperwork and to get my things back. Once it was done, a nurse made me sit in a wheelchair. I thought it was silly, I'd already been all over the hospital on foot, but who was I to argue with Muldoon staring me down.

"I know you're mad at me. I can tell." We'd just entered the elevator to go down—Muldoon, me and my own private chauffeur.

"I'm not mad. I'm considering putting a tracking device in your ass."

"You're gonna LoJack me, Detective?" I snorted. And if I wasn't mistaken, the nurse/chauffeur giggled. "What was I supposed to do? They told me I could leave. I thought you abandoned me."

"I didn't leave. Not far. I was arranging to have your car towed back to Peytonville and get my car to the hospital so I can take you home."

"Oh." We reached the bottom floor and the doors hissed open. I was wheeled to a service-looking entrance. "Why are we going out here?"

"There are reporters everywhere out front."

"Gotcha." All I needed was more scrutiny, though I had promised Kellen an interview. Did I ever have a doozy of a tale for him.

I snuggled into the passenger seat of Muldoon's police-issued sedan. He walked around and got in behind the wheel. "Ready?"

"Yep." I yawned. "It's much nicer sitting up in the front seat rather than handcuffed in the back."

He chuckled but didn't comment.

"Did you get the 4-1-1?"

"What?" Muldoon looked at me like I'd lost my mind.

"Did you find out any information? On Danny."

"Oh. It was all tied to the professor, his mother. He was six when she hung herself and even though he was so young, he'd heard enough to think Jones and the others were completely responsible. He was put into foster care, later adopted. He'd been working on a plan to get even." He paused for a moment. "When the detective was talking to him—"

"You got to see him getting interrogated?"

"Yes. He told the detective he initially wanted to make the men lose any and all credibility, lose their jobs and whatnot. It had been unintentional killing Carpenter. He'd been trying to scare the man, but it had gone too far and he died. Once it was ruled a suicide and he'd been left out of the investigation entirely, Danny couldn't—I believe his actual words were *didn't want to*—turn back. He decided to go after the other two."

"What about Kelsey?"

Muldoon tightened his hands on the steering wheel. "Danny didn't know about Jones's…operation with the video cameras. He killed Jones and staged it to look like a suicide. Best as we can tell, Kelsey had gone to the office to get the equipment and make sure there wasn't any other evidence of what Jones did. Instead she found the DVD in the camera with the killing. She decided to blackmail Danny."

"So he killed her."

"Looks that way."

"Why me?"

"He saw the two of you outside the building the night she grabbed the equipment."

I shook my head slowly. "And he thought I was in on it too?"

"Yes."

I shuddered. Here he'd been coming after me this whole time and I hadn't had the slightest clue. "Why did he tell y'all all this? Why did he confess?"

"Aside from you knocking his nuts up into his nose?' Muldoon shrugged. "Might have been a combo of guilt. And the painkillers."

"Will that hold up in court? Y'all drugging a suspect to get a confession out of him?"

"I didn't drug him."

"Semantics."

"They found his apartment here in Dallas while he was being interviewed. Found his address in the employment records from Henderson's. They recovered the DVDs with Jones's death. He'll be charged with attempted murder of you in the stairwell. If we can physically tie him to any of the other attempts on you, the charges will keep piling up."

"No thanks to me. I just got in the way and almost got myself killed."

"You probably saved Henderson's life. Danny had a plane ticket flying out next week. A day or two more and it'd be too late."

"For Henderson, maybe. Danny still thought I could bust him."

"I don't know that it mattered once he got to Henderson. It's over now. So you don't need to worry." He patted my knee.

"Good." Too many thoughts to ponder, my brain slowed to a crawl. I watched the scenery fly by. The pain pill was making it harder and harder to keep my eyes open. But the last time I closed them, Muldoon'd gone—even if only to make transportation arrangements.

I woke but this time Muldoon was still by my side. Sometime while I was sleeping we started holding hands. His fingers were laced with mine on the center console. "Was I snoring?"

Muldoon glanced over at me and squeezed my hand. "Naw. Talked a little, but you swore me to secrecy, so we're good."

"Cute and funny." I grimaced as soon as the words left my mouth, but thankfully Muldoon didn't say a word.

Not one for uncomfortable quiet, I began to chatter away. "So I guess it's all over now, huh? They have Danny locked up in Dallas." I released his hand and sat a little straighter in the seat. "Life can get back to normal now that I don't have anyone gunning after me. And you can stop running over to my house to see if I'm knee-deep in someone else's troubles. That's got to be a huge relief for you."

He pulled into my neighborhood. And still hadn't said a word. As we neared my street, the little butterflies in my tummy swarmed. After all we'd been through, why was I nervous to be alone with the man?

Muldoon pulled into the driveway and shifted the car into park. "I will be stopping by."

I couldn't stop the smile that spread across my face. "Oh?"

"There may be follow-up questions between Danny's trial and Jerry Pullman's."

The smile slid from my face. "Sure." Here I thought he could leave the shield aside yet he was still thinking cop duties. I was still an "on the job" responsibility despite his stopping by comment. "I want to put it all behind me. I just want to grab my daughter and get my life back on track. No more sticking my nose into anyone else's business."

Muldoon nodded and got out of the car. Despite the sling, I was out the passenger side before he could get around to open the door. He walked me up to the house. The two of us stared at one another. "Well…" he said at the same time I said, "… Um."

The front door whisked open. "There you are. Oh my gawd. He-woman." Levi wrapped me up in his arms and hugged until I squirmed. "Thank you for bringing her back safe, Detective."

"I didn't do anything. She took care of herself. She needs to thank whoever taught her karate."

"Wha…?" Levi eyed me. "Re-eally?" One blond eyebrow arched upward.

"What can I say?" I winked up at my friend. "I picked up a few things from you."

Levi threw his head back and laughed. "Indeed. Well don't just stand there. I have dinner set out for you. There's plenty to go around, Detective." Levi leaned around me and slapped Muldoon on the shoulder, then turned to go, calling over his shoulder, "You're welcome to stay."

"No, thanks. I have to get back to the station to finish up some paperwork." He waved at Levi's departing back, then turned to me. "Nice of him to invite me to *your* house."

I shrugged with a slight grimace. "That's Levi."

"Hmm." Muldoon shook his head. "So."

"So." I leaned against the doorframe.

Muldoon gazed at me for a long minute, then leaned forward and planted a sweet kiss on my lips.

I swayed a little, but it might have been as much from the fall as the kiss.

Muldoon pulled away. "You need to take it easy." He tapped the tip of my nose. "I'll call you. Soon."

Muldoon turned to go.

That was it? He was going to "call me" and that was it? I'd faced down a serial killer, taken a lump or twelve in the process, and he was just going to walk away and *call me*. Um. No.

"That doesn't work for me," I said aloud. "Hey, Shaw. Wait a sec."

He stopped halfway up the sidewalk and glanced back over his shoulder. "Hmm?"

I was going to walk over to him, but things ached that I hadn't realized could ache and I was a little dizzier than I might want to admit. Instead, I stayed up against the doorframe in what I hoped looked sexy with a twist of come-hither and motioned for him to come back to me, but as long as I stayed upright I wasn't too concerned with what it actually looked like.

He eyed me with a curious gaze as he retraced his steps. When he got within arm's reach, I snagged the front of his shirt and pulled him down for a long-over-due, toe-curling kiss. I moaned as much from his magnificent touch as from the tenderness of my stupid lips. But it was oh-so-worth the little bit of pain when he deepened the kiss. His hands gentled at my waist as he eased closer. Kissing him could become my new favorite thing, right above coffee—that's how good it was.

When he finally drew back, his eyes were clouded over.

I released his shirt but kept my hand on his chest. "No. No phone call. No checking up. Saturday night you come by here around seven. Pick me up. We're going out on an actual date." I playfully slapped his cheek then pushed him back toward the street where he'd parked.

He didn't say a word, just stared at me a little dumb-struck as he walked away.

Levi was at my elbow before Muldoon even reached the car. He led me into the house and back to the kitchen. "That was some kiss."

"It's not nice to spy, Levi."

"*Moi*? I'd never. And y'all weren't talking loud enough to hear. What did you say?"

"I told him when to pick me up for our date."

"Look at you." He shook his head with a laugh. "Come sit, eat. Food's getting cold."

The entire table was covered with food. He'd bought Thai takeout as well as a pizza and two heaping bowls of pasta salad. "Are you expecting company?"

"Only one—"

"Mom!" Paige came barreling in from the hallway. "I've missed you so much." She threw her arms around my waist. "What did you do to your arm? Were you scared? I can't wait for you to tell me everything that happened." She chatted away a mile a minute—a mini-version of me.

Tears filled my eyes. I'd missed my munchkin so much. Over the top of her head, I mouthed, "Thanks, Levi. I love you."

"You too, sweets," he mouthed back then pulled out a chair for me. "Sit."

Over dinner, Paige asked question after question. I gave her a *very* diluted version of my encounter with Danny, enough for her to think I was wonderful but not enough to know how perilously close she came to losing me. When we finished eating, Paige wanted to call her dad and tell him of my heroism. Who was I to stop her?

A FEW DAYS LATER, we were sitting at my dinner table having a repeat of the feast from hell—Levi didn't think

we were eating enough with my arm still in a sling—
when the phone rang. It was Colin wanting to talk to
Paige. Even though he saw her every day at school, he'd
called every single night, usually about the time we sat
down to dinner. I wondered if something was going on
with him, but not my monkey, not my circus.

"Sweet pea, it's Daddy." I handed her the phone and
snagged the last egg roll from the table. "Oh, guess
what."

"Hmm?" Levi looked up from his cell phone.

"Coz called me earlier today. The school agreed to
the severance package he drew up." I nibbled on the
end of the egg roll, but was too full to eat another bite.
I dropped it to my plate and leaned back in my chair.
"He said the school *may* have been under the impression that I *might* sue and take it to the media if they
drew this out."

"So when do you start at the playhouse?"

"Monday morning."

Levi made a face.

"What?"

"You and access to all those costumes." He shuddered but a huge smile split across his face.

Paige came bounding back into the room. It did my
heart good when she acted like an actual ten-year-old.
"He wants to talk to you." She held the phone out to me.

Why me? I shook my head before I put the phone to
my ear. "Yes?"

"Hey, Celeste. How are you doing tonight?" You
could almost hear the smile in his voice.

My Spidey sense alerted. Colin was being far too
congenial. "I'm fine." I toyed with the egg roll on my
plate. When he didn't speak right away I rolled my

eyes. "Did you need something? Besides asking how my night is?"

"I, um…"

Great. Colin was about to hit me up for something big. Shades of our conversation right before Chad's death flashed through my brain. A chill scampered down my spine. Not again.

I don't know if I was frowning or what but Levi reached across the table and squeezed my hand before he mouthed, "Everything okay?"

I nodded, though I wasn't entirely sure. "Spit it out, Colin."

"The last time Paige was over she was talking up your playhouse."

I closed my eyes.

"Naomi—"

"Don't you dare say it," I said almost under my breath.

"—would like to try out for the play, but the director told her auditions were closed."

"Then they probably are," I said with clenched teeth.

"But you can get her to make an exception, right?" He paused. "C'mon, Celeste. All you have to do is put in a good word for Naomi."

"You must be insane." Like I would ask Annabelle to cast Naomi. Not even for an ensemble role. "I haven't even started working there, yet."

"Do it as a favor. For me."

I rolled my eyes. Help her? As if.

* * * * *

Get 2 Free Books,
Plus 2 Free Gifts—
just for trying the Reader Service!

Get 2 Free Books,
Plus 2 Free Gifts—
just for trying the Reader Service!

Get 2 Free Books,
Plus <u>2 Free Gifts</u> -

just for
trying the
*Reader
Service!*

STRS17

READERSERVICE.COM

Manage your account online!

- Review your order history
- Manage your payments
- Update your address

> **We've designed the Reader Service website just for you.**

Enjoy all the features!

- Discover new series available to you, and read excerpts from any series.
- Respond to mailings and special monthly offers.
- Browse the Bonus Bucks catalog and online-only exculsives.
- Share your feedback.

Visit us at:

ReaderService.com

RS16R

Get 2 Free Books,
Plus 2 Free Gifts—
just for trying the
Reader Service!